Carrasco '67

A harrowing tale of an Imperialist Pig

Elaine Broun

Thank you to all the nameless heroes who selflessly assist those at their most desperate hour. The events in this book are a fictitious interpretation based on a true story.

Elaine Broun

Prologue

You might say it was destined to be or perhaps a mere coincidence, but for whatever reason, their lives were forever changed.

Chapter 1

Montevideo, Uruguay. 1967.

Across the house, a distant ring resounded from the telephone as the sound of a vacuum cleaner whirred, zigzagging back and forth across the floor. Immediately, the soft cadence of a woman's high heels clicked upon the wooden floors, joining the warring noises as she gracefully made her way towards the telephone, oblivious of the peril soon at hand. Picking up the receiver with her delicately manicured hand, Paula Gray slowly brought it up to her ear. "Hell—oh," she finished with a faint exhaust of air as she was sharply interrupted by her husband, Peter.

"Don't—" his voice broke. Regaining his composure, he continued with measured force, "don't talk. Just listen! The children—us—we are in danger!" Instantly, her skin prickled, and the room buzzed as she felt it implode, growing smaller by the second. The stress in his voice was biting. Peter wasn't the type of man that raised his voice to anyone. "Do you know where the children are?"

"Why yes, I—" Once again, he butted in.

"No, Paula, I mean now, at this exact moment?"

"Yes-yes, I do—but Peter, what's happening?"

"Not now, I don't have time to explain, Paula!" He knew he was being harsh and rather dickish, but time was of the essence. "I need you to go get the kids right now! This is serious. When you leave the school, take the route we normally take via the Rambla whenever we go to the beach and meet me at the first place we stayed in when we arrived."

Paula said, "You mean the ho—" She started to say the name of the hotel, but he stopped her.

"Don't! Don't say anything over the phone. Somebody could be listening in!" For a second, he was beating himself up as he realized he himself had divulged the name of the road, but it was the shortest route, and he couldn't take it back now. "Paula, wear a scarf and make sure none of your red hair is visible. Go as fast as you can. I will be waiting for you at the hotel. One more thing, when you arrive at the school, pull around back, load the kids, and have them crouch down on the floorboards out of sight. Be sure to check the gas gage that you have enough gas. I'll let the school know you are on your way… and Paula…" There was a brief pause. Clearing his throat, he said in a stifled voice, "I love you with all my heart! Please… hurry!"

Chapter 2

Carrasco, an affluent neighborhood in Montevideo, Uruguay.

His words sliced through the stagnant silence. "Idiota-idiot!" Mata was pissed. Miguel de Luna had screwed up. An unfortunate breach of anonymity earlier that day had cost them dearly.

"Como tú eres un idiota!? You're such an idiot! Do you want to blow our cover and expose us?" He bellowed. "Your job was to infiltrate the company of Indústria Fontes, obtain information, and report back! That's it! Are you a part-time idiot or just totally fucking stupid?" Mata ran his fingers through his tightly cropped hair. His muscles in his chiseled cheek twitched as Miguel suppressed his anger. His temper was his nemesis, and so was his arrogance. It truly was a toss-up, and each had a tendency to get the best of the other. This situation strained all his limits. Mata was relentless in his barrage, emphasizing each word with a low guttural cadence. "You-are-responsible-for-only-two, TWO assignments, and you already are screwing that up!"

Miguel waited until he felt he could interject, "Things are fine. I still have my ways."

Mata barked, "Como, how?"

Miguel—caught off guard—was stumped. Providing a plausible bullshit line that he thought Mata would buy, bluffing, he straight-faced said, "Why it is simple really, simply by using fear as the unknown. They certainly are afraid of our cause so let's say if they truly do discover who I am, then at that point fear is our guaranteed method to control the situation." As ideas came into his head, his arrogance surged. "After all," Miguel continued, "WE," he emphatically stressed, "are The Movimiento de la Liberación Nacional! The National Liberation Movement! WE," he emphasized, "are the Tupamáros! The people of Uruguay are genuinely *afraid!* With everyone on edge this is advantageous to us. Don't you agree? Frightened people are controllable, they become weak."

An oscillating fan hummed in the background. The basement had two rooms, both small. One of the 8x8 coffin-sized rooms was carved out as an office, so small the air tended to be a bit dank, despite the fan. Devoid of any décor, the room at best only met the basic necessities at hand: a desk with a chair on one side, and on the other, a worn-out love seat with the cushions sinking in from age. Off to the side was another room that he had never been allowed to enter. Ironically, a solitary picture of a Madonna and baby hung cockeyed on the wall next to a beat-up metal cabinet with its door permanently ajar. Above, a single light bulb slowly swayed from left to right caught in the draft from the oscillating fan. In the corner as it moved, the same fan occasionally captured the reflection of metal from the rifles stacked against the wall.

Mata tapped the old wooden desk emphatically with his middle finger as he clasped an unlit cigar between his fingers. "Without money, without information that you obtain while working there, you imbecile, we are nothing!" Tracing a worn groove on the wooden tabletop with his finger, he asked, "Tell me, how do you expect to finance this movement?" He leaned back in his chair gesturing in the air with his hand. "—everyone contributes! My suggestion is for you to return to the office tomorrow and do some serious damage control. Here's a warning: if unsuccessful—and you better not be—let's just say this. If you are ever exposed, I can assure you that you will be on your own as far as we are concerned. Spelling it out for you more explicitly means no protection whatsoever! However, in the event you are fired and there are financial losses involved but no exposure, your status will be demoted to that of a woman amongst us until I see fit to override my decision! If you are exposed, well then—" He didn't finish, leaving Miguel to all kinds of assumptions. Mata was as male chauvinistic as they came, and he wasn't above humiliating anyone profusely when administering punishment. That was precisely how he treated all his subordinates. Miguel was a bit rattled at this point with his confidence waning and his over inflated ego bruised. He waited until the opportune moment and then said, "As I gave my oath to the movimiento—the movement, I promise to rectify the situation."

"You better hope so!" Mata spouted. Without another word, Mata left. Entering the only other room in the bunker, he closed the door, leaving Miguel to his thoughts. Slowly, Miguel slid down as if his legs could not sustain his weight, dropping down on to the worn leather couch. Lowering his head between his hands, his thoughts raced. Sweat that was building began trickling down his back as he wiped the beads of perspiration off his upper lip with the back side of his hand. Right now, he wanted a drink, a stiff one at that, but he knew that was one of the forbidden vices as a Tupamáro, and now definitely wasn't the time to risk adding to his troubles. The Tupamáros collectively viewed a loose tongue as a risk to the anonymity of anyone and/or mission and then what? *Now what? God! What was I thinking?* Miguel mulled over the recent events. *I should have kept my mouth shut,* he badgered himself, *and not have pressured my "illustrious boss."*

Miguel was referring to Emilio Fonte, for whom he presently worked and was the president of Indústria Fontes. As powerful as he was, Miguel made the mistake of viewing him as a pliable stool pigeon. Time would tell. He hated working for Gringos, and Emilio hired a bunch of them. He wished all Gringos— a disrespectful way of saying Americans—would all leave Uruguay.

Earlier, Emilio Fonte was telling Miguel a meeting was scheduled for the next day to discuss some inconsistencies in certain accounts but he hadn't figured out exactly where the inconsistencies came from. When he did, the persons responsible would be placed on a termination warning—albeit, not realizing that this was the worst-case scenario unfolding. Unbeknownst to Miguel, Fontes had hired one of the silent soldiers from the Tupamáros Terrorist Movement. As soon as Fontes found the accounts where the numbers were not adding up or, for that matter, the other company that the work was done for figured out, then Miguel's number would be up! Fonte would regret it if things fell through. That summed it up as far as Miguel was concerned. This was exactly where he didn't want to be, and yet, it was exactly what he got off on: the adrenaline surge of being on the edge and the power trip he took while instilling fear. Things were going to unfold—it already had, and now, he spent his time pensively formulating his next steps. Threatening families was normally the mode of operation. He knew that the first plan of action was threatening the lives of Fonte's kids and wife. Most caved at this, and Fonte was no different than the average man. He would have no choice. He would willingly tow the line to spare his family.

Not wanting to risk Mata coming back out of the side room, he stood up slowly, still not trusting his legs, and while his confidence was a bit breached, he shrugged his concerns off and walked towards the exit. Nothing got to him really except where Mata was concerned. Let's just say that Mata was the only person for whom Miguel had any inkling of what might be close to a sense of respect, and while he respected him, the rest of the populace just tolerated his asinine countenance.

He began climbing the staircase in the basement. At the top of the staircase was a false door, and the view from the other side appeared to be a tired looking armoire that had seen better days, disguising the inner makings of the hidden doorway. The entire armoire was built with a hidden hinge support so that it could easily be swung open. Behind it, a small, false paneled wall could be pushed open, and one could exit the underground bunker. Looking through the peep hole on the panel, he visually swept the room. Determining the room was clear, he proceeded to leave. Facing the back panel, he unlatched the door, gently pushing the panel inward and swinging the armoire to the right. Stepping up and over the lower half of the opening in the panel, he exited through the armoire. Standing erect, he proceeded to close and secure the panel, pulling it into place, awaiting the sound of the first locking click. Next, he returned the heavy wooden armoire to its rightful spot, pushing it back into place, listening for the second click. As always, extra precaution was made to ensure that all the surroundings were as they had been, and only then did he leave.

Feeling generally annoyed, Miguel walked through the residential area to the nearest cross street to hail a taxi. Paper advertisements were glued to the walls of the corner neighborhood bar, one in particular protesting the killing of a leftist college student stood out. These were volatile times, and he was one of many that were to blame. The sky above was gray. The smell of impending rain permeated the air, and the wind was picking up. Spotting a taxi, he placed his two fingers at the corners of his mouth while his tongue arched and made contact behind his teeth. Then, he let out a sharp high-pitched whistle as he gestured at the taxi driver, getting his attention. The taxi had seen better days at best. The breaks squealed as the taxi rolled to a stop. The motor was loud, and the exhaust was pungent. *Beggars can't be choosers,* he thought to himself. Revving the motor back up, the driver slipped the gear into first. Lifting his foot off the clutch while applying his foot to the accelerator, he urged his taxi forward. The muffler sputtered and rebelled at the mere effort. Miguel gave the driver a bogus address that was blocks from his house, which took about twenty minutes or so to get there. He leaned back and propped his arm across the back of the seat for the remainder of the ride. The driver slowed to a stop. Leaning over, he slid the meter handle to the right to calculate the value of the trip and the amount owed. Handing the money through the window partition, Miguel climbed out onto the sidewalk.

A slow drizzle began to fall, making his mood morose. He so disliked rain. Flipping up the collar of his coat, he pushed his hat down, securing it around his head a little better to counter the wind and started walking towards his apartment. As he walked, the drizzle morphed slowly into full blown raindrops, and by the time he made it home, it had transformed into a full-on downpour. Quickening his footsteps as he neared his home, all kinds of thoughts ran through his mind. Miguel was not looking forward to the next day. He was grateful that he didn't have the baggage of a wife nor kids.

Tonight, he planned to organize his thoughts and formulate his strategy for the next day, proving to Mata and the other members of his cell—as they called their individual groups—that he had it under control, that he was leader material. He had always envisioned meeting their leader, Rufo, whose real name was Sendic, under a bogus occasion for something he did. However, at this rate, providing he didn't fix this fiasco, it was going to be a disastrous meeting! The problem with Miguel was he was a bonafide psychopath. As is typical behavior of a psychopath, his daily life revolved around him. Miguel had constant narcissistic fantasies of grandeur, and envisioned himself being revered by the organization and others, going down in history. Realistically, if and when he went out, it would more than likely be by a bullet. The reality was this: Miguel mentally always overrated his efforts, his net value, and most of all, his shrewdness.

Chapter 3

Yesterday, Miguel sensed something was off. Typically, he was somewhat a paranoid individual, so he always suspected that he was being watched and now even more so at the office, but he just couldn't put his finger on it. Earlier the day before, when he observed the internal auditor coming to see Sr. Fonte, his suspicions went on alert. At that very moment he made plans to return later that evening after he was sure that the cleaning crew and any staff members had left. Sneaking back in, he could do some necessary investigative espionage. His preliminary homework was done since arriving on the job. He knew the crew's schedules, when they arrived, when they left for the day, lunch and break times, days off, and even their family members or significant others! He didn't stop at that. It was his business to know every detail of all the staff that worked at Indústria Fontes. Nothing was overlooked or considered unimportant. Even though he didn't anticipate anyone being there, he would still proceed with caution—just in case.

As dusk waned and night cloaked the evening sky, Miguel sat patiently, biding his time in his car, while observing the entrance to the building. He took a long drag of his cigarette and exhaled, blowing smoke rings. When the last of the cleaning crew exited the building, he grabbed the door handle, shoved the door open and stepped out of his car as he tossed the butt of his cigarette on the stone mosaic sidewalk. Dressed in dark clothing to blend into the night, he walked around the side of the building, hugging the shadows, using them as a protective cover. Reaching the object of his interest just outside the service entrance, he opened the circuit box. He noted the careless practice of the electric company leaving the electrical box unlocked. Pulling the wires out, he carefully inspected each of them. Finding the one he needed, he snipped the line to the power for the building.

Miguel made his way to the door, using his own office key, to enter and then locked the door behind him. Inching his way towards the staircase, he began his quiet ascent, stopping at each floor to peer through the window, checking to see if he overlooked anyone that remained in the building. As an added measure, he waited a few minutes, listening on each level before proceeding to the next floor, thus repeating the same process until he reached the seventh floor.

Capturing some movement on the right side, he rapidly ducked down, pressing his back against the wall while unsheathing his pistol. His adrenaline shot through his veins like an out-of-control freight train. This was his drug of choice; he loved living on the edge. What a fool. The last thing he needed was someone to recognize him. Moments ticked by, and nothing happened, so he slowly raised his head. With his back pressed to the wall, he craned his neck up to take a look into the office reception area, discovering no one except the light shining through the window coming from the flashing business sign across the street. Feeling foolish for mistaking the flashing light as a person, he silently cursed himself for the waste of precious time. His heart beat was certainly elevated as he returned the gun to the holster and resumed his ascent up the staircase, finally making it to the eighth floor where he pushed the door gently open.

Prior to leaving work, he had taped down the latch so that the door would not lock. Thinking back, that blasted secretary just would not leave! He finally had to assure her that she would not get in any trouble if she left before he did—only after he had to work the flirting angle to manipulate her. It is admirable to be dedicated but insufferable when a person is trying to get rid of someone. Then, it can become quite annoying! *Like she even had a chance with me!* He could tell she was afraid since he had seniority, yet she was attracted to him. He didn't miss the irony of the situation. Remaining focused upon arriving at the eighth floor, he went straight towards the office of Sr. Fontes. This would be challenging as he was aware that there was a double lock and an alarm to contend with; however, the latter was now useless, knowing he had cut the lines. Time was of the essence before people would come in droves once the breach was discovered. His calculations gave him precisely fifteen minutes from the time he cut the alarm wire until a notification would reach the police department plus the ten-mile distance of travel to the nearest station. In total, he had thirty minutes to execute his mission.

Miguel got his tool bag out of his back pocket. Untying the leather straps that secured it, he rolled it open pulling out a tension wrench and a couple picks in varying lengths. Using the tension wrench to stabilize the lock, while he inserted the slender pick, he lifted the pins, and he was in. The first one was a fairly simple mechanism, but the second had a delayed relay on it imposing a greater challenge in the dark. Sweat began to trickle down his arms since the air to the building had shut down once he had cut the wires. The humidity blanketed the air. Only in Uruguay can someone sweat in the early spring due to the humidity. The marble floors helped to retain the coolness especially since the hallways didn't have an air unit in every area. In the silence of the room, he could hear the whoosh in his head from his blood pressure rising. The final click resounded, and he knew he was in!

Every time he had been in this office, he took mental pictures where everything was located. He counted the steps to the door and the window, noting the location of the file cabinets and all other furnishings. He already knew the inner workings of the office routine. People are so trusting when they think they have all the facts and a false perception of knowing someone. Once their trust is gained, it was like tipping dominoes in a row: one after another would blab, and the rest followed. Fontes, however, only trusted a select few that were in his small circle of higher-ups. Miguel knew this, and he had been working diligently towards gaining his trust, for longer than his ego normally permitted. He was a tough one; his wall was impenetrable. Unfortunately, his calculations went wrong, and now that Fontes decided to get involved, all his future plans were teetering on crashing down around him if he were exposed:

what he could gain by reaching this upper echelon, the accolades and financial gains he potentially could earn for the cause; it would all be for not. Rummaging through the papers, nothing of importance was found on the surface of his desk—which Miguel expected—so he began the task of picking the lock on the drawer.

Earlier in the week, Fontes slipped up after summoning Miguel to his office to suggest that he pull all the tax reports for the accounts. He overlooked completely closing a secret compartment under his desk, revealing its existence. Feigning ignorance when Fontes became aware of his mistake, he discreetly slid it closed with his foot. Miguel let him believe that he was admiring the painting on the wall behind him by one of his favorite artists completely unaware. It was a typical rural Gaucho scene around a campfire. Having noticed the secret compartment, he tucked this information away, knowing this could come in handy. Generally speaking, there was only one reason to have a secret compartment, and that was to hide something of value. The thing he had to figure out was the triggering mechanism to open the latched door, and then he would be in.

Most secret doors in furniture did not function like your typical lock and key, but by a type of mechanism. Feeling his way around the ornamental wood trim, he kept coming up empty-handed. Finally, he slipped his fingers directly underneath the inner central trim and heard a click. Pushing in on the side panel, it opened easily. A groove large enough to slip one's fingers in allowed access to a slim hidden alcove where several folders or a couple of two-inch manuals could easily fit.

Miguel removed two folders from their hiding place, revealing the papers within. The top report was marked confidential. On the memo line in bold black ink was written 'Miguel de Luna.' Pulling out a slim, miniature camera from his inside pocket, he removed the elastic side that bound the folder shut and began taking snap shots of the entire report, piece by piece. When finished, he carefully returned everything to its rightful place. Glancing at the second folder, he saw it was regarding an upcoming proposal, which, at the moment, did not matter much to him, but he went ahead and documented it. All surfaces were then wiped clean and re-locked. Listening at the door, he heard voices. The bottom lock of the office door was standard and could be re-locked from inside, but the upper one could only be done with time that he didn't have since he didn't have the original key. This would raise flags tomorrow when it was discovered to be unlocked. Most likely, it would be blamed on the secretary. The little scapegoat might be useful to him after all.

Miguel darted across the hallway and wound up underneath the secretary's desk. The night security men came in through the stairwell and proceeded to inspect the offices. He could hear them talking about who they thought were responsible for the power outage, blaming the government for being lax or the idiots running the electrical company. The minute they turned the corner to check the back hallway and breakroom, he darted towards the stairwell door that they had left opened. Taking the stairs two at a time, he made his way down at a rapid rate. A small echo resounded occasionally, letting him know to slow down to avoid divulging his presence. Once at ground level, he allowed himself precious minutes to observe his surroundings. Removing his concealing outerwear, he stuffed the items in his backpack with the intent to blend in on the street. Assured there weren't any policía yet, he hurried now hearing the faint sounds of sirens in the near distance.

Determining all was clear, he exited the side door between the buildings. Stepping out of his concealed corner between the buildings, he walked towards the street, crossing over to the other sidewalk and proceeded to walk at a normal pace as to not attract attention. A half block down from the Fontes offices, his luck came in the form of a bus just as sirens could be heard a block away. If he rode a bus, he could disappear in plain sight. The bus line ran like clockwork, so he knew one would show up shortly according to his calculations of its schedule. It didn't matter where it was going just as long as he could get away, and then, he could deal with the rest. Ten minutes further down the road was the shopping district Arocena in Carrasco. Pulling the cord, it rang the buzzer, advising the bus driver to make a stop. Miguel stepped down from the bus while expelling a small sigh of relief. Moving forward, he walked until he made it to the busier side of town with the plan to hail a cab home. Curiosity was eating at him, and he couldn't wait to know what was in the reports; only then would he be able to formulate his next move.

A bit haggard from the adrenaline letdown, upon arriving home, he climbed the stairs to his apartment. Entering his apartment, he went straight to the shower to wash off the gross feeling from sweating so much in the hot building. Walking into his small bathroom, he turned the hot water handle on to heat up the water. The tile around the shower was pale yellow, and the grout was riddled with mold all over from the moisture, while many of the floor tiles were fractured. He cracked open the small window above the shower and then proceeded to wipe the fog building up on the mirror. Staring at his reflection, he noticed how he looked like his father's side of the family: strong Uruguayan-Italians coming from a long line of handsome men, tall by South American standards. He further noticed he already needed to shave again. He also felt like he had run a marathon—chalk it up to the hazards of his recent cocktail of stress and adrenaline. He let the water run as he waited for it to turn clear. This had a tendency to take a while until all the rust-colored water poured out of the shower head; only then would clearer water follow due to the old, rusted pipes. Stepping down into the shower, he proceeded to sit down on the little built-in bench to absorb the steam. As he began to relax, he mentally planned his next moves. Fifteen minutes later, the hot water began to run out, so he grabbed the bar of soap and quickly scrubbed his body and washed his hair with the final rinse already turning to cold water. Quickly, he shut the water off and stepped out, grabbing a towel and wrapping it around his waist—caring not that as he walked, large droplets cascaded down from his hair to his chest and down his muscular legs, landing all over the floor and making little offset puddles from each step he took. Stepping into the kitchen, he grabbed a beer out of the refrigerator. Positioning the cap on the side of the counter, he hit the top of the cap with the side of his palm, popping it off before taking a long cold swig. Retrieving the camera out of the backpack, he went to develop the film, beer in hand. Flipping the light on in his room he closed the door. Sensing that he was about to be fired, he was anxious to develop the film so that he could find out, perhaps once and for all, what they knew and what lurked ahead for his future.

Chapter 4

Emilio Fonte sat in the back of his limousine with his trusted chauffeur of fourteen years at the wheel. The limo had blacked-out, bulletproof windows and a black exterior with a cream-colored Italian leather interior. It had all the things most limos had: TV, stereo system, bar, a telephone to speak with the driver and, of course, the separation glass between the driver and its occupants. There was no detail omitted. Together, they traveled the same route daily in quiet union. Emilio rarely closed the separation glass, for he and his chauffeur had developed a mutual respect and friendship due to many years together. No matter how important or how much wealth he gained, he never lost touch with his origins nor did he carry himself to be above another human being.

Emilio did not look forward to this morning's most pressing agenda, which was potentially removing Miguel from the firm based on the outcome of the internal audit just completed. Angry at himself, he pondered, how could a man that he handpicked be possibly embezzling on some of his accounts? Knowing something wasn't adding up, he wanted to get to the bottom of it as quickly as possible, so he had requested that his Department of Internal Audits do further investigations of their own. This took about two painstaking months of long hours poring through account after account, ledgers, bank statements, tax documents, etc. The report, finally complete, was placed on his desk just yesterday. He was fully aware if he waited, it would just allow time for more prejudice to come upon the company that couldn't be rectified easily; the report findings were serious money laundering on some of his best accounts. When Emilio finished reading the report for the second time, he leaned back in his chair, exhaling slowly. Slipping his glasses off, he rested his arm on the armrest, dangling his glasses from between his fingertips, while rubbing his eyes with his other hand. He pondered every angle as his anger got the best of him. Leaning forward, he pounded his fist on the desk, exclaiming out loud, "That bastard is done!"

Calling his secretary over the intercom, Emilio asked Marta to locate Mr. De Luna and ask if he could come a bit earlier to his office. A short while later, a soft rap was heard on the door and Marta announced, "Señor Fontes, Señor De Luna is here to see you." Emilio motioned with his hand to send him in, saying, "That will be all. Thank you, Marta. And Marta, make sure under no circumstance are we interrupted."

"Yes, sir, as you wish." Exiting, De Luna gave Marta a little smile, feigning all was cool with him as she softly closed the door while lowering her head timidly, really not wanting to make eye contact.

"Mr. De Luna, sit down." Once seated, Emilio began. "It has come to my attention that many inconsistencies have been happening on several of my biggest accounts. Mind you, these clients... many of them have been with our firm for years." He paused and then slid the report across the desk at Miguel. "I requested detailed reports of all your day-to-day activities and any transactions that you had where monies were exchanged between the bank and our clients' accounts, so that we could review them together. Take a look if you wish and then if you could explain yourself regarding the discrepancies listed, now is your time?"

Miguel stood up and interjected. "Is this some kind of a bad joke? This is insulting at best!"

Emilio cut in, "Miguel, insulted or not, you have this one opportunity to speak upon your behalf in order to redeem yourself in the eyes of this firm. First of all, I'll have you know the reports were done with the intention of finding an innocent, man-made error. However, what has been unveiled is bonafide corruption and deceit!"

Miguel acted indignant and began his tirade again, hoping to put doubt in Emilio's mind. "Why would you discredit my dedication to this company like this? How can you question my loyalty, especially by a mere report that is biased by someone else, probably with their own ambitious agenda in this company?" Emilio replied, "I seriously doubt someone upon my request would use this to climb the ladder, and anyway, this is with good reason; the evidence speaks for itself. Reports don't lie, Miguel."

Trying to deflect, Miguel threw in, "Did I not bring in the Mendelsohn account? That alone netted a profit of one million American dollars a year! Someone bringing in business isn't exactly demonstrating that they are trying to undermine a business."

This time, it was Fontes that was showing signs of strain, of being close to losing his patience. "Mr. De Luna, sit down and lower your voice. I have brought you in solely to tell you my findings, not to debate them. We are aware of your actions and how far your role in all of this plays out. It is obvious to me that you do not have one iota of a defense, and all this loud rhetoric and gesturing is wasting your time and definitely-mine. As we speak, a guard is waiting for you outside to escort you out of the building. Nothing else applies, and nothing you can say now will change my mind. My decision has been made." He picked up the phone and dialed Marta, giving her instructions. "Your belongings will be gathered by my secretary and brought to you."

Miguel spoke, his voice becoming cold and detached. "Hang up the phone." Emilio froze. He could hear Marta saying "Sr Fontes?" repeatedly, but he didn't answer and then hung the phone up as Miguel continued. "Do you have any idea whom you are dealing with? Do you love your wife? Think about it, caro amigo—dear friend. How about your wife Ana and your children? Beatriz, I believe? She is seventeen by now? Beautiful girl," he continued smugly, "and I believe she attends Escuela Santa Rita, is it not? Then, there is Ricardo, your son. Now, he, I believe, should be nineteen by now and in his first year at University?"

The more Miguel went on, his voice became more sinister, an occasional hint of a maniacal lilt setting in. "You, sir, are not dealing with just me, you fool." *He came close to revealing who he was associated with and yet fell short of actually telling him.* "I have plenty of connections-big ones!" This was enough for

Emilio; he didn't need to say anything further. He had a gut feeling he was alluding to the Tupamáros and yet he didn't quite say this.

"So, I ask you again, do you love your children? Your wife? How much do you value them?" Miguel said seriously.

Emilio's mind was reeling from the informational bomb that was just dropped, but quickly regrouped himself. He spoke with such rage that he almost didn't recognize the ferociousness of his own voice. "Don't you even think of threatening me or my family. It is you that has been caught! Don't think that we are so weak and ignorant. I as well have my trusted people and have all the information I need to put you away in the penitenciária. The penitentiary will keep you until you are an old man!"

"You are the only old man here, and you are delusional if you think you are in control!" Miguel answered. However, being cautious, he listened at that point to what Emilio had to say. He needed as much detail of what they were up to so that he could formulate a counter plan.

Emilio continued, "I also have many important people that with one phone call, your life would be mine!"

"If you think I will let this be, you are the greater fool then!"

Devoid of fear, Emilio said, "I suspect you do not want the publicity, am I right? If I denounce you, it will expose you, right? If I call the police, they will arrest you and that would bring a lot of attention. At a loss for words, Miguel?" He had hit close to home, but Miguel maintained a stoically silent façade. Borderline losing to the mental warring that was taking place in his brain, he had struck a chord. Emilio continued, "So may I make a suggestion in return?" De Luna nodded and gestured with an open hand as he swept the air as if saying "go on."

"So, it seems we both are at some sort of an impasse—wouldn't you agree? We both have much to lose and much more to gain by a truce amongst ourselves, so I propose this." Speaking in a formidable voice of authority, he continued, feeling a smidgen more in control, "You get out immediately and leave my family alone, and in return, I give you my word that I will not expose you to the media, the policía, or the military—agreed?"

Miguel sat there, mulling over his options, knowing that—at the present—there really were none. They both had much to lose, and it pissed him off that Fontes had the upper hand at this juncture.

"As much as I would like to tell you what you could do with this proposition of yours, I find that, in the long run, this benefits me, so for this reason only, I will give you my word; no harm will come to your family, and I will agree to your terms for the time being as long as you keep your word—and only because it suits my agenda. I will, however, expect a rather sizable last paycheck." He paused as he stood up and walked towards the door, only then turning around and saying, "However, I will leave you with this thought: I will still be watching you if but from afar. I have many eyes everywhere, maybe even still in this building. How well do you know your secretary, the elevator attendant, or the maids? So, my dear friend, caro amigo, be careful of your conversations. The wrong word to the wrong ears and you might find your daughter's body in the trunk of your car! We have our ways."

Opening Emilio's office door, Miguel exited. Passing the secretary's' desk, he took the box with his things from Marta's hands and arrogantly blew a kiss to her. She nervously smiled back, embarrassed, assuming he knew she had been the one to pack up his belongings. With a smirk on his lips, he said, "I hope you were careful. I wouldn't want anything I treasure to be broken." Turning away from her, he began to laugh, first softly before building to a loud guffaw. He left her feeling uneasy. The man scared every fiber of her being. She sensed he was crazy, and this terrified her. Trying to refocus on her work, she regretted the day he had come into her life. He already had caused her nothing but grief, and she bitterly hoped that he would never be back. Marta wasn't a young woman, so with years of experience, she was quite good at reading people, and this was a bad hombre.

Chapter 5

Peter Gray exited his 1932 Mercedes Benz. He was exceedingly tall, blonde, blue-eyed, and extremely handsome. His face was chiseled as was his body under his custom-tailored suit. Trying to avoid the rain, he sprinted into the building owned by Pradman Industries. It still felt surreal; a hum of excitement ran through his veins every time he walked in. Partner! He was a partner for one of the top two accounting firms in the world! It was just six months ago in Rio de Janeiro when he got the final word. With the support of his wife Paula, he and his three children—Dane, the eldest at thirteen; Jack, twelve; and Bergen, his only daughter who was eight—packed and moved less than six weeks later to Uruguay.

The receptionist greeted him as he walked in. "Good morning, Mr. Gray!"

He reciprocated her greeting in perfect Spanish as he passed by, entering the elevator. The attendant sat inside the elevator with the door open: uniform pressed, shoes shined, and white gloves without a stain on the fingertips anywhere. There was a small black stool he could fold down from the inside wall for those long days. Upon seeing Peter enter, he didn't hesitate. In an instant, he immediately stood and punched the buttons, selecting the floor and then holding the door open until he passed through. These actions were done in a fluid motion of repetitive experience. Peter never mentioned the floor he wanted, but the senior attendant already knew where his destination lay. The carriage dinged, announcing their arrival to the eighth floor. The doors slid open, and he politely thanked the elevator attendant who grabbed the brim of his uniformed hat with his thumb and two fingers. With his other hand behind his back, he tipped his head with a respectful gesture. Peter thanked the attendant as he stepped out—which wasn't expected—but Peter was the epitome of always being a consummate gentleman.

Proceeding with the start of his day, he politely greeted anyone he came across as he made his way to his office. The path was well appointed with the usual plants, wall décor, and a random grouping of dark, heavy, wooden furniture made to last for the vast number of visitors that passed through these corridors. Approaching his office, Peter Gray observed his secretary Lucia at her desk.

Lucia was a recent hire, a petite brunette with timid mannerisms but proving to be an exceptionally good choice. Looking up, she saw him as he approached her desk; she stood, greeting him first, "Good morning, Mr. Gray." He greeted her as well with a genuine smile, and kind words. In the short span of time that she had been employed, they had established a copacetic relationship with a mutual respect. "I have your agenda for today..." Gathering her notepad and pencil, she stepped from behind her desk, and her high heels made rapid little clicking sounds as she walked across the wood floor with her short little legs, trying to keep up with Peter's long ones. Every morning, they began as such. Speaking first, she inhaled deeply and then rattled off, "Sir, you have a meeting at 1:00 with the Mastos clients. Señora Batista called regarding the dogs; the litter was born the night before, and there are five to pick from, but she would like you to wait three weeks at least to give the mother a chance to recover and be more receptive to visitors. Annnd..." she paused, looking down at her notes to make certain nothing was overlooked, "Don't forget about the Association for International Businessmen (IBA) dinner tonight at 7:00 at the Playa Hotel. Can I still confirm that you and your wife will be in attendance?" He nodded in agreement. "You will be seated with Mr. and Mrs. Schaffer and Mr. and Mrs. Jones."

"Yes, that is fine. Do you know who the presenter of this evening is?" Peter added, without looking up as he shuffled through his papers.

"Yes, it is Dan Mitrione, Mr. Gray. If you recall, he is the former CIA/FBI man that is in Uruguay to teach counter insurgency techniques to the policía." Lucia flipped through her calendar one more time, once again triple checking she hadn't missed anything. His schedule was always top heavy, and things were constantly rearranging. "Oh, and one last thing I almost over-looked, Sr Jairo stopped by and said to tell you that the additional payment has been received by the tax office regarding the underpayment error that was uncovered on the Pontificia account." Jairo Castellan was Pradman's resident senior company lawyer, a regular ace in the field. Peter unbuttoned his coat as he sat down.

"Very good, Lucia. If there isn't anything else, then that will be all for now, thank you." Peter reached over and clicked on his desk lamp as Lucia quietly closed his office door behind her. The lighting in his office throughout the day wasn't always the best, even with the curtains open he kept a lamp lit on his desk, to avoid getting drowsy. This was a small price to pay; it was the best office on his floor. The view from the window was incredible: he could see two different streets. Being one of the few tall buildings on the block, his view wasn't completely obstructed, but enough to play with the lighting in his office. After Lucia had closed the door, he got on the phone to put in a call to Paula. The concierge at the hotel answered, where upon Peter asked to be transferred to room #263.

"Hello?" he heard his wife say in her southern accent.

"Paula, it's your boyfriend."

"Peter, stop that!" she said. "You embarrass me. What if one of the children had answered?"

"They wouldn't. They're in school! Anyway, I have got to get moving here, but I am just touching base with you. I will be by to get you at the hotel at 6:15 so we can get over to the dinner. Be gorgeous, my favorite little red head!"

The phone clicked. She smiled and returned the receiver to its cradle. She surveyed the hotel room as her thoughts lingered on Peter. Glancing towards the window, she was drawn to the front balcony that overlooked the Atlantic Ocean. Taking her cup of coffee, she stepped out onto the balcony and sat down as she did every morning. Staring at the sea in its grand panoramic grandeur was something she would never get enough of. The sound of the waves rushing in and out with the occasional sounds of the birds was so relaxing. She earned this time; it wasn't easy getting children ready for school out of suitcases. Paula began mentally running through her outfits, trying to decide what to wear before finally picking an off the shoulder, gold-shimmering gown. Gold was always a great color for her since it played well, accentuating her flaming red hair and its subtle golden highlights. She continued to take in all the beauty of the ocean and all the white sand; even this early, it was fun to people watch. This was heaven, pure eye candy, and she would miss this view once they moved into a house, and yet, she was anxious to do so for the benefit of the children. They needed room to run around, but meanwhile, she would enjoy every minute as long it lasted. Looking down at her watch, she was startled, realizing how much time she had allowed to slip by! Jumping up, she hurried, ringing the chamber maid so that they could freshen up her dress with a light steaming in order to get it back in time for the evening dinner. After arranging this, Paula showered, dressed, tied a scarf around her head, and left for her appointment at the Beauty Salon. The previous week, she had made the appointment for a haircut and style, followed by a manicure and pedicure. As far as make-up was concerned, Paula was very particular, preferring to do her own. Life was good.

Chapter 6

By mid-morning, Peter had worked up a list of prospective clients he wanted to bring on board to Pradman Industries. His wish list was shaping up as he put them in numerical priority order. At the top of his list was Indústrias Fontes, which was run by Emilio Fontes. There was always one client that was the prized catch to many companies, and he was determined to land them. Fontes wasn't the type of person you could just go after. One had to court them slowly and know when to and when not to approach. Having a history of accomplishments that carried weight and personal interactions with the man was the cautious way. He was a savvy, no-bull type of businessman. His medium stature did not take away from his power.

Peter had first met Mr. Fontes when he attended a previous IBA dinner, and he thought they had hit it off fairly well, so tonight, at this month's IBA dinner, he looked forward to further building on a potential relationship and using Paula as a pretty diversion. Not wanting to look desperate, he strategically took time before approaching him. He wanted this evening to be about social interaction, deterring the thought that they were needy. Indústrias Fontes' numbers were impressive, and it would be an ace in his deck if he could land such a prestigious client in such a short time.

"Mr. Fontes, good morning. Peter Gray here," he said after Lucia connected their call. I was wanting to know if you would be available to meet within the near future. Perhaps, over lunch?"

Mr. Fontes replied, "Peter, that seems feasible. I read your brief summative assessment, by the way, that you sent over, and I have to say my curiosity has been piqued. Let's let our secretaries get together on the phone, and I am sure between the two of them, they can carve out an afternoon between our schedules. I really apologize that I need to cut this short, but I am expected in a board meeting. Pleasure doing business."

"The pleasure is all mine, Mr. Fontes."

"Call me Emilio."

"Thank you very much, Emilio. I will certainly get my secretary right on this. Good day to you, sir!" Peter hardly suppressed his excitement.

"And to you as well," replied Emilio.

It was a peculiar phone call at best, but Peter wasn't going to complain; his foot was in the door. He expected Mr. Fontes to be more stand-offish, hard-nosed type of guy, but he was actually an alright chap. Tonight, however at the IBA Dinner if he had the opportunity to speak with him, he remained decided that business talks would wait until their meeting and that only social pleasantries would be exchanged.

Peter buzzed his secretary. "Lucia?"

"Yes, Mr. Gray?"

"I want you to make another call to speak with Mr. Fontes' secretary and schedule a meeting for us. See what he has going on. Find out if he golfs. If so, make it a morning game of golf followed by lunch if possible."

"Very good, Mr. Gray," Lucia spoke as she cradled the phone between her chin, ear and shoulder, supporting it as she took notes on her notepad. "I will get right on it for you."

Peter felt that jittery excitement whenever he arrived at work. He didn't get to where he was without some huge sacrifices, but now, the paybacks for all the years of toeing the line while climbing the business ladder was paying off. He had a gorgeous wife that turned heads when she walked into a room, three great kids, a fantastic job, and if all went well, he would land this account and move out of the hotel into a new home—with luck, all within the same month!

In the meantime, while the kids were at school, Paula would spend her days with the realtor, hopefully securing a home soon. Paula learned early in this search that American and Uruguayan realtors operated things quite differently from one another. Just because a client found a place first and put a contract on it didn't mean that before the signing of said contract, someone couldn't come in and trump them by bidding higher. First come, first acceptance was an American thing, so Paula diligently kept looking, hoping their days at the hotel would end soon. It seemed trivial, but she was terrified that the people doing the laundry at the hotel were going to ruin an item of clothing by washing or drying it the wrong way, but most importantly, she was ready for privacy, and the children were overdue for a backyard to play in. It was lovely having room service, not having to clean or cook, and the gorgeous Atlantic Ocean as your panoramic view was divine. However, there were limitations on keeping three active kids occupied. One only could go to the beach so many times in cold weather, and even the gorgeous parks were just too chilly to be outside, and with the frequent rain, plans were ruined on many occasions. Luckily, Paula found out about the local bowling alley in Arocena, a sub-district near Carrasco. From then on, the kids went there often, especially if it was raining, or they would go to an occasional movie or to shop when the beach wasn't an option. Uruguay was turning out to be a very family-orientated, awesome place to live.

Chapter 7

Good evening, Señores y Señoras! Bienvenidos, welcome to the eighth annual meeting of the for International Businessmen Association. I am your host, Sr. Edson Alves." Polite clapping rose in volume and softened as he raised his hand, acknowledging the crowd. "Tonight, while you are dining on our finest Uruguayan cuisine by our top chefs, our illustrious guest speaker will be none other than Sr. Dan Mitrione, as some of you are already aware!" Everyone began really applauding at this. During the applause, Peter leaned over and whispered to his wife, "Supposedly, he has a serious take regarding safety—probably overkill." Paula looked at Peter alarmed. Realizing his error in his choice of words, he quickly smiled to deflect any tension while giving her a comforting pat on the hand. He was about to say something when the guest speaker began speaking at the podium.

"Buenas noches, good evening. Thank you for being so gracious," said Dan Mitrione. "Many of you may not know who I am, so therefore, I would like to introduce myself to you, and for those that do know me, well, just bear with me a bit." He politely gave a short laugh. "To begin, my family immigrated to the United States from Italy many years ago. After getting my education, I began my career as a policeman in Richmond, Indiana. Soon, I joined the Federal Bureau of Investigation (FBI), where I was later assigned to the State Department's International Cooperation Administration through the Central Intelligence Association (CIA). It was here in this capacity that I began my journey to South America." The waiters began serving drinks, as he continued. "I recently finished helping the Brazilians with the aftermath of the overturn of their government and the precarious situation that this created, so let's see." He laughed again, saying, "Sometimes, I don't know if I am coming or if I am going; things have been so busy for me. Um, so…" losing track of what he was about to say he continued. "Oh, yes! So, after that, I returned to the United States in Washington—to be exact—with my newest project being working on updating the Agency for International Development (AID). Next, I was asked by the Office of Public Safety (OPS) on behalf of the Uruguayan government to help teach counter guerrilla warfare techniques, and so, there you have it! I have been somewhat busy."

He scratched the back of his head, and laughter erupted from the crowd. Señor Mitrione went on, "And so, this is what leads me to tonight's topic at hand. You are not strangers to the subject of the Tupamáros; this name is a play on the official Indian name of Tupac Amarú. The newspapers have been filled for a long time about their activities, so I will get to the purpose of my presence here tonight. My purpose is not to alarm you but to empower you with knowledge for the safety of you and your family while you are living in Uruguay. Some, I suppose, are here for temporary purposes, and others may be permanent foreigners, ex-pats as they are so called, so I will address both scenarios. Either way, things have changed, and unfortunately, my news isn't all good. Why, you might be wondering? I will explain. The Tupamáros movement began originally as a peaceful approach to inform and encourage the need for social reform—a change, we shall say. What originally began as a political view to help the common, every day, less-fortunate person or persons without the support of the governing populace has changed, continues to change, and has become a more threatening stance. There has been an insurgence of violent tactics, especially after Mr. Raul Sendic, their leader, went underground with his group known as the Movimiento de Liberación Nacional. In English, it is the National Liberation Movement, aka Tupamáros. How do they remain at large?" He asked the audience, not expecting an answer from them.

He continued. "The brilliance of the Tupamáros, so far as we know, is that they seem to have limited knowledge of one another, so the head person of one 'group' may not know the head of another group. They all work together but separately so that if one is caught, only a small cell (as their group is called) of five to seven men are compromised, and it does not hinder the entire operation. Another fact about them is their organization leans towards being Marxist—a leftist group, so to speak. What began as a somewhat noble cause has now evolved to less than reputable acts of violence. I am not sure if this is a temporary thing or if this is a sign that things could escalate; time will tell on that front. What I do know about the movement is that kidnappings are up, especially for those that are perceived to have an advantageous financial value to their cause, and they are not above aiming for children." With that comment, the gasps of many of the women present could be heard, but he did not stop. "The terrorists are of all walks of life. Can you believe it? There are even rumors of females." With that, some of the women at the table began whispering amongst each other, demonstrating their abhorrence at the thought! Dan waited for the room to quiet down. "Ladies and gentlemen, what I would like to impress upon you are a few points, the first one being you must be aware of your environment! Your nice neighbor that you've known for the last year—or maybe even just met—could very well be a Tupamáro. Have you thought of that? Second, and this will be a difficult task, but be very careful of whom you hire, both at work and as staff in your home. If something seems odd, do not take a chance; listen to your instincts. No reference is unimportant. Take the time to check. Try to blend in. When in large groups, try and avoid speaking English, drawing attention to yourselves. I recommend that, for now, you do not go out after dark. If you must socialize, do it in the privacy of your homes and be very alert to your surroundings. Ladies, if out shopping, look around to see if anything looks odd or out of place before entering your car. If you feel uneasy, go back into the store and wait."

Peter thought to himself, *If this guy doesn't want to alarm the wives, he was doing a poor job of it.* He toyed with his drink in hand as Mr. Mitrione continued his discourse.

"Observe! Once again, be observant. I urge you, until further notice, to be very alert. Now, for the men, many have inquired about obtaining a gun for your homes; feel free to call me and ask about the requirements. I may be reached at the contact number listed in the brochures found at each of your tables. At this time, I will accept any questions you might have. Yes?" he said as he pointed at a gentleman. The man asked his question about protection. Several wives asked about protection for their children, and several more questions were discussed and answered after that. "I don't believe we are at a point where you need to panic, hiring bodyguards and those sorts of things, but what I am trying to do is make you aware and alert that some of the recent occurrences seem to be of a serious nature. Men, there are brochures outside if you would like further tactical protection trainings for you and your family." Finally, Dan Mitrione's portion of the evening concluded as he said, "Thank you for your time. Good evening."

The invited guests applauded as Sr. Alves walked up to the podium, clapping as well, and then shook Mr. Mitrione's hand. "Ladies and Gentlemen, Mr. Mitrione." He open-handedly acknowledged Mr. Mitrione and continued clapping. Several people stood. "Mr. Mitrione, we thank you for your words of wisdom and your guidance, and I am sure that all your knowledge and advice will be taken to heart," said Sr. Alves. "Now, moving on to our next order of business, we would like to welcome our newest members. Please, remain standing when I call your names: Mr. Olag Vereschildt from Amsterdam, who has joined Martinez & Milton's Industries…" He went on, mentioning a few more businessman and companies that had joined, but Peter knew by watching the animated conversation between women in the room the fire had been stoked. This included his wife and her friend, Anne Schaffer, who was seated at the same table along with her husband Mark, a colleague. A whirlpool of nerves, a regular hornets' nest had been stirred up in a twenty-minute period of time. Wiping away tears, Anne asked to be excused to the lady's room, and Paula went with her to be of some comfort. Fear had set in. No matter how reassuring the husbands might have tried to be, when someone gets between a woman and her family, he has rocked her world, bringing out her momma bear response, defending her cubs. The rest of the evening, at best, had a bit of a somber pall. Mr. Alves could be heard saying, "…and after the dessert that is being delivered, you are welcome to stay for drinks and dancing. For those that have other obligations, we thank you for coming and look forward to seeing you at the next meeting. Good night!"

Mark leaned over to Peter as they stood and applauded and said, "I did not care to hear risk to our families. This is going to be a difficult sell to convince Anne to remain here in Uruguay, no matter how wonderful it has been up until tonight."

Peter replied, "Our appearance is what gives us away. You heard him. We just need to take his advice: make ourselves less conspicuous and lower our profile. It's a good thing our accents in Spanish are spot on and we can blend in better than most of our colleagues. Except for your youngest, Mark, our kids are in private schools. Perhaps, we individually need to have a meeting with the director to just alert him as to what was said tonight. What do you think?" The applause subsided, and one by one, those in attendance sat down.

Mark responded, "That is a good idea—" Just then, he noticed Anne and Paula approaching the table, so he was momentarily distracted from what he was going to say, but Anne had heard him.

"What is a good idea, Mark?"

Mark looked over at Peter, making eye contact with him. If his expression could speak, it would be saying to go along with him on this. "Having Peter and Paula over for a cookout, darling." Continuing, he didn't skip a beat. "We could even invite George and Barbara Jones, and their kids. You know George from the British Embassy?"

"Right, right," Anne said. "It would be good to get the dreadful topic of this evening out of my mind and have some fun! Say, I'll start organizing it, and I will let you know when, Paula, if that is okay?" Thank God the diversion worked. Paula agreed to Anne's suggestion. As a good portion of the room had already cleared into the foyer of the building, the rest of the crowd remaining were still caught up at the time, saying their goodbyes, some as they were walking towards the elevators.

Peter placed Paula's mink stole around her shoulders as they began walking. The men fell back behind their wives so they could exchange a few words out of the range of their wives. Peter started, "About what I said earlier, let's first suggest that the schools might increase their guards, at least until things settle down." Mark nodded in agreement as they caught up with their wives entering the elevator. Each stood in a momentary silence, lost in their own thoughts as the doors to the elevator slid closed—as if foreshadowing this chapter in their gilded lives coming to a close as well. As the elevator moved between floors, the whir and occasional clacking noise could be heard. Times had changed. Innocence lost. Was evil prevailing?

Chapter 8

The little boy extended his small, frail hand. "Señor, please, spare some centavos?" Being poor was rough. Getting a token tip from Miguel was seemingly harder. He was a selfish bastard.

After being handed the cryptic note, Miguel barked at the kid, saying, "Get out! Go!" Safest way to deliver a note was to send it via a poor, illiterate child. Having dismissed the kid brusquely without giving him a coin, he unfolded the note. The message read, *"The bougainvillea are in bloom. Stop by to see."* He knew this was a summons for a meeting by the coded words. The locale of the home on the outskirts of the meat-packing district to which they were referring was familiar. Each of their home-base houses was marked by a specific flower planted to identify it in the front yard. One house was the bougainvillea, and there were some with names of different shades of roses and orchids. He waited until afternoon when it was busy with folks trying to get home before he started to the rendezvous. That way he could easily get lost in the crowds and not risk being followed. He wondered if he would be there before their leader—but probably not. He wasn't one of the elites yet, but in his mind, he was almost there. Soon, he believed, he would be done proving his loyalty and worthiness; then, no one would question him ever. He was ambitious to say the least, wanting to move up the ladder, but recently, it seemed things had slowed down, and he wondered if it was due to this recent incident which came at a bad time. Impatience also messed with his self-control.

Miguel walked up to a little stone house. The home was recessed from the street for privacy, and for security; a tall wrought iron gate surrounded its boundaries. Bougainvillea were found to be growing across the front, cascading over and through the fence, blocking visibility from the street. This wasn't the best area of town, so many of the homes had the added security of a fence. It wasn't just the fence, but the wicked thorns on the bushes deterred anyone from entering as well. Two large Dobermans were loose on the property as an added deterrent. If one paid close attention, they would notice the strategically placed cacti plants set beneath each of the windows, assuring no one would attempt to breach entry through them. The house had two different points of entry before reaching the front door. Ringing the outer bell, he knew they were looking to see who was there from some vantage point, but he knew not where, nor could he see from the two-way windows within. What appeared to be a maid in uniform was actually a female Tupamára disguised as a maid who came to let him in. The Tupamára then locked the gate behind him. She muttered something about removing any dirt from his shoes before entering, which seemed odd, but at this point he wasn't going to rock the boat—though, he bristled at taking orders from a female; why the leader allowed them to be soldiers he never understood. To Miguel, a woman's place was only in the home, and an education was a waste on them.

After checking his shoes, as he was bid, and ascertaining they were acceptable, he entered the house. Following the Tupamára, they walked down the hall to one of the back bedrooms. He noted she had a nice little ass. He wished he could show her what her real purpose in life was. She signaled for him to stop. From what he could see from his vantage point, it looked like an ordinary room. The Tupamára asked him to wait and closed the door, leaving him in the hallway. He heard her footsteps, but that was it. What seemed like a few seconds later, she was back, beckoning him to enter. Closing the door, she locked it. Without a word, she walked over and pulled the armoire away from the wall. It moved silently and effortlessly. From his vantage point he was unable to see what exactly she did next, but it triggered the wall panel to open inwardly revealing the staircase which led down to the basement. Pointing to the opening, she bade him to enter. Stepping in, he stooped over to avoid hitting his head, and after stepping down a few steps, he was able to straighten back up as he descended the rest of the staircase. He was impressed to say the least; this security measure was not like the other homes he had been to that they used, but then again, this one was one of the ones used as a "People's Prison," where their hostages were held. Just like any basement, the lighting was minimal, the air thick with a musty smell. This seemed to be a somewhat normal basement: an office with two additional rooms and nothing unusual. However, one room was soundproof and had bars. He was tempted to ask questions but chose to be silent until spoken to. Silence was the art of observance, and here, it was always best to wait until spoken to. Waiting for him, was someone he had never met before. This older man appeared as innocent as one's favorite grandpa, and yet, looks—he was about to find out—were deceiving.

The man spoke, cutting to the heart of the topic. "What solutions have you tonight for us?"

Miguel, still trying to process his surroundings, was taken aback at the abruptness of the questioning without introductions, but he sensed this was someone he didn't question, but did their bidding. Miguel spoke up, "All is well as I said it would be. Sr. Fontes agrees that his family would benefit well if I were allowed a peaceful transition to my next post." The older man rapped his fingers on the wooden arm of his chair, then lazily with his middle finger began to draw imaginary circles over and over on the arm rest. He appeared to be in deep thought and never looked up at him the entire time. Miguel could feel himself tensing up as seconds felt like hours.

Eventually, the man spoke, "You say that with the confidence of a priest saying that the Lord will come again. Seems very arrogant to place so much confidence in the word of a man who isn't one of us. Wouldn't you agree, Sr. De Luna?"

Miguel pondered an acceptable reply. He knew that his words weighed heavily on the outcome of today. He didn't want to end up being "detained" here for an indeterminate amount of time. Detainment should be left up to the hostages only. "Señor, I have been careful with my communication. I can assure you," Miguel conveyed with sincerity. "Sr. Fontes knows that the continued safety of his family solely depends on his anonymity and to the anonymity of our cause; he understood he would be watched and so would his family. If any breach were made, it would mean instant harm or possibly even the death of his entire family!"

The elderly man stood up and walked towards the doorway of one of the rooms. With his back to Sr. De Luna, he spoke not to him but to the Tupamára. "Soldada, soldier, escort him to the street and make it clear to him that he is to do nothing but search for a replacement job." With that he left the room, swinging the door behind him with force. Miguel was surprised how that, of all things, unnerved him most. He could hear her climbing the stairs but had yet to follow.

With growing impatience, the soldada snapped a command to follow: "Viene!"

Turning, Miguel picked up his pace and followed her up the same staircase from earlier. The Tupamára reached for something along the wall in the dim light. Once again, he couldn't see exactly what she touched, but it seemed to release the mechanism connecting to the outer-paneled wall. Just before she did, she first looked through a peephole with the purpose of assuring the room was clear before the final step was taken to exit the bunker. Without a sound, the unlocked secret door slowly and silently popped open. They each took their turn stepping out into the bedroom. Pushing the panel back into place, she readjusted the armoire, wiped any traces of shoe prints or dust, closed the outer door as it had popped open with the movement, and then proceeded to straighten the braided rug on the floor.

The Tupamára methodically went through the motions, continuing to refrain from exhibiting any sort of emotion nor engaging in any conversation with him. Miguel walked back down the same hallway as before, all the while, he was curious why this woman was so cold and devoid of warmth. Christ, she acted like a cold, calculating bitch, and it pissed him off that he was being escorted and bossed around by a freaking woman! After being led out the front gate and without any parting words other than "Find a job," she closed the gate, locked it, slipped the keys back in her pocket, and walked away. That was it: cold, calculating, and to the point. At least, that part was done. He interpreted this visit as a direct message that he would be able to continue in the organization, so long as he found another job, so he believed...

Chapter 9

Peter passed through the hotel's interconnecting door between his suite and the children's rooms. Upon seeing Dane, he instructed, "Hurry up, your mother is waiting for us in the dining room for breakfast. I told her I would drop you all off at school today."

Dane answered, "I'm ready, Dad. Just need to grab my school valise." Peter stood at the door of the suite, ushering his son out. They both walked down the hallway towards the lift, joining the rest of the family downstairs.

As they sat at the table, eating freshly made croissants with apricot jam, eggs, and bacon, Peter made an announcement. "Kids, remember I told you that you would be able to have a dog when we moved here?" That got their attention as the three children snapped their heads in their father's direction.

The boys, Dane and Jack, spoke the loudest "Yes" in unison while Bergen shrieked with excitement. Paula quickly sprang into action with profound embarrassment, hushing them all.

"Okay, okay, don't stress your mother out. This isn't how we behave, is it?"

The children, beginning first with Dane, then Jack, and finishing with Bergen, replied woefully, "No, no, Dad, I'm sorry. We won't ever again." Dane asserted himself saying, "Just, Dad, can we please not have one of those sissy type of small dogs?"

Knowing that was a stretch of the imagination, he continued. "To answer your question, it depends on the breed. I got a call yesterday from a breeder, a breeder of Boxers, to whom I had made an inquiry when we first arrived. She said that a litter of puppies were born yesterday. She has several brindled ones from which I was wanting to choose."

Bergen couldn't resist. "Daddy, when can I hold her?"

"Her?" Jack barked with disgust. "Dad, it's gotta be a boy!"

"Jack, it 'has to be,' not 'gotta,' and Bergen, we will see." said Peter. "They were just born, so we have to give them a few weeks for the mom to be more agreeable to people touching her babies."

Jack spoke up again, "Well, we're in a hotel. They won't let us have one here, will they?"

Peter answered, "Very astute observation. However, the breeder said once the puppy is about four weeks of age, we could bring it home one night a week overnight and feed it with a baby bottle. Your mom and I thought we might sneak it into the hotel, but we would need to get the puppy back the next day quickly to make sure it is getting enough to eat from its mother; if we did everyone would need to make sure that puppy doesn't make any noise."

Bergen busted out with enthusiasm, "Oh, Daddy, this is the bestest day ever!"

Grinning, Peter bent down and gave his little girl a kiss on the top of her head, running his hand gently down the side of her hair, cupping her chin gently in his hand. He didn't have the heart to correct her grammar and squelch her exited enthusiasm.

"Go on now. We have to hurry. Give your mother a kiss goodbye and let's get this show on the road." A big production of hugs and kisses went on as they said their goodbyes to Paula.

The Gray family all walked through the lobby together to the entrance of the hotel where Jose Martinez met them outside. He was the concierge, bellboy, elevator man: you name it. He was a man who wore many hats, for he had worked for the Rambla Hotel since he was a young boy, beginning as a dishwasher and errand boy and then working his way up. Speaking to Mr. Gray, he greeted him first. "Buenos días, Sr. Gray." Then, he nodded and smiled at the kids, saying, "Buenos días, Señores Duny-Jacky, y la bella Señorita, Berrrjeans." The kids got a giggle out of that, for no matter how long they had been there, he had the hardest time pronouncing their names, especially Bergen's. It sounded almost like saying the word bear-jeans. Dane had observed how any name with an e on the end they added a "y" sound to it too; this made his name sound feminine and that he didn't exactly care about. Peter then gave them an admonishing look, and so Dane being the eldest, and ever the protector, grabbed Bergen's hand and squeezed a soft warning of silence, while he bugged his eyes towards Jack with a warning.

Sr. Martinez let Peter know that the car was ready out front and pointed politely with an open palm hand. Suggesting they walk outside to the car followed by a respectful tip to his hat with a partial bow, also a sign of respect, he then handed Peter the keys to his Mercedes. Peter drove down the Rambla, which was the main street following the ocean front. The ocean was beautiful to look at, and many of the homes, he noted, were of a Dutch architectural influence. They were beautiful but odd, being here in Uruguay, seemingly out of place. Turning left onto one of the side streets, Peter drove towards the center of town, first passing through parts of the outskirts. Ahead was the sign indicating "The British Schools" which was a mile away. Entering the school's compound, he pulled up and parked. The boys immediately jumped out while chiming their goodbyes as they ran on to join their friends. Being shy-natured, Bergen fell behind, still having the need to be walked in—at least to the corridor near her classroom. Turning towards her dad, she suggested, "Don't forget to call that lady and tell her I want a girl puppy!"

"I am not sure what is still available, but I do believe there are at least three girls, so I really don't think we will have a problem. Now, give me a hug and scoot on to class." She gave him a quick hug and then, grabbing her valise again, turned towards her classroom where the teacher was waiting at the door. Nearing the door and seeing one her friends, she squealed in her excitement that she was getting a new puppy! Peter smiled, and yet, his heart was heavy, for he originally wanted a dog just for the kids to play with for companionship, but now, what the children didn't realize, was the true significance of having a dog was to have a future alarm system, which consisted of a large, barking dog, which hopefully would announce any nighttime visitors. He was toying with this idea because of the occasional news articles, but then, he had to admit to himself that he was now a bit on edge after listening to Mitrione's speech at the IBA dinner last night, which made the rumors now seem like a possible nightmare.

Should they have moved here? By all evidence, it appeared that the children were adjusting well: they seemed very happy and were already being invited places. Paula, in the meantime, had joined the Women's League, hosted an Ambassador's Ball, and found a dear friend in Anne Schaffer. On the other hand, for him personally, what Peter recalled that Mitrione discussed last night... Wow, that threw him a curve ball! He hadn't been particularly worried before, and yet, he now realized the seriousness of the subject which left him antsy. They hadn't experienced anything but wonderful things since arriving. The people were friendly and kind, the views were gorgeous, the restaurants were fantastic, and the Carrasco neighborhood—he already knew—was where he wanted to live. He was mulling over so many things in his mind that he didn't even realize he had already made his way to the director's office at the school. Speaking to the secretary, he identified himself, "Good morning. If you recall, I am Peter Gray, the father of Bergen, Jack, and Dane Gray. I would like to ask if I might have a word with Dr. Miller, please?" Dr. Nigel Miller was the Director of the British Schools. "I know I do not have an appointment," he continued, "but something came up that I feel most urgent that I might have a word with him?" Dr. Miller's secretary replied with a thick British accent, asking him to please have a seat while she spoke to Dr. Miller. Not very long after she had completed the call did Dr. Miller appear.

"Mr. Gray, how are you? Such a pleasure to see you this morning!" Without stopping, he continued, "So it is my understanding you would like to have a small chat. By all means, come into my office." He gestured for Peter to enter his office. Once the door was closed, Peter began relaying what had transpired at the International Businessmen's dinner the night before. "I see," said Dr. Miller, "grave, very grave indeed. Peter, we have had a few board meetings in the most recent months to discuss the alarming increase of violence and kidnappings, and what effect that could maybe have on our school. For that very reason, we made the decision to hire an additional security guard for the back gate. Naturally, we are aware that foreign children are prized targets for kidnappings. Always has been a sad fact, especially the rich ones. However, I will make all the necessary phone calls requesting an emergency board meeting to discuss this subject further. Perhaps now, there is a reason to modify our strategies and increase our security even further." Peter was pressed to get to work by then, so he thanked Dr. Miller for his time and asked if he would let him know the outcome.

Back in the car, for the moment, Peter needed to quit thinking about this and trust that all would be okay. It was hard to focus on work while presently being distracted by worry. Worry that your children were safe on one side of town and your wife on the other. He was glad Dr. Miller appeared to take his concerns to heart, but the depressing reality was, no matter how much security was put into place, it just might not ever be enough.

Chapter 10

Miguel had cleared the first two hurdles towards landing the position of an upper-level auditor for Pradman Industries. Today, he finally had a scheduled interview with Sr. Peter Gray. This interview would be the second one and the first with Peter. You only arrived at Peter's doorstep if you passed the previous hurdles.

Home base had prepared excellent references and bogus employment histories. Any reference calls would be re-routed to one of the many homes serving as command centers throughout Montevideo. Of course, all his references were confirmed with impeccable reviews. Miguel, now using a new identity, went by the name of Pedro Conche. Originally, while a student at the Universidad de la República in Montevideo, he was approached by the Tupamáros because of his brilliant mind and his leftist views as many young men were being groomed for the role. Presently, this job provided him the chance to redeem himself. Screw the Emilio's of this world; they, to him, were simpleminded, nón-visionary people. He was the mercenary for the lower class. No more would the upper rich crush and oppress people like him, which came from the lower middle class and below. His involvement would last as long as it took to ensure the current corrupt political leaders who, in his mind, no longer had the ability to squander money lining their own pockets.

Standing as Peter walked in, he offered his hand towards him. "Good morning," the two said, greeting one another in unison.

"Please, have a seat." Peter gestured to the chair on the other side of his desk. "Would you like some coffee?"

"No, I just had some before coming. Thank you, sir," said Pedro.

"Your references have checked out well. Your former employers have positive things to say about your contributions to their companies, along with many innovative ideas. So, tell me, Pedro, what is your policy on confidentiality?"

Pedro answered with a sincere thoughtful expression, "Sir, if I may, without confidentiality, without extreme trust in your fellow teammate, then no one should ever hire anyone. Ultimate respect for your clients should be a priority. What benefits them benefits us."

Peter liked what he heard. He liked that he viewed his co-worker as a teammate. This implied unity in his eyes. The young man before him, was in his early thirties, had youth, intelligence, an education, and the more they talked, he was impressed how a young guy had built such a formidable work history; in such a short period of time since finishing the university. Pedro, he also noted had only been in the work force for just seven years. Peter saw a drive in Pedro that reminded him a little of himself as he began his career. The interview continued for another hour.

Taking a brief interval, Peter gave him a tour of the office. As he did, he pointed out the different departments and briefly touched on the main accounts assigned to them for auditing. Besides auditing for businesses, many of the junior auditors had accounts just for preparing tax documents for small businesses and general bookkeeping. Pedro's first interview was a preliminary screening. Normally for auditors, this entailed checking out credentials, determining their level of experience for the areas needed, and then culminated with an auditing exam. This type of exam was grueling which was impossible to finish in days, much less in hours. The exam typically constituted being giving an actual auditing job, recently completed. The candidate would work throughout the day until they were asked to stop. The purpose of the exam was the ability to study their approach to auditing, and to see how accurate their responses were step by step. Peter would review the candidates work. If he approved, it signified that they would have the opportunity of a second interview with Peter, who was the final word on any hire.

Returning to Peter's office after the tour, he asked Pedro to see examples of some of his flow charts and some examples of financial reports that he had been responsible for. He didn't quite have the grasp that Peter did, this was expected due to his limited years of experience, and yet he showed more promise than anyone Peter had interviewed so far. The pressure was on to get a viable source of help that was a quick learner. Business had grown exponentially since Peter took over the office and he needed more help. Unfortunately for Peter, he wasn't aware of the mole working within his very own company. This mole had furnished Mata with all the names of the interviewing candidates, where they lived and the telephone numbers. All but a few low-level performers were paid to go away and the rest were just dummies chosen to purposely blow their interviews. Performing strongly so far, Pedro ticked all the boxes.

Nearing lunch time, Lucia called a longtime Pradman auditor Edson Silva, reminding him that it was time for him to accompany Pedro to lunch. While away, Lucia would collect Pedro's paperwork bringing it to Peter. She also had organized a lunch delivery so he could have a working lunch while he began the tedious task of reviewing what Pedro had accomplished so far that morning.

If you ever had the opportunity to have a meal at a restaurant in a Latin country, it became immediately apparent that time was *not a factor of import!* So, two hours later, Pedro and Edson made their way back to Pradman Industries. The afternoon agenda presented, he now had to navigate through two more business account scenarios. The task was to troubleshoot, balance, and present the results as the final test. One account had some serious infractions that would cause a company serious problems, and the other was just a busy audit with a few unique requirements for a large company. When Peter finished reviewing the paperwork from the first exam, he asked Lucia to bring the paperwork from the first business account Pedro had worked on, and so he began checking this out. Three hours later he asked Lucia to retrieve the work from the afternoon, so that he could review it, even if he wasn't finished; also asking her to serve Pedro some coffee and a small snack while he waited to be summoned.

"Pedro, I thank you for coming. Please have a seat, make yourself comfortable," he gestured to the elegant chair opposite his desk. Pedro was nervously optimistic by his performance so far. Being invited back to Peter's office he hoped was indicative that he would be hired or offered yet a third challenge to remain a contender for the job.

"My decision is rarely made this quickly, but I like what I see. Of all the candidates you proved yourself to be the strongest. I think with some training, teaching you techniques I have developed, you will prove to be a strong asset. The tax season will be upon us soon, and I will need strong reliable auditors to help ease the burden. I would like to offer you the position." Peter looked to see Pedro's expression.

With a smile, he answered, "Yes, I would be honored to work for Pradman Industries! Thank you." Pedro felt like yelling "Yes!" as loud as he could, but he kept his cool demeanor and asked when he would be needed, along with other necessary questions. This was the most prestigious position he had to date, so to say he was enthused was an understatement. "Now, regarding salary," Peter slipped a paper across the desk for him to read. "At the top is the starting salary based on your experience and years of service. On the left side shows years of service versus the potential growth for your salary, pending certain milestones are met. This isn't written in stone as we know the markets change, the economy etc. Do you have any questions?"

Wrapping up this portion of the interview, Pedro was escorted by Lucia to his new office and informed that he could have the rest of the week to set up his office. Lucia passed on the information that he could spend the time familiarizing himself with the first two accounts to which he was assigned, and that he could begin officially first thing Monday morning. Finished, Lucia left, closing his door behind her. Walking over to his new desk, he pulled the chair out and sat down. Propping his feet up on the desk, he raised his hands interlacing his fingers together behind his head, he leaned back as he erupted quietly with laughter.

Chapter 11

Weeks later, on a Saturday morning, a confused hotel attendant had just brought a very odd "breakfast request" to the Gray family's room. The request was typical breakfast fare, followed by an empty bowl and a large quantity of milk, which absolutely perplexed the attendant. It wasn't his position to question, but he thought these Americans were a strange lot. Dutifully, without questions, he set up the breakfast table in the hotel room. Leaving the rolling cart to the side, he left and closed the door. The wicker picnic basket on the bed started to rock a little, and a whimpering could be heard. Paula opened the top and picked the puppy out of the basket. She spoke to the puppy as if it were a real baby.

"You were such a good little girl, Loba! Yes, you were! We can't let them know you are here, can we? No, we can't!" Bergen giggled at that as they both walked through the connecting door into Paula's room.

"Mommy, you're funny," Bergen giggled. Paula let her hold Loba while she made a baby bottle for the puppy. The breeder finally allowed the overnight stay, but early the next morning, she had to be returned promptly to her mom for nursing purposes, being that she was only four weeks old. Paula tied a bib around the neck of the puppy while Bergen held her. Lifting Loba out of Bergen's arms, she cradled the puppy in her arms and proceeded to feed her a bottle, just like a baby.

Carrasco '67

Some of the fear from the night at the IBA dinner seemed to dissipate. Since arriving in Uruguay, nothing really had gone on, so Paula had begun to relax and almost forgot about her earlier fears. Since everything seemed normal; innocently, she reverted to putting it out of sight, out of mind. So, they continued their daily comings and goings, enjoyed the new puppy, and continued searching for their first home.

Chapter 12

Paula found a house in Carrasco. She was ecstatic about it, and so was Peter. The house had belonged to the president of one of the largest carbonated beverage manufacturers. This house had all the bells and whistles that someone on the corporate rise of Peter Gray's level would expect: a beautiful brick home with thick terracotta tiles on the roof, a circular driveway made with huge flagstones, elegant front door with expensive beveled glass, spacious rooms, a beautiful backyard, maid's quarters, a garage and a side driveway entrance for staff to unload groceries straight from the car into the kitchen, which was top of the line. The architect designed the cutest banquette nook that was built into a corner of the kitchen, making mornings very practical if Paula wanted to cook privately for the family and dismiss the cook for the meal. It certainly was a posh neighborhood. Could they want for anything else?

The ship containers had finally arrived with their belongings, and the contents were delivered to the house, allowing them to finally move in. At this juncture, the first order of business on Peter's agenda was finding all the parts and assembling the beds, while Paula searched for the bed linens, pillows, and some necessary kitchen items. The boys were to help Peter assemble the beds, while Bergen helped Paula find what they needed and, after a quick jaunt to the local market for the basics, she began to cook dinner. The rest would be a slow process. The movers sliced open the furniture boxes, and Peter directed them to which room their contents belonged. The following days, while the kids were at school, Paula soldiered on, unpacking box after box, determined to host a party the minute that monumental job was done. She was excited to show off their new home. The day the bicycles were found, however, the boys had another agenda. They pumped air into the tires, tightened the pedals, and then immediately took off to explore the neighborhood. They had waited so long while being cooped up in the hotel, and so Peter said helping with chores could wait as long as their rooms were picked up. The boys came back later, tired and thrilled. They discovered the bowling alley in Arocena wasn't that far from their new home, and they already made plans to go again with money as soon as they were allowed. Life was good!

Chapter 13

Paula turned into their front circular driveway while the boys stood in the yard hammering her to hurry up. The all-important day at the bowling alley had arrived. As she stepped out of the car beginning to retrieve her packages, Jack started in, "Mom, remember you promised we could have extra money for snacks and not just bowling?"

Paula laughed. "Jack, when have I ever forgotten to feed you boys? Let's get inside. You cannot go like this. Go change out of your uniforms, make sure you place your uniforms nicely on the bed for Claudia, and not all over the floor and then you can get going to the bowling alley."

Jack started to complain, but Dane grabbed his arm and drug him down the hall towards their room—ever the diplomat—whispering, "You want to go, don't you? Don't blow it for us! Mom can change her mind, doofus!"

When they were ready to go, Paula handed the money to Dane, being that he was the eldest, and then asked, "Boys, when are you supposed to be home?"

In unison, Dane and Jack answered, "Six o'clock."

"Are you to go anywhere else?"

"No, Mom," they both chanted.

"Good! Glad you remembered. Now, go have fun! Don't forget to look both ways and get off your bike at street corners and walk them across."

"Yes, Mom," said Dane.

"We will," said Jack as they both pedaled off. She still worried as they sped away. Their bikes were different. They stood out like a sore thumb, being that they were American, and painted with bright colors with striping. Since they were so close to the bowling alley, and that they would be going with friends, she felt somewhat comfortable letting them go.

Chapter 14

A Year Later

Time had marched on. Peter was amazed that they were celebrating their first year since arriving in Montevideo. Things had gone relatively smooth since the move, getting the kids adjusted in school and his successful first hire, Pedro. Bergen got her "girl" dog, and the boys had made a lot of friends in the neighborhood. Even Paula had trained the dog to wipe its front paws, walk forward, and wipe her back paws before entering the house! Paula also had made her mark within the British Women's League of Uruguay and had made many friends as reflected by her social life. Life was good.

There were so many beautiful places to explore, restaurants to try, and still they continued to find different things to do. The people were so warm and friendly. Peter never felt better than he did now, both professionally and personally. He had just about decided that this was the place he wanted to raise the kids permanently, and to grow old with Paula. Musing aside, Peter was pumped. After going back and forth for some time, he finally secured one of his biggest goals. He had landed the contract linking Pradman Industries and Fontes Industries as their newest account. It was the crowning jewel of all his achievements! Emilio was to arrive shortly to finalize signatures, but before Peter was going to take him to lunch and then give him a tour of the different departments. Lunch was at a local hotel, which was one of Peter's favorites of the local hot spots. Being that he was quite the regular, they always catered to him, making it easy for him to get in and out quickly during the workday. For this reason, he tended to go there often. They feasted over some excellent

Paella and finished off with an after-meal coffee, with flan for dessert.

Upon returning to work Peter began by taking Emilio by the auditing department. As they toured the different departments, Peter would stop, explain exactly what their specific jobs were, and introduce as many as he could that were available to meet him. Across the corridors from where they stood, there was another office. Emilio saw a profile that looked very familiar, but he dismissed the thought as ludicrous. Peter observed Emilio looking in Pedro's direction. Thinking he showed interest, he offered to introduce him to Pedro the minute he was off the long-distance call with a client. Wrapping up the tour they headed back to Peter's office. The profile of that man he'd seen kept eating away at Emilio. If it was Miguel, he would warn Peter that this guy was not who he said he was. If possible, he would try again to get a glance. A chance came as they worked their way back to Peter's office. Emilio was blown away! He couldn't believe he was seeing that scumbag again! Peter had meant to introduce them, but things didn't work out as planned for the business call ran long. Thank God for that! It was imperative that he warn Peter before the day's end. He doubted that he would have hired someone of that caliber if he had had all the facts.

After they returned to Peter's office, Emilio asked, "May I close the door?"

"Absolutely, may I prepare you a coffee?"

"No, no thank you," Emilio said. "Listen," speaking softly almost at a whisper, he asked, "How well do you know this man you call Pedro?"

Peter replied, "Well he is a recent hire, great references, sharp, eager to learn and a hard worker. Why do you ask, if you don't mind my asking?"

"Peter I will answer all this later. I am going back to my office. Stay here, I will call you the minute I get there." With that he thanked him for the tour and took off as if he could not wait to get away. Odd-how very odd.

Chapter 15

The mood amongst the ex-pats was euphoric over Peter's firm landing the Fontes account. Celebrations were being held at the Jones's house later that evening. Being a small, multi-international community, getting together meant so much to all of them. It was a bit like having a surrogate family when most of their loved ones lived in other countries, so everyone looked forward to the times that they could gather. George and Barbara Jones wanted to host this evening to celebrate their close friend, Peter Gray's success.

George Jones held a high position within the British Embassy which allowed them to have a huge home. In the back was an enormous yard, a custom pool with a catwalk bridge that crossed over the center, and a soccer field set up to the side. It was one of the many grand perks of being with the Embassy which benefited the entire family. They could also be entertained by going to the basement of the Embassy whenever they wanted and watch any of the latest English or American movies too, including football games! The perks were great! Bobby, Barbara and George's son, was the same age as Dane, and they had hit it off well when Dane first moved to Uruguay. It was a mutual, great-buddy-bonding, so to speak. They were avid football and soccer players, so tonight was right up their alley! The adults had their area, and the kids had an entire area of the yard designated for them with junk food to eat to their hearts' desire: hot dogs, burgers, pizza, and ice cream! This was not always a good combination since the kids had a football game set for right after dinner in which all the school-age kids would play. The evening was not about rules, but about having fun and making memories.

Meanwhile, over in the adult area, there was a huge patio with lights strung across the trees lighting the patio. Tables were set up all around. George stood up to make a toast. "To our friend, Peter Gray, and his beautiful wife, Paula, who we still do not understand how he got her to say yes!" This got some good-natured whistles and catcalls, sparking a lot of laughter amongst the group. George continued, "We are so glad that life brought you here. You have already made your mark; you are definitely a powerhouse to be reckoned with, and we look forward to many years of friendship, alongside our business relationship as well. Not to mention seeing your wife and all, sure makes up for your ugly puss…" Raising his glass, he yelled out, "Here, here!" Everyone had busted out laughing and stood to reciprocate by raising their glasses with their standing ovation—ironic since he was also a good-looking man.

Pointing at George, Peter wagged his finger as he mouthed while laughing, "I'll get you!" George was most definitely the comedian of the group! When dinner finished, groups broke up into mixed pairs to play croquet away from the flying football area.

The boys were three-fourths into their game of football with Dane's team winning by a touchdown. The ball was snapped, and Bobby caught the pass. He charged down the field. This group of boys was made up of young, competitive athletes!

Bobby collided with another player, fighting to maintain his balance, while trying to keep the play in bounds. It was at that moment from the right side that Dane tackled him, following the first collision, denying him a first down. The combined impact of the first hit, then Dane and hitting the ground dislocated Bobby's kneecap instantly. Down on the ground, he was writhing in pain. Dane was horrified, seeing the gruesome sight of his kneecap. Seeing the large bulge on the side of Bobby's leg was more than

Dane could handle; he had a weak stomach for injuries and blood. He didn't want the fellow guys to know, but Dane felt like he was going to throw up!

Bergen started yelling, "Bobby's hurt!"

Dane looked at Bobby and stated, "I'm getting your dad!"

Bobby, groaning in pain, answered, "Hurry."

He felt awful. Jack, having heard the commotion, approached with his buddy to see what was going on. Hearing his brother's voice, Dane looked up and asked him to go get Marco's dad. Jack asked him "Why?"

"He's a doctor—that's why—and get Bobby's dad too. That way, I can stay here with him!"

"Okay, okay, you don't have to snap!" Jack fired back.

A few minutes went by before Dr. Marcos Savério showed up. It wasn't pretty. Dr. Savério told Bobby that he needed to reposition his kneecap back into place, warning him that it would hurt. Bobby tried to be manly, but this was more than he was able to handle. Tears streamed down his face as Dr. Savério popped the kneecap back in place. Bobby angrily wiped the tears off his face. He was angry that this happened, knowing it would keep him from being able to play football for a while, but more so because he just humiliated himself by crying in front of the guys. His leg was immobilized with a splint and some torn bed sheets Mrs. Jones had cut into long strips. By then, others were around to help Dr. Savério. Mr. Jones, Peter Gray, and even Dane assisted lifting Bobby up so that they could take him to his parents' car. Bobby groaned in pain as they carried him, even though they were trying carefully not to jostle him. George tried to comfort his son. It was rough seeing him in so much pain, but they needed to transport him to the hospital to make sure he had not torn his ACL or fractured anything as well. Bobby was placed in the back seat of the car so he could extend his leg and a pillow that was brought by one of the maids was placed behind his back so he could lean back comfortably.

Peter turned to Barbara and George. "Don't worry, we'll take care of your guests and see to everyone." Barbara and George thanked him as they climbed into the car and left with their son. Dane had asked to go, but Peter and Paula both told him that this was not the time and that, when possible, he would get to see him.

Due to the hosts of the party having to depart, the evening ended abruptly. Meanwhile, the Jones' nanny corralled the younger children to keep an eye on them while the staff, with many of the guests, helped clean up. Each guest present, in their own way, wanted to feel like they were supporting George and Barbara by helping. One by one, each couple collected their children, quietly saying their goodbyes with Paula and Peter seeing them all out.

Chapter 16

What a rat race driving to work could be. *One thing about the Uruguayan culture,* Peter thought, *Boy, do they like to use their horns a lot.* God forbid you take too long once a light turned green to move forward! He had a headache that morning, so the honking was not helping. Normally, he didn't drink much, but the number of cocktails he had last night was in keeping with the celebration! Too bad it was cut short. *Well, fun's over, back to work, as they say.* Today's agenda was the weekly meeting, but before that, he had asked his secretary to send some flowers to Barbara and George, thanking them for the evening, hoping this would make Barbara feel a little better. He also asked Lucia to pick up a gift for Bobby as he recovered.

The meeting was about to start in the conference room. Peter caught up to Miguel, aka Pedro, as he was walking in. The conference table was a sleek modern style, made from the wood of Eucalyptus trees, with huge chunky pieces of raw wood for the legs. The chairs were also elegantly appointed with tall backs, and soft cushions in a matching shade of brown were on the seats to absorb the brunt of sitting on wood for potentially long meetings. Water and coffee carafes were placed strategically down the center of the elongated table so that all could have easy access. Glasses, coffee cups, and saucers were placed to the top right of each seating area, as if set for a dinner table. Bowls of mixed peanuts were also provided since most of their meetings tended to over run their scheduled time frame, and the final touch was the meeting agenda booklets with the company logo in silver offsetting the navy-blue booklet, carefully centered on the table directly in front of each chair.

One by one, the rest of the auditors filed in with a couple of the company lawyers, and the meeting began. Oscar, one of the senior auditors, brought up the first order of business. "I have noticed our numbers have been off on one of our accounts bank-wise that is, and yet, all the paperwork indicates as though things are in order on reports. I want to get to the bottom of this and all present will continue to investigate this until we have an answer. I don't care for sloppy work." Pedro looked up and just gave a blank look of indifference yet feigning concern. Inside... boy, inside was a different thing. He was feeling that jittery anxiousness one got when you were at risk of getting in serious trouble. Oscar continued, "Specifically, if you skip the intro and will turn to page fifteen, we can always get back to the rest of the topics. Detailed is the individual entries and all the column totals versus the transferred monies, acquisitions, monies paid, invested, returns, sold shares, net profits of the company and actual accountabilities from the bank side." The meeting droned on, repetitively going over all aspects associated with this issue. Oscar didn't get to where he was without being someone that was attentive to every single detail. This is what made him good; this is what made him great in his field. Finally, the last page of the agenda, was to be the itinerary for the future actions in the company.

Peter turned to Juan, a junior auditor, asking, "Do you have anything to add?"

Juan answered, "No, not really. Nothing different than what was already covered. We just haven't had the manpower to give our undivided attention to the money discrepancies since it is tax season, and the Mendelsohn account has been consuming our time. We were hoping now that Peter had brought on a few extra accountants, that we could reassign a few men to focus solely on this problem."

Oscar asked Peter, "Who all has worked on this account? I am seeing initials of several I recognize but the PDC, is that Pedro's?"

"Yes, if you will recall he began with us a few months ago and also Erik Jorgensen, who has been a tremendous asset with our International Danish accounts."

They continued covering several other minor subjects, including organizing topics for a pamphlet template for new foreign hires. The purpose of the pamphlet was to cover all kinds of topics such as best places for groceries, car repairs, schools, dealing with the real estate market and, lastly, security and the Tupamáro threat. Most of Pradman Industries upper-level hires were originally from many different countries. Being that they were an international firm, they needed bilingual employees from all walks of life. It was important to understand the culture of the person you were doing business with, just as much as one knew their language. Therefore, it was equally vital to give them the necessary tools to wade through the uncertainties of a new country by helping them acclimate. The sooner the new hires settled in with their family, the quicker they became focused and productive. After devising a strategy regarding the investigation due to accounts in question and organizing the draft of the new hire pamphlet they adjourned just in time for a late lunch.

Descending the granite staircase instead of using the elevator, Pedro chose to leave the building in this manner to avoid small talk with anyone that was in attendance of the meeting. He remained deep in thought. Red flags for him were raised when the accounts he had worked on were brought up during the meeting. Not overly concerned just yet, he believed he had covered his tracks; this was just another classic example of his overrated sense of self. He was convinced those idiots did not have a clue! At lunch, he ordered a big steak and a beer, and began to read the paper. Newspapers were the best! On a grand scale, messages could be passed across Uruguay quickly if needed. No method was untapped for the Tupamáros. Today, he needed to see if there were any cryptic messages that he needed to know about as he focused on the different story lines in the newspaper. If there was anything, it normally would be thrown in the human-interest section. Unbeknownst to him, today would be his ultimate unveiling!

Chapter 17

Gray was on the move, heading across town to meet with Sr. Fontes. He was nervous due to Emilio being so vague on the phone call yesterday. The minute he got back to his office he had wasted no time calling him back, leading him to believe that there possibly could be an issue affecting their recent partnership. It was a few minutes before two the following afternoon, when Peter stepped off the elevator on the floor that housed the directors of Fontes Industries. He walked straight ahead towards the receptionist's desk, announcing himself for his scheduled meeting. Confirming he had an appointment, the receptionist directed him to the sitting area near Emilio's secretary, Marta, who instantly acknowledged him with a greeting and a smile. Marta explained that if he wanted, he could enter Emilio's private elevator which opened directly into his office and wait for him there. Marta punched in a code, which allowed the doors to sweep open. Entering, the door after a couple of seconds began to close and began moving upward. He took in the interior of the elevator. There were no buttons to select any floors, for it only opened into Emilio's office so there wasn't a need. The intricate wooden accents on the molding within the building carried through, matching the inside of the elevator in a more delicate diminutive form, adding to the overall elegance of the surroundings.

Not long after Peter sat down in the chair by his desk, the elevator doors closed only to return with Emilio. Stepping out he greeted him, "Peter, so glad you could come. I do not want to waste your time or mine, so I want to get directly to the point. I specifically asked you what you knew about the young man I saw in your office yesterday for a reason."

"You mean Pedro, Pedro Conche, the one I mentioned."

Continuing, Emilio added, "Yes, Peter, we caught him embezzling in our company and I don't know how else to break this to you, um- he's a Tupamáro! Were you aware of that?"

Peter was dumbfounded as he processed that information. Seeking composure, he paused a bit before speaking. "How do you know that? Are you sure?"

"Unfortunately, I am positive!" Emilio replied stoically. "I too hired him a while ago, but he was caught stealing monies, and I had to let him go. I could not fire him. I had to amicably let him go for the sake of the safety of my family. I just had to warn you. Obviously, I was threatened and so was my company. I didn't want history to repeat itself. Since I had caught him, it did give me a small leverage since he doesn't want publicity nor to be detained by the police. My family, however, is still being watched; I feel like I am being watched regularly at home and at work. We are living in a regular fishbowl. I don't want this for you, for your family. These people are dangerous, Peter, very dangerous. Be very careful if he is working for you, I can bet you he is already doing damage and it is up to you to thwart that with damage control. The trick is finding out to what extent he had infiltrated, where, and the problems that he has caused so far."

"Get advice from your bosses and please do not let Miguel—as I knew him to be or, as you call him, Pedro—know that we ever had this conversation! Will you give me your word? He has threatened my family. I will not risk their safety!"

Peter got up slowly and began to walk with restless energy. "You absolutely do not need to fear for your family because of me. Remember I also am a family man. This actually makes sense. I have been questioning some things and couldn't quite put my finger on it. This could very well be the missing piece to the puzzle. So, your coming in has saved me possibly a lot of wasted time. I've noticed money has been disappearing in small but inconsistent quantities." Peter mentioned, "Thank you so very much. I know this was very difficult for you. I'll let you know what comes of this, but this gives me a starting point at least so that I will begin checking all of the accounts associated with Pedro."

Emilio stayed long enough to give Peter a better understanding of the types of accounts Pedro had been assigned at his company. Next, he went over what they had discovered since he left and the conclusions they arrived at - how he managed to pull this embezzlement off. Borrowing Emilio's phone, he called back to the office. Speaking to Lucia he gave explicit instruction's not to talk to anyone about what he was about to say, and to go directly to Jairo's office. He wanted her to tell him that he was on his way back and that it was imperative that he wait for him so they could speak. This became the first step, a starting point. He would remain hot on Pedro's trail. Peter took the opportunity, not missing the chance of trying to obtain one of Emilio's accounts in spite of the situation they were in. The men had covered all that needed to be discussed for one day, so they decided to call it a day. Sr. Fontes returned to his office at Fontes Industries, and Peter returned to work, hot on the trail of Pedro.

Fortunately for Peter, no pretenses were needed regarding the scheduled meeting, for senior partners conducted their meetings every Monday, so nothing seemed out of the norm. He worked like a madman all weekend, bringing in only Jairo to help from the legal aspect. They had both come by taxi because they did not want to alert anyone of their presence in the building. All documentation pertaining to Pedro was collected and categorized. All his activities, as best as they could trace, were painstakingly accounted for. Peter and Jairo split the list of all the company lawyers from the different companies they served and the senior partners at Pradman. One by one they reached out alerting them that an emergency meeting was scheduled at eight o'clock in the morning. They were clear that any conflicting appointments must be canceled, and that all summoned needed to be in attendance. It was a monumental task to expect all would be in attendance, but they did their best to convey how crucial this meeting was for the firm. They both managed to compile a vast amount of pertinent, detailed information, which they believed would help ascertain which breaches were actively in process or already had already been breached.

Once again, those relevant to the meeting filed into the conference room, and once the cordial greetings had been exchanged, Peter began the meeting behind closed doors. "Gentlemen, I came from a meeting with Emilio Fontes on Friday. No explanations are necessary as to who he is or how important this is to our firm as we desire to maintain him as one of our biggest clients to date. "I unfortunately bear bad news. It seems using the headhunters for my search for an auditing assistant was a horrible mistake. The man that I hired, Pedro Conche, is an active Tupamáro! He also has another alias formally known as Miguel de Luna when he worked for Emilio Fontes."

Sr. Jorges, a senior partner with Pradman Industries, interjected, "What?! Are you sure?"

"Unfortunately, yes. Emilio Fontes was the one that let me know about his involvement. If you recall he was on my agenda last Friday for a meeting. It was during the tour that he noticed Pedro at his desk. After I completed the tour and we were back in my office, he divulged the unsettling information. Not wanting to stay a minute longer, he asked that I stay put until he returned to his office; he stated he would call immediately. It was in this phone call that he asked me to meet as soon as possible in his office. He filled me in on every little detail of all his activities while at Indústria Fontes."

Sr. Jorges once again interjected "How is this possible? Surely, he must be mistaken."

Rubbing the back of his neck, Peter felt one of those doozies of a headache coming on. He had to get through this meeting— hopefully without it affecting his vision. Whenever he got these bad headaches, his vision could be messed up for hours at a time. Wouldn't that be great?

"Gentleman, it is very much true. The reason he kept it under wraps was due to whom he was dealing with. He requests total anonymity, out of fear for the safety of his family. He has already been threatened. Out of respect for our long working relationship, he wanted us to know also for our very own protection. Now, you know why I insisted the lawyers attend. We need advice on how to proceed. Jairo, what do you say?" Peter directed the question to one of his company lawyers, Jairo Castellan.

Jairo proceeded to drop a bomb shell, "We cannot fire him!"

"What? Why?" said Sr. Jorges. "I don't want that type here. He will ruin everything I have worked for, everything my father worked for!"

"It is exactly for that reason. We do not need bad press, and as of right now, we do not have any concrete evidence," Jairo said. "What we have is hearsay, and in a court of law, that would be thrown out. We must have concrete proof before we make any moves, and this has not been established as of yet. If we have something to pin on him, we can fire him legally."

Peter added, "These people are cunning… calculated… They have people on board just as sharp as we are. Let me remind you we are not mercenaries or soldiers of any kind; we push pencils. We must be patient and reduce all access to bank accounts and anything of great substance without his knowing we suspect him. We must operate this way, or it could be detrimental to us. Only when we have something concrete, as Jairo suggested, do we move forward. None of us want our families or anyone here at work to be harmed. We must be careful plotting our next moves. Please, study these reports I have handed you. We all must look for anything that we might have overlooked. We must not act on impulse. We must continue as though naught were amiss. However, we are under the microscope, must I remind you, and this must change. We will assign Pedro to several bogus accounts that we create: one seemingly a major one and another few minor ones which he will be unable to damage. All the while, we will monitor him: his every step will be followed and documented as to how he is managing to operate right under our noses, in case he tries to mess with any other accounts."

The meeting drug on as they created the bogus accounts, setting up false contacts, logos, purchase orders, and banking logs. It was well into the wee hours of the morning when they felt they had things relatively in place. During the meeting, Peter had sent out for food from a local eatery that was known for being open at odd hours so they could eat while they worked. After a little more tweaking, they would be ready. Then, the waiting would begin. Patience was a definite virtue, and this would be their way of catching him in the act. So, by the ample amount of rope being supplied, he eventually would trip up and be hung by his own actions. At least he hoped, and when he did, Pradman and Fontes Industries would be there to make sure the rope did not give any slack!

Chapter 18

Three weeks later, at precisely 3:20 in the afternoon, Peter received the first of several phone calls. Apparently, it didn't take long before Pedro's comings and goings began to unravel. One of the senior partners of Fiesta Rójo, a certain Fernando Magia was on the phone and none too pleased. He began by saying, "Peter, I understand that you sent in an addendum regarding the underpayment error listed on our tax return. Even though we have already corrected the issue, it seems that your employee, Señor. Conche, has another agenda that I do not believe you are aware of. I would have called earlier, but we had one last meeting with our lawyers about this, after I terminated a phone call with Señor. Conche. I wanted to make sure I was proceeding with their knowledge before doing anything."

"Wait a minute," Peter blurted out, "seriously? Fernando, what are you talking about?"

"I received a phone call last week from Pedro." He hesitated, his words catching in his throat, but he managed to go on. "Peter, he is blackmailing us! He said that he will not report us to the IRS and to the Board of the International Business Association if we provide him with 20,000 US dollars in small bills. That is what I am saying. I believe that is extortion, is it not? I want that man turned into the authorities as soon as possible, or I guarantee you we will take our business elsewhere. I am giving you the benefit of the doubt since our company has been doing business with yours even long before you arrived. To be exact, it has been eighteen years, and we have had full confidence in your company—at least, we did until now. I do not need this blackmail against the integrity of our company. Understood?"

Peter cleared his throat. "Understood," he replied, "I appreciate your giving us the benefit of doubt due to our long-standing history. I assure you the matter *will be* rectified." Peter had a hard time with his emotions. It made him sick on one hand, yet on the other, he was pleased they finally had something solid to pin on him. Realizing he paused, he resumed his train of thought vocally, "Please, accept my assurances that this matter will be resolved, and there will not, I assure you, be any negative repercussions on your behalf. Recent events made us aware of Señor. Conche and we at Pradman Industries assure you that the matter will be dealt with and resolved to your satisfaction!"

Señor. Magia interjected, "I will send our team of lawyers over and my accountant that manages the Fiesta Rójo account. I need peace of mind, make sure you allow them to work with your men. I trust that your word will remain solid?"

"Of course! Please, this would be most welcome. Just let me know as soon as you know the day and time, and I will make sure my men are here, ready to work. It will be good to have both sides together and on the same page. Both sides legally need to be on the same page."

After the phone call ended, Peter felt rather defeated; never in his imagination did he think that, in his lifetime, he would be entangled in a situation such as this! To him, it was a personal humiliation and a negative blot on his career. Most people got up and went to work, worrying about did I forget to pay my bill, or did I remember to send my wife flowers for her birthday? Him? No! Of course, not that would be considered normal. He went to work to hire a terrorist!

Another emergency board meeting was held at Pradman Industries several days later. Peter wanted him out, but several of the senior auditors were reluctant to fire him. They too were scared for their families. So he came up with the idea of inviting Emilio to speak briefly at a meeting. He felt by him sharing directly what he knew and seeing his obvious disdain for the man, that this, perhaps would sway the board towards making a definitive decision regarding firing Pedro. Emilio only stayed long enough to say his peace. When he finished speaking, he excused himself leaving the rest of the meeting in the hands of Peter, the board, and the lawyers.

"Twice in three weeks is twice too many," voiced Enrique Cabral, another senior partner at Pradman's, speaking to those that remained in the conference room.

"I am not concerned about anything but our reputation. Financially, we can recoup the damages, but what we cannot recoup is loss of our reputation and the confidence that security and privacy of our clients' companies are indeed safe in the hands of the auditors at Pradman. Pedro is to be removed immediately so that we can show our clients our moral stance, and then, we can begin to repair this damaging blow! I want that ass out of here! That is an order from your senior partner!"

Peter dared to speak up, "I am alarmed by the turn of events, and I do agree the longer we have him here, the more damages will mount. This was like having a worm in a bowl full of apples, never knowing where it would end up and how much internal damage it inflicted as well." Peter added, "I am just concerned. We have made progress compiling evidence, but I am unsure that we have enough to hold against him. I worry if we are acting prematurely."

Jairo took over as head legal counsel during the meeting, "No Peter, you are not premature about this, he needs to go. My suggestion is wait until tomorrow. When he arrives, you will tell him what we know and terminate him. Afterwards, he will be escorted out, and a call will be made to Señor. Magias, letting him know that Pedro was terminated. I cannot speculate what the outcome might be: it's one or the other. Either he will want to remain anonymous or retaliate—we must be prepared either way. My suggestion is to implement a hiring freeze for any new employees for an indeterminable amount of time. This will give us the ability to regroup and see if there are any other employees subject to suspicion. Pedro might have an accomplice within our walls. I am not sure of this, but we need to eliminate that as a possible threat. If all in agreement, say, 'Aye.'"

"Aye," they all said in unison.

"Know this, by his being fired," Jairo continued, "the potential of any of you becoming a target increases exponentially. Do not underestimate anyone else as well. Before the meeting, I drew up an idea for a plan of action as detailed in the briefs before you. I do want to go over this and accept all comments. I want to emphasize that before we go into that, all of you, and especially you Peter, since you are directly involved, are to conduct all business within our building minimizing any outside vulnerability, whenever possible. My advice, do not conduct business where you must travel to our clients' businesses. I know this is asking a lot and many may not like this. We will cross that bridge if it becomes an issue. Last, tomorrow I will be available for anything, and I expect everyone to be here just in case Peter needs assistance. Peter, if he reaches out again, keep it simple and do not let him know what we know. Once he has been terminated if he communicates with you let us handle him. Everybody, go home, get some sleep, we have a big day ahead of us."

Chapter 19

Peter left early for work. He was exhausted to say the least. Most people had more than two hours of sleep. Lucia was dependably punctual, so Peter waited by her desk asking her to hurry in, for he had a lot to discuss. Without delay, she followed him into his office with a pen and a tablet. He brought her up to speed, carefully explaining exactly what her role would be from here on out.

One by one, the employees of the building began arriving as did Pedro. Lucia did exactly what she was instructed to do and let him know that Sr. Gray wanted to see him. He looked as if his skin had an immediate reaction, prickling at the back of his neck—a sinking apprehension hit him in the gut. However, he remained expressionless, as he was admitted into Peter's office. Following a short rap on the door a few minutes later, Jairo joined them. Pedro observed Peter's body language, noting that he was tense. Peter cut him off as he tried to greet them. "Sit down, Pedro—or whatever your real name is."

"What—what's going on?"

Once again, Peter cut him off. "Listen, I am not one for idle chitchat, and I won't begin to beat around the bush, so I'll get to the point. The purpose of this impromptu meeting is to make you aware that we know what you stand for, where your loyalties lie, and apparently what you have been up to within these walls and Indústria Fontes. Is this clear enough for you?" Glaring at Pedro, he kept on, "It has been brought to our attention who you really are." Pedro's eyes darted back and forth between Peter and Jairo. Both sides trying to read each other. Peter and Jairo focused on Pedro's body language and facial expressions. Pedro remained stoic; it was an ingrained response as he felt more in control, plus he had been trained for these types of situations. In most situations, this procured him more time to react. In the event things went south, he had a backup plan: a gun which was kept in his briefcase for 'emergency purposes.' "Is there anything you would like to share with us that you have been up to, Señor Conche?" Peter said acidly.

"It seems you have convicted me without a trial, Mr. Gray. Isn't that rather un-American? You Americans boast on freedom of speech, isn't that right? Innocent, I believe, until proven guilty?"

"That's providing that the innocent isn't caught in the act! Enough of this mierda. You have been caught misappropriating funds on one of our accounts and that is reason for immediate termination. So, I will keep this simple, we have our proof, we have our answers. Collect your things, you are as of this moment terminated from Pradman!"

Stunned considering Pedro normally was the one in control, he felt cornered, which inadvertently brought out the ugly in him. It was naturally easy to surmise why he never had any successful personal relationships—call it the anti-social defect of which sociopaths were made. Most people in this line of work weren't exactly cut out to mingle amongst society. Sociopaths usually cared less and were devoid of pathos. If someone was in the way, they soon would be reassigned positions, for the good or the bad.

Pedro stood up to leave then froze for a second, pivoting slowly until he again faced Peter. "Just letting you know by the way; we are very much not done. I don't really think you know what I am capable of and what it truly would mean to you to *'send me away,'* do you? I have means to make you regret these types of impulsive decisions."

"Impulsive?" Peter said with contempt. "Impulsive or not, your position has been terminated! Your moral fiber and work ethics here at Pradman Industries was found lacking, and I *will not* have the likes of you here compromising our good name by embezzling our clients' accounts. Just grab your crap and get out!" Purely disgusted, he rendered a hand gesture in the air as if pushing him away.

Seething with anger, Pedro wanted to lash out, but remained impassive, biding his time. He despised foreigners with a passion. It was enough to keep up the charade for the cause, but now Pedro swore his vengeance on him and it would be exactly where it counted. Mr. Gray was known as a family man—well, perhaps, not for long, not when he was through with him, more like devoid of a family.

Chapter 20

It is said that patience is a virtue. Unfortunately for Pedro, he fell short in that respect. His disquiet was building daily as he awaited news from somebody— anybody for that matter— affiliated with his sub-group. Always in the dark, he was pressed to know when or by whom a communication might arrive, thus ensuring the protection and the continued anonymity within the ranks of their Marxist, urban- guerrilla organization. The group did not play games, but if one considered manipulating and toying with victims a game, then this was exactly the type of play he looked forward to, especially when it involved the lives of the Família Gray, which presently so happened to be his retaliatory obsession!

What a sick, twisted bastard! Several weeks had passed. By now, Pedro felt he should have received orders. Being antsy, he decided to burn up some of his idle energy by going for a jog. Standing on the stoop of his place, he bent down to secure the laces on his tennis shoes. Dismissing the benefit of a warm-up, he took off. Turning at the corner, he headed further into the residential area to avoid the traffic of people. Loners never cared much for people. It required too much. It required what Miguel wasn't willing to give. There are basic requirements, such as manners, idle chitchat, and especially affection, the latter he had no use for either unless it benefited him. Sweat beaded on his forehead and upper lip. He got off by the endorphins as they kicked in. This gave him a false sense of invincibility, of power. A good workout for him was about a five-mile jog. Next to his missions, the only thing that had equal standing of importance was his workouts. Pumping his arms and legs, he moved up one of the biggest hills in the barrio. As he crested the top, he turned around, noticing the tall grass blowing in the wind and how all the buildings below were smaller in stature from his vantage point. Not wanting to cool down too fast, he started a slower pace as he began his descent, using a different direction. Upon reaching the bottom of the hill, he began his cool down phase for the rest of the way back. He took a short cut across the field below, and then he descended the shorter hill where it intersected with the main road further down near his home. As he approached his place, he watched a young beggar child ring his doorbell. Getting closer he summoned the child over. The child asked him if he was Miguel, all the while insisting that the letter in his hand could only be given to Miguel and no one else! Leaning forward, Miguel yanked the note from the boy's small hand, leaving him shaken in a panic. "You've delivered your note. Now get!" His barking totally unnerved the child to the extent he backed away, flinching in fear. Tripping as he walked backwards, the boy regained his footing, pivoted and then took off running. Amused by scaring the boy, he chuckled as he entered his living room. He used his foot to swing the door shut behind him, leaving his hands free to tear open the envelope.

The note read, *Come to the Plaza at 9:00.* No other instructions or where it originated from were included. When summoned in a delivered note, it meant one did not fail to appear. Flipping his zippo lighter open with his calloused thumb, he flicked the gear until a flame popped to life. Lighting the note on one corner, he gazed at the ember, mesmerized as it came to life. Angling the paper in different directions, he controlled the burn to avoid getting burnt. Deep in thought, he watched the paper slowly disappear. As the note reduced in size, the flame's heat increased and the early sensations of discomfort were felt, so he tossed the remnants into a bowl, where it soon burned out.

Not waiting to ensure that the flame was completely out, he got up and began stripping off his clothes, throwing them down as he went. Stepping into the shower, he jerked the shower head to a better angle and lathered up. He wasn't the type that lingered in the shower, he always got the job done and cut off the water. Doing a half-assed job at toweling his body, he walked into his bedroom, throwing the dingy white towel to the floor. The built-in closets filled one entire wall. Opening the second set of closet doors, he grabbed some underwear and socks out of the drawer and took a couple of hangers from above, which held up a thin black turtleneck and some slacks. He released the clothing from their confinement on the hangers and cast the hangers to the floor, as he had the towel earlier. Once dressed, he slipped his wallet in his back pocket, picked up his keys, and headed out for his encounter.

Meetings were always such clandestine feats. His curiosity always piqued at the anticipation of who his contact might turn out to be. He had always hoped it would be someone he knew, but up until now, it was always a stranger. Sitting at his usual table, he waited, all the while knowing that he was being watched and that his contact would be there as soon as they determined he was not followed. Not being sure what the topic at hand would be, he hoped that this would be the go ahead for retaliation measures towards Señor Gray, who he now mentally dubbed "The Imperialist Pig." He wished he could just blow a hole in his head. This measure would be even more gratifying if it were done in front of his wife, but he knew the operation had to go off inconspicuously. A man approached casually and sat down. He looked rough around the edges, as if he led a simple life. Pedro was surprised when an eloquent voice began to speak with an upper crust Castilian accent. His orders were given. A future mission was mapped out and he was given the green light on making covert communications with his target Mr. Gray. It was also ascertained exactly what he could say and the limits as to how persuasive he could be. The man glanced down at his coffee cup, feigning as if he was really into the preparation of it, all the while dictating his instructions. He added sugar, swirled the cup with the spoon, and laughed while looking at Pedro. Pedro played right along. They stayed long enough to wrap things up, shook hands, and parted ways.

Back at home, Pedro opened and slammed drawers, pulling items out and stuffing them into a knapsack. Packing finished, he closed the closet doors and threw the knapsack over his shoulder while grabbing his keys off the bed. He made sure all was secured before locking the front door and left to catch a bus. The main bus station was located a block away from the closest city bus line stop. After ten minutes in line, he purchased a ticket to the neighboring town of Pando. Business was business. He was asked to survey the city of Pando for a future mission. This meant mapping out the city and its businesses and observing the comings and goings of the general populace. The mission was to eventually cut off all roads to Pando and to take over the town. There, he would have the ability to make phone calls that would not be tracked back to him, so his first order of business was to find a phone booth to let his head cell leader know that he arrived. After the call, he walked around town before eventually settling on a simple hotel, checking in under yet another assumed name. It was nothing to write home about, but it was simple enough that he would be forgotten after he left. He chose this particular hotel since it seemed to be the busiest. The worker was visibly overworked having to multitask solo. Since he was working so distractedly, once checked in, Pedro would be but a fleeting memory. His reward tonight for doing this side job was the go ahead to make the initial threatening contact towards Peter Gray.

Chapter 21

Peter stood at the window, looking out while adding sugar to his coffee cup and saucer Lucia had just handed him. The bone-colored china was of a fine quality: a slender silver rim around the edge. Just the words "Pradman Industry" were written beneath their logo. Now was the end of the busiest quarter of the year. Long hours plus the stress of damage control these last few weeks had really made him long for a vacation! Unfortunately, the kids were still in school, and the situation he found himself in did not bode well for taking time off, so that was not going to happen.

The phone on his desk rang. "Mr. Gray?" Lucia said meekly. "A Señor Célsio Marcos is on the phone for you. Will you take the call?"

Not recognizing the name, Peter asked, "Do I know him?"

Lucia replied, "I do not believe so. He appears to be a prospective new client wanting a basic audit."

"Very well," he answered, "transfer it in please." Seconds ticked followed by a series of clicks as she made the phone transfer complete. Lifting the hand piece, he announced himself. "Peter Gray, speaking."

The voice on the other end began. "You made a big mistake firing me, you *Imperialist Pig!*" What began as a familiar voice morphed into a voice with a thick, guttural accent that did not match Pedro's normal voice. The longer he spoke, the more pronounced it became, no longer the familiar educated accent, but the real Pedro—or Miguel or whoever the hell he really was—emerged. Peter was amazed at the duplicity, that he could have such a normal voice at work and then revert to this ethnic sound. "I don't think you should have let me go, you *Imperialist Pig.* I have connections, shall we say, and they all could potentially end in a bad way. Let me translate that for you: the severance pay I received does not cut it. I do believe it is time for you to correct this oversight, wouldn't you agree? Here is how it's going to be: you will get me the money I want, except this time, I want double your little measly pittance by tomorrow."

Peter was frustrated but tried to keep his voice level under control. He knew the last check they paid him was half the amount. However, he didn't work the full month and so he did not earn it, and he did not deserve a severance package either! "Pedro, what you ask for is not the norm. I, cannot make any promises, call me back this afternoon, maybe I'll have an answer."

Pedro added, "Seriously? This isn't exactly debatable," amused, he continued, "but okay, we'll play it your way - for now... I have time, and anyways, *WE know where you are.* If we don't like your response..."-The line went dead leaving the threat open ended.

Peter started to ask him what he meant by the underhanded threat, but he knew, and then, all he heard was the click on the line and pure silence. The bastard hung up on him. He did not need to guess what his threat meant; he wasn't a complete moron. The asshole just threatened him! Peter sat there for a minute digesting this, before asking Lucia to find Jairo.

Jairo didn't hesitate; he sensed the urgency of the matter, for Peter never asked anyone to come right away to his office-ever! Peter was the type that had all his ducks in a row and things were methodically thought out ahead of time, always precisely calculated and organized. This summons was different. It felt different. Lucia's voice had been strained over the phone. Uncharacteristically, without waiting for a greeting, Jairo entered the office without knocking and closed the door behind him. Upon seeing Jairo, Peter spoke into the intercom, telling Lucia they were not to be disturbed. Then, he began the litany of describing every detail of what had transpired on the phone call with Pedro.

Jairo began with a suggestion. "Do not pay him anything just yet."

"Why? Peter asked.

"Don't be naïve, Gray! The threats, the insinuations… I do not need to spell it out for you. This guy is a Tupamáro, he will not stop after a singular payment. I will bet my Mercedes on that. You have angered him. I guarantee you this is not over yet. Blackmail and theft alone are reasons for imprisonment. Cases like this, with the present climate here in Uruguay, are reason enough why we need to employ some protection for you. A, what we call, 'thug-type' material that would pose a threat to him. They can throw their weight around too. When he calls, just keep him going and stall him on the line. Barter back and forth on the amount. Make him take you seriously and do not back down. Do not appear easy nor agree too quickly, but in time agree to a certain amount. While you have his attention, see if you can get him to openly say who he is directly involved with— *if* he is working with anyone we know. Maybe I am grasping at straws and giving him more credit than credit is due; he just may be your average crook with an education. I just do not want to risk underestimating him either. So, let's set a plan in place. Agree on a time for him to meet you this evening in your office. Make sure it is after the staff normally leave. Have the draperies drawn shut in your office and just have your lamp on. Being that the lighting in your office tends to be low, this will help conceal the guards I will have for you hiding." Jairo pointed at the corners to the left and right of the door. "We don't need to risk anyone else's safety, so really check that everyone is gone. Meanwhile, I am going back to my office to call my contacts at the police department, and I am going to reach out to Dan Mitrione too. You remember him, right? The speaker at the International Businessman's dinner?"

"Yes, I remember him," Peter replied.

"Good. Okay." He thought to himself for a second as if he were running through all the steps mentally. "I will get them to send some men over so we can set up this sting and arrest this asshole for embezzling and threatening you. We do not have anything else to pin on him. Just because he threatened you does not mean he will go through with it, but we need to send a clear message that he is on our radar."

Right now, Peter was just so grateful for Jairo's presence. Jairo—having been ex-military—had his tactical knowledge, and right now, it benefited him greatly!

Peter hung up the phone. Via the intercom, he summoned Lucia again. It was only then that Peter began to let her in on some of what was going on. She was already stressed out this week. Usually when she was like this, it tended to have something to do with her ongoing problems with her boyfriend. As far as Peter was concerned, she should dump him after he'd recently observed some fresh bruises on her arm, and that did not sit well with him. He wanted to address the issue with her, but now was definitely not the time. Lucia seemed taken aback by what he was telling her regarding Pedro, and yet, surprisingly, she didn't say much. That seemed odd, but he dismissed the thought; Lucia was trustworthy. Peter had kept it simple, instructing her to stay long enough to usher Pedro in when he arrived and to act normal, as if nothing was out of the ordinary. The moment she ushered him in, she was to leave immediately. Although extremely curious and having a million questions, she didn't dare ask, for it would stand out blatantly that she was stepping out of line. Needing this job as much as she did, she wouldn't risk losing it for anything or anyone, so she truly believed at the moment.

Chapter 22

Five o'clock that afternoon, two beefy-looking guys dressed in regular street wear walked into Pradman Industries. Looking a little out of place, everyone was too busy in their day-to-day routine to pay heed, so they were easily forgotten. Proceeding towards the elevators, they entered and hit the button selecting the eighth floor after booting the elevator attendant out. As the door was closing, they could hear his clamoring protests, demanding that they stop the elevator. No words were exchanged on the ride up. They were from a rough cut, and not much for conversation. The elevator played a jazz rendition of "The Girl from Ipanema" in the background. The paneling in the elevator was elegantly carved, and it intricately framed the antique glass on the walls. The reflection of these guys didn't match the elegance of their surroundings. When the men showed up at her desk, Lucia looked up. Her eyes did not mask her surprise very well, but she reigned her composure as best she could. Surprisingly, they weren't at all what she expected. One could bounce a quarter on their abs. Even though they looked cleaned up, it was obvious that they were in no shape or form businessmen. The first one spoke up, not rudely but definitely devoid of general pleasantries —not as much as a 'Hi,' 'Good afternoon?' or 'Would you mind?' but, "Show me which door is Señor Gray's office." This was said with a commanding directive, and being rather dumbfounded, she pointed at the door, without realizing she had, nor did she stand up or try to stop them. The same guy who seemed to be the one in charge did not wait to be announced. He rapped twice on the door and just walked in! They didn't even wait for what proper etiquette deemed appropriate; where Peter would have received a call on the intercom and then given the okay for them to enter. Lucia increasingly felt rattled, but she knew she couldn't have controlled the situation even if she had tried any differently. This was a bit nerve-racking, and she despised confrontational issues anyway. She was increasingly afraid of what this might mean in the long run for herself, being that she worked so close to Mr. Gray.

Peter didn't fault her for allowing them through, nor did he care for their lack of tact, but he realized they weren't here for their manners or good looks. They were here because he had got himself in a serious mess. The main one spoke up, pointing at himself and then his partner. "I am Pineda, and that's Coimbra. Let's move these chairs. They are in the way. When he arrives, I want you to be sitting at your desk, pretending to be doing some work. We will be standing inside your bathroom. When he enters, we want you to remain at your desk, get him to agree on the payment and hand him the cash. We will be listening and let us do our business when the moment is right. Got all that, Gringo?" Peter seethed on that white American insult. The jerk continued, "Oh, and close the drapery. Keep it closed. I do not want anyone to be able to look in from the other building."

Peter wasn't liking the way Pineda callously spoke to him, but then he needed them more at the moment than they needed to be bothered with his affront. "Fine," Peter said with suppressed irritation to his voice.

"Also," Pineda added, "I have been assigned to you during the day, at work only. We will work out the details later." Peter asked them if they wanted some coffee, but they refused, choosing instead to inspect the entire floor of the office. They ended up asking for the key to the stairwell doors so they could be locked. The only way Pedro could enter or exit now would be through the elevator. So, in the event he tried to make a break, the elevator would be his only perceived option. Pineda added that the situation might get messy, but he would not get far.

Now, the wait began. They had at least an hour left before Miguel arrived, and these guys were already on his nerves. They were cutting up back and forth, talking about sports and women and not the least bit concerned by the events about to take place. Pineda threw himself down on the couch to wait. Turning to Peter, he patted the cushion. "Can you get me another couch this week? This one isn't very comfortable. If I am going to be here, I want something more comfortable."

"I didn't buy it." He stopped, took in a deep, self-calming breath, and then replied, "It came with the office, so no. You are hired to protect me, not lie down on the job." *Jerk*, he thought to himself. Peter despised the present situation. Under normal circumstances, he would have told them to screw themselves. Currently his only option was -well there weren't any options, because he wasn't in a position to argue. He found himself proverbially between a rock and a hard place, so the saying goes.

As the hours ticked by, Peter's apprehension grew. Knowing it was just the stress of everything playing havoc on him, he tried to shake it off, but this was a different kind of stress, in which he found himself feeling ill-equipped to deal with. Thoughts racing, Peter wondered if Pedro was still going to show up and what next if he didn't? He did arrive but was late. Naively, he thought if they got him tonight that this all would be over. Hearing the ding in the distance, Peter recognized the elevator's announcement as it arrived. Moments after hearing the elevator doors slide closed, Lucia called in Peter's office, announcing Pedro's arrival, wherein he bid her to let him pass. The minute he entered, she hightailed it out of the building. Lucia did not like Pedro at all and he scared her to death, so she wanted to be as far away from him as possible. As Lucia was leaving, Peter returned the phone to the cradle, eyes darting towards the bathroom door, nerves on edge, pulse racing, he moved his attention to watch as the doorknob began slowly turning. About to be tested to the limit, he tried to appear as if nothing were amiss. It was amazing how adrenaline could pump from zero to a hundred in a split second, coursing through one's body.

As soon as Pedro cleared the threshold of the doorway, all hell broke loose. The two guards hidden in the restroom waited for Pedro to take the bait. The minute he did, they made their move. Bursting out of Peter's personal bathroom, they tackled him to the ground, in the process knocking over a side table and sending a lamp careening and crashing to the floor. Pedro rolled over the broken ceramic shards, slicing through his shirt and into his arm. A large shard stuck out from the newly opened wound. Spewing vulgarities, he grasped the chin of one of the guys and was shoving it up with all his might. The shorter of the two guys had lost his grip when they landed, but he too regrouped and grabbed onto Pedro's arm. Pedro did a sideswipe kick to his head, knocking him into the desk. The guy wiped the blood off his lip and grinned while saying "Tú quieres mas? Want more?" Pineda lunged at him. This time, with the help of his partner, he pinned him down while the other snapped a cuff on one wrist and twisted his arm behind his back, trying to get to the other hand. Pedro strained, thrashing and kicking. He broke loose and grabbed the handle of Peter's black graphite phone off its cradle and swung hard, making impact and breaking Coimbra's nose. Blood spewed. Coimbra touched his nose. Wiping it, he looked down for a quick second. Oblivious to the pain, he looked at the blood that covered his fingers and became enraged. In a fit of rage, he swung, landing a right hook to Pedro's chin, and then pounded—blow after blow after blow, and yet Pedro held his own. He was in optimal physical shape. The only difference was he wasn't as beefy of a guy as Coimbra.

Distracted by Coimbra's blows, Pineda decided to end this circus. Coming from behind, he struck a mind-dizzying blow to the back of Pedro's head. He wasn't going down easy, but like it or not, he had lost his edge. After the devastating blow, which brought him abruptly still, they took the opportunity to pin him. He was screaming at Peter, "You'll pay for this! I'll kill you!" He still thrashed with all his might as if he had a chance. He kicked the armchair, sending it flying, knocking it into the shelf behind it. The coffee service went every which way and spilled the contents of its hot, aromatic liquid, while the coffee cups and saucers shattered as they landed one after another on the wooden floor resonating repetitive crashing sounds as the porcelain shattered into pieces. All Peter could do was stare as if he were watching a movie playing out before him. Pedro obviously had been trained to fight. The way he fought back, did not fall under the category that came naturally but was born of a vigilante lifestyle. Coimbra was finally able to pin his head down to the ground, sitting on his back, immobilizing him while Pineda cuffed the other hand. Two against one wasn't favorable odds for Pedro.

Coimbra looked at Peter. "Give me your handkerchief." Peter grabbed the one out of his pocket and handed it to him. Coimbra proceeded to tie it around the wound on Pedro's arm to stymie the blood flow. Pedro continued thrashing while screaming obscenities, making the task all that more difficult. Grabbing him under the arms and not too gently, they hauled him to his feet, dragging him out of the office. The entire time, he strained, kicked, and yelled, not giving up and still trying to get loose. The men grunted under the exertion as they tried to maneuver Pedro towards the elevator.

Pedro screamed, "You piece of shit! I'll kill you! All of you are dead! No one messes with us!" Peter got up and closed the door, but the last comment didn't go unheard. He up righted the end table and walked over to the couch to sit down. Leaning his head backwards, he closed his eyes and exhaled slowly. *What have I done? Oh God!* Now doubting their decision to catch him. He shouldn't second guess himself for helping a criminal be brought to justice, but if there were repercussions from this, he could be the target. Slowly, his breathing returned to normal, he opened his eyes and surveyed the damage in the room. The office was trashed. He could still hear Pedro's rants down the hallway. The elevator had just arrived, and they were having trouble getting him into it. With nerves rattled, Peter got up and began the task of trying to straighten up the mess. He did not want to explain this to anyone tomorrow.

He walked down the hall to the custodial closet. By now, they probably were loading Pedro into the police van, preparing to transport him to the jail. Peter could no longer hear him. Thank God! Grabbing a cleaning cart from the custodial closet, he returned to his office. He did everything he possibly could to right the room, but the coffee stains, the broken leg on the chair, and the blood were a lost cause. Before tossing the items out, he got his swiss army knife out of his desk and used it to cut out the blooded area from the carpet, tied it up in a trash bag, and hide it under the trash in the outdoor dumpsters. Without a choice, he loaded the damaged sofa chair and the rug into the service elevator to transport to the trash collection area in the back of the building. Lifting them one at time, he threw them inside the trash receptacle. Just in case someone had questions, he had decided that he would tell folks he accidentally tripped, causing the chair to break or something believable like that. Next, he went searching for matching replacement pieces from unoccupied offices. Luck had it that he knew where he could get an identical chair, but he was out of luck as far as the carpet was concerned. He went back and forth between offices until he made a decision on one that at least coordinated with the colors of his office. Sitting down for a moment, he penned a note to Lucia for her to reorder a replacement chair and carpet to replace the ones he now had, and at the bottom he wrote "ask me later."

Next, he went to the kitchen area and collected a replacement set of dishes for his side table. Peter took the custodial cart back to where it belonged, and then returned to his office, locking the door. When he felt like the room was once again presentable, he focused on himself. As he entered his private restroom and began to freshen up, he tore off his shirt and began washing the sweat off his face, neck, armpits, and chest. On the shelf, he kept deodorant and a bottle of cologne. He put both on but only a hint of the cologne since normally it would have worn down its potency by this time of day. Selecting a shirt out of the bathroom closet, he began to re-dress. When he got home, he wanted to be absolutely sure Paula would think he was wearing what he had left in that morning, so he grabbed the same tie and began the process of tying it around his neck. Once he felt like he had it together, he bent down, picked up the bloodied shirt, and wadded it into a knot, careful not to expose the bloodied areas. How he managed to get blood on his shirt, he wasn't sure, but needless to say, it was evident that he couldn't go home to Paula in that condition. He quickly passed a comb through his hair and after flipping off the lights, he went back down the service elevator, threw the shirt out with the rest of the trash, and headed for home.

Chapter 23

The police van stopped. Pedro wasn't sure where he was. They were at a standstill longer than it normally took for a traffic light to change so he assumed this meant that they had arrived at the police station. It was stifling in the back without proper ventilation. Voices approached and the door to the van opened. *Assholes, all of them! No matter, I won't be here long,* he arrogantly believed. *Word will get out.* They jerked him out of the back of the vehicle and onto his feet. His eyes were having trouble adjusting to the lights outside the police precinct since the inside of the van had been pitch dark. The heavy wooden doors were not only protection but a natural noise barrier as he soon learned. It seemed rather desolate as they stood outside with only the occasional noise of a distant train following its lonely route. Announcing himself, the officer bid that they open the door. He was genuinely surprised at the level of activity going on. Pedro could tell they recognized the "Sergeant," as he had all his puppet boys surrounding him. *So, this was the Sergeant,* he thought to himself. His expression was one that meant business. He was taller than the average Uruguayan—solid too. He spoke up, "Trága el prisionéro. Bring the prisoner in and let's get him processed."

The first guard went to grab Pedro's arm, but he headbutted him. If he was going down, he wasn't going down easy, nor was he going to present himself as a weakling. He wanted people to fear him. The scuffle began again. He loved a good fight, although it would have had better results if his hands weren't cuffed. The Sergeant came over and whacked him on the side of the head with the baton he kept always hooked on his belt. Pedro saw stars and was immediately stunned by the blow to the head. They got him inside the rest of the way without any resistance, putting him in a holding cell facing the booking desk. Slowly as his wits returned, he began mouthing off again. "You might as well let me out. You are wasting your time." This guy was relentlessly annoying! The guard at the desk yelled at him to shut up. He needed to take a leak, but that would have to wait. He looked around to see if he recognized anyone or if anybody's language might reveal a fellow sympathizer. Forty-five minutes later, two guards escorted him into the inner sanctum of the jail. A knot had already emerged where he had received the blow from the baton and his head throbbed. He was put in solitary confinement. It was better that way. He was determined to find a way out, and he didn't need anyone bothering him. Pedro, as he was trained, from the time they brought him in, began tracking his surroundings. How many corridors he passed through, all the while keeping a mental check of all the turns they had made.

On his way to the cell, the guards were mouthing off at him. "Not such a tough guy now, are you? Where are your friends? If they are so powerful, why are you here?"

Pedro seethed. If looks could kill, his stare would have taken out this particular guard. It didn't make much of an effect on the second guard, but the first one kept his next comment to himself. Pedro succeeded rattling the guy, although it wasn't necessarily a good idea to make enemies with him. As it were, the Tupamáros infiltrated everywhere, and one could never tell who was one. The second guard tossed the typical uniform garb of an inmate at him: pants, a thin shirt, and flip-flops. Since Pedro made no attempt to catch them, they landed onto the dusty floor of the cell at his feet, however one of the flip flops ricocheted off the concrete bed built into the wall, landing in one corner with just enough force to cause the red urinal bucket to wobble upon impact.

Pedro scanned the small cell, taking it all in—so far, it wasn't much: crappy clothes that retained the aromatic funk of clothes that remained wet too long before completely drying, a cement bed, a bucket, and a weathered blanket that he picked up after noticing it on the floor. Flipping it open, he noticed that it had been heavily patched in several areas where previous holes were rendered aid by needle and thread.

The guard reappeared, rapping the bars with his club and commanding Pedro to hurry up getting changed and to shove his street clothes and shoes out through the bars. Pedro was ready for a fight with the first person that tried to touch him. The only problem was what stood between him and anyone—metal and lots of it. For now, he was better off if he was ignored, left alone and unnoticed! He had a lot to weigh. Mata was probably getting wind of this through the chain of communication. Even though he found himself incarcerated, it was imperative that his resolve remained unshaken. He grabbed the collar of his shirt at the nape of the neck and pulled it up and over his head, sticking his hand through the bars, tossing it on the ground. Next came his pants and shoes, but his socks—well, that was a passive aggressive move on his part, for he decided to keep them on his feet, testing the waters in a minor way, knowing they would expect him to give those up too. Finally dressed, he unfolded and smoothed the blanket upon the cold concrete slab of a bed and laid down using his hands, cradling the back of his head as a pillow.

Staring at the ceiling, he just remained stoic with his slow, even breathing. Rolling to his side, he repositioned his body using his left hand to hold his head up. His eyes moved slowly from surface to surface, continuing to take stock of his surroundings, then turning his attention to the noises surrounding him that were in and out of sight - noises beyond the grid of the bars, his new norm. As a trained Tupamáro soldier, he was prepared physically and mentally for situations as these. Systematically, he became engaged in a data-logging process; every movement by the guards, no matter the reason nor the time, he mentally noted, knowing this information could help him or anyone from his group now or in the future.

He played the part of a compliant inmate to facilitate being forgettable. He listened to some conversations that were intermittently dropped. For days, nothing happened, and nothing came from any conversation he heard, so he began to reach out, first communicating with the people in the cells adjacent to his left and right. Whenever a guard came by, he avoided eye contact and answered with few words. The place was noisy. It stunk. It was during one of the cell checks on the fifth day that the thinnest of mattresses was brought in for him, which he immediately put on the on top of his cinder blocks. He actually was excited about this, for it would be another barrier between the cold of the concrete and his body. Now, he would have the ability to use the blanket to cover himself.

Peter would pay. His only mission was to break out and eliminate that pig. Ever determined, he vowed Peter *would be* the newest tenant in one of the people's prisons! Pedro got up, took a piss and then laid back down as the night call had just been ordered for lights out. As he had done the last five nights, he lay there, staring up at the ceiling, all the while listening to all the conversation's he was capable of hearing. He already got some info out of some of the guys about what they had been up too and heard names dropped of people he assumed they feared. He was hungry again, but dinner had already been served in the jail, and the portions were small at best. Sometimes, even if one were still hungry, it was difficult to stomach some of the slop that was served. Worn out and sore from not being used to a stone bed, he stood up again. Stretching at first, he then paced around his little 4x5 area, trying to exert some of his unspent energy until sleep finally beckoned him.

Chapter 24

The phone rang, ending the silence within the bunker. A voice on the line said, "I need to speak to el jefe now. It's Lobo."

The female voice asked him to wait. She knew no one risked calling unless it was vital. The retaliation was severe if anyone wasted any of the leader's time, so they didn't. "This better be good," Mata warned.

The man spoke in a quiet voice. "One of our brothers has been imprisoned due to a foreign businessman. I need money to pay off the head guard and get him out."

"Who is it?"

"He says his name is Miguel de Luna."

"Damn it!" Mata growled.

"I was able to visit him yesterday. He mentioned he remains in possession of a set of keys to the Pradman building. He wants to get out fast so that he can get into Pradman before they think to change the locks. At this rate, he believes that they will think he has no way of getting out anytime soon. The equipment alone in the building that he can swipe can net repayment of the money we have to use getting him out, along with a neat little profit for us."

Mata, after a small silence, replied, "Fine, you will meet Sergio at the museum, and you will get your money. The minute he is out, have him call me." All Lobo heard was a click, and the line went dead.

Pedro didn't realize he had fallen asleep until someone woke him by touching his arm with one hand and covering his mouth with the other. He jumped up in protective attack position as the man whispered, "Hush, brother." That got his attention. "Follow me. We are leaving."

Pedro clapped his hands silently together and laughed softly. "Yes!" he said. "I knew it!"

The man spoke, "One of ours will not stay oppressed." He handed him clothes and told him to get dressed. "Follow me and do not make a noise. Do not speak; let me do all the talking." The officer on the morning shift had just arrived at the desk, beginning to process the current paperwork. He wasn't aware of the full details involving Pedro, and frankly, if he was, he didn't care. He was here to bring home a check, and the minimal effort involved was fine by him. What he did know was that if he got this done fast, a little token of their appreciation was coming his way, and he was a whore for money. He had been bought before. They all had a price. The Lieutenant at the desk looked up as he passed by the booking desk with Miguel. Nodding at the guard it was as if to communicate the coast was clear and to go! Slipping out the side door, the guard slipped him a phone number with instructions to call it immediately, and that there was a taxi waiting for him around the corner to take him home.

Pedro was out! Once home, he unfolded the note and called the number.

"Give me the telephone!" Mata commanded. Speaking into the phone, he said, "You are more of a liability to me than an asset, Luna!" Without giving him the opportunity to reply, he continued. He knew the phone call was a short privilege. "Can you assure me that you can get in and out without suspicion?"

"Yes, they forgot to ask me for my keys, and I doubt that they thought to change all the locks. I know I can get in through the service area."

"Very well, arrangements will be made. Stand down for now."

Lobo, another Tupamáro, mentally replayed the last conversation he had with another anonymous person on the phone. He was instructed to show up to the Bar Zona Sul within the hour, wear a red handkerchief in his coat pocket, and look out for someone with a red handkerchief as well. In order to make it all fall into place, Lobo had to hurry.

Chapter 25

Pineda was already in Peter's office when he arrived. Taken aback at the sight, he turned, closed the door, and walked to his desk. *This is going to take some getting used to,* he thought to himself as Pineda began his delivery.

"Let's go over a few things. We need to make sure your drapes are always closed, and your furniture must be moved in different positions every day. This will include the couch—just in case any sharp shooters are out there. Also, you have an appointment with the police headquarters today at two o'clock."

"Right, like I can work in the dark like this. There isn't enough light," Peter complained rather curtly. "We have to at least leave the curtains open a hair."

"Your skin," Pineda said flippantly, "but need I remind you if you do, they will have views from two different angles. That is a lot of territory to protect you from and a great vantage point for you to be picked off—and me as well. I refuse to go out for that reason. So, the curtains stay closed!"

Peter actually looked forward to the meeting just to get away from this ass they had assigned him to. He did however have a point, stating he was a target from two directions. He had not thought of this before. He tried to concentrate on his current project, but he could feel himself being stared at. He looked up at Pineda. "What?"

"I was thinking," Pineda added as he scratched his unshaven face, "what's it worth to you?"

"What's what worth to me? What are you talking about?"

"Getting rid of your problem is what I mean. As you can see," he boasted, "I am armed, and I am a good shot. I can get him for you." Waving his hand in the air, he made his hand look like a pistol and, pointing it to his arm, made a sound as if a gunshot was fired. Continuing without a pause, he said, "Then, I graze a bullet to my arm to make it look like self-defense, and voila, your problem is solved—for the right price, of course."

"*This* is what you call protection? Let me get this straight: you are assigned to me, which is your obligation, and then, you are bribing me on top of this to ensure my protection is successful, making you my personal hitman? Incredulous! You are a real piece of work." This time, Peter spoke in English so he would not understand.

"Go ahead and don't speak Spanish, Gringo. Anyway, it is your life that will be hell if he gets out. Word around is that he may already be out. Just give me the signal, and I will take care of it."

Peter responded fluently in Spanish, devoid of an accent. "No, no thanks. I don't operate like that. I am just going to have to pass on this." Peter kept writing on his flow chart.

"Come on, you want this over with, don't you?" He just wouldn't let it go.

"Just drop it!" Peter said emphatically.

Pineda put both his palms up in the air, gesturing a surrender. Pineda flopped down on the couch again and kept on jabbering. Peter pretended to work, ignoring him. After a while, he heard sounds of snoring. He looked over at the big lummox on the couch. *Great. What a piece of work they got me as a bodyguard,* he thought. *They said they needed to send someone that was ruthless in situations as this.* Taking the opportunity while the big ox was asleep, he picked up the phone to call Jairo. "Jairo, do me a favor. Can you use your contacts and see if Pedro is still locked up? Pineda thinks he might have been released."

"Jesus Christ!" said Jairo, exasperated. "Is this for real?"

Peter replied, "Afraid so. My so-called bodyguard is taking a nap right now as we speak, and frankly, I don't know what's worse: listening to his snoring or listening to him when he's awake! God, he's obnoxious."

"I'll find out and get back to you."

Peter hung up and took advantage of the time to get some work done. At times it was difficult to concentrate through the snoring. It was like a freight train coming from the couch. He had a few minutes anyway and then he was going to go grab lunch. Afterwards, he decided to risk things and keep one of his designated appointments before he remained entombed within Pradman Industries.

Peter pulled into the closest parking spot he could find. He entered the police department with purpose and walked up to the counter. The place was active. Several people were already standing in line, waiting, he assumed, to try and visit a family member or to bail them out. The tick tacking of typewriters could be heard over the sounds of their voices, as well as intermittent phones ringing. He stood in line. Looking around, he noticed a woman sitting at a desk in the distance crying. Wondering what caused her distress distracted him for a bit. He always had a soft spot for women and just could not stand to see them weep. Sweeping his eyes to the other side, he saw a bunch of uniformed guys just talking it up, as if there wasn't a line or any sense of urgency on their part. At the counter, some young man was arguing his case to the officer. This was frustrating as all get out. Twenty minutes had passed, and he still hadn't moved up much. Seemed like everyone had a problem today. Eventually, another officer did come up to the counter, and some signs of movement began. "Señor." The guy signaled him to come forward.

Peter began, "I am needing to speak with someone about extra protection. I have a situation that is becoming more threatening, so I have an appointment to speak to someone in Señor Mitrione's office, but I prefer to speak with Señor Mitrione directly if possible."

"Wait a moment." The officer went over to one of the adjacent rooms and spoke to another officer. They exchanged words for a while, and then he returned. "You do need to speak with Mr. Mitrione. If you will follow me por favor." They walked down a corridor and turned, walking ahead. After several more twists and turns in what seemed to be a maze, they eventually arrived at Mitrione's office. Knocking, he heard a man's voice saying to enter. He turned, saying, "Wait here please." The officer went in and went over the small details that he knew before he came back out to usher Peter in. Introductions were made before he closed the door and exited. Clicking his heals, the officer tipped the brim of his hat and left.

Peter observed this man before him. He looked to be highly intelligent and had the best poker face. Peter was having a tough time reading him. He wasn't overly tall, yet not short either. He seemed to be the type that was serious and always in control. Mr. Mitrione began, "Please, sit and make yourself comfortable. Now, you are asking for extra protection I hear." He recognized Peter from the IBA dinner, so he switched from Spanish to English without missing a beat. "Seems you have had a little run in with a possible Tupamáro. You know this is going to be rough if he really turns out to be one. I just want you to mentally prepare for the ramifications." Not waiting for a real response, he continued. "Let's start. I need you to tell me everything that led up to this moment. Do not leave any detail out, however unimportant as it may seem. Also, what we need is to get you prepared. First, I will need to train you on how to carry yourself when out and about, and how to scope out to make sure the area is secure before entering. Also, I need to show you how to make sure you are not being followed. Have you ever used a gun before?"

"Well, yes. As a matter of fact, I have," Peter said soberly. "I was in the Brazilian Army and also grew up hunting."

"Good, that gets us further ahead." Dan walked over to a cabinet and unlocked it. He took out a revolver and handed it to Peter. "This was purchased off an American in the military that just returned to the USA. We acquire many of our firearms second hand that way." Dan handed him a box of bullets too. "I will assign two guards to your home: two by day and two by night. I will introduce you to them before you leave."

"What about my wife and kids?" Peter asked.

"If they leave the house, one guard is to go with them wherever they go. In fact, he will be the driver, in case something was to happen—just until we figure out if this is for real or not. They are trained for high-speed chases. Make sure your car is in good condition and that it always has a full tank of petrol. If you find yourself needing to make a run for it, you don't need to be running out of gas. They will also check the car constantly to make sure it hasn't been tampered with during the night or during the day while it isn't in your sight. Normally we would have you protect your car by keeping it in the garage. For your protection, you also need it out and ready, just in case the need arose that you might need to make a run for it. Now, if you will please follow me as we walk, I will fill you in on a few more things." Peter reached down to grab his coat. "You can leave your coat. We can return for it later." Nodding, Peter followed him out. "Okay, I am going to begin with showing you how to check corners, making sure that you are clear. Get close like I am with your back to the wall. Move close to the edge, quickly look from left to right, and take in all that you see first before you poke your head out to look. Check the drivers in their cars, both those that are parked and those moving. You are looking for out of the ordinary things."

Dan continued saying, "Look for things that seem odd, out of place. If it is warm weather, do they have a coat on? Is a car parked where it shouldn't be? Groups of people that do not look right together or in a spot you would not expect them to be? Someone that is out of place, stuff like that, or has a car been there for too long without moving." They continued through several drills and combat maneuvers in the hallways as well. "Now, I want you to park in a different location every day and every time you leave or come back. Take a different route to work every day. Break up the routine constantly. Always park your car facing out towards the street so if you need to run for it, you can. Before you leave to enter your car, wait thirty minutes at least and watch what is going on outside. Take in who is out there and what they are doing. Take notice of anyone hanging around. Remember not just to watch the males but watch the women too! The Tupamáros have women working for them too! If anyone is suspicious, it warrants waiting, so stay put. It is better to be safe than sorry, so to speak. Now, if you feel that someone might be following you, here's what I want you to do. This is a way to quickly figure out if they are for real. First, casually cross the street. Using your peripheral vision, check to see if anyone crossed the street following you. If they did, walk a bit and then do the same again: cross the street back over, but this time, aim for a group or a crowd of people and stay there until they go away, or you see a guard—if indeed someone is following. I cannot emphasize enough you must be alert at all times. Call me *any time* if you feel the need."

"What if my wife needs the car to go shopping? What measures do I take then?" Peter asked. They walked back into Dan's office.

"I have an idea. Let me make a phone call." He picked up his telephone and dialed the number to his assistant, "Armando, I need you to call the taxi office. Have them select three of their most trusted drivers that we can assign to a case and send them over right away please."

"Can they actually do this?" Armando asked.

"They have done this before for me, just ask for Luis Rivera. He will take care of things. I have used him in this capacity before. Get back with me when you have word. Thank you, Luis." Getting back to Peter, he said, "They will get back with us. Let me explain how this works. On the days you know you will need one of the drivers, call the day before and place the request with Luis. You will be provided with the names of three individuals to select from. Only accept rides with one of the three. They will be someone you can trust and will be dispatched to you for the day. If they are not available, then Paula will have to reschedule her outing. It can get expensive, but they will be at your disposal to wait if need be and to get you to multiple places within the same day. If we end up dealing with Tupamáros, Peter, no dollar is too much to pay."

"Thank you very much, for everything. I cannot tell you how stressful this is for me and my wife. We have received a few phone calls to the house this week and yet no one speaks, and now, the last two nights we've had glass bottles thrown on our roof, of course when they land on the ground they've shattered leaving glass everywhere and scaring my family. Last night it was rocks and bottles. At first, I thought it was just kids that were bored, but I am starting to believe this is more sinister. I have no real proof, but my gut tells me it has to do with my firing Pedro. He mentioned we would regret it. I do not want this to make my wife want to move. One of our closest friends just decided to leave Uruguay. His wife, being emotionally delicate, couldn't take the stress any longer. I believe this is beginning for us. The irony for them, they weren't even having any issues with a Tupamáro. The wife was simply scared." Peter became silently pensive. The phone on Dan's desk rang breaking the momentary lull in conversation. He picked up the phone and listened. "Great!" He replied, "go ahead and send them on over." Putting the phone back on the cradle he relayed to Peter, "The drivers are here to introduce themselves to you. I will have them write their names down so you will have it handy."

A sharp rap on the door announced their arrival. "Come in!" Mitrione responded. One by one the guys filed in. You could tell they were honest hard-working guys. Pleasantries were exchanged with a lot of "mucho gustos" going around. "Take a good look at their faces Peter," Dan added. "I want you to be able to recognize them easily. These are the only three you will ask for by name. You will preferably call the day before you know that you will need their services, ensure one of them is scheduled. Payment will not be dealt with but at the end of each week. They will tally it and send a bill to the office. Fair enough?"

"Yes, absolutely."

For now, just follow my advice. Go home, try and relax. I will give you my private number as well. As for today I am sending two guards to follow you home. Do not hesitate to call if you need anything—day or night!"

"Dan, one more thing. I would like to obtain more guns or rifles if any become available. I want to place them strategically throughout the house. That way, no matter where I am, I can get to one. I don't want the children to see me carrying one around if at all possible. That would scare them and set Paula off."

"I should be able to. Just be patient, and I will be back in touch the minute I have some. All right, I think we have more than covered enough for today. I will walk you to the door." Both men stood up. Exchanging normal courtesies, they bid each other goodbye. Turning to the driver's he shook each one of their hands personally thanking them. Unused to this demonstration of respect towards someone of their stature, they awkwardly responded with embarrassment. Dan opened the door, waiting for all to pass. Peter, being last to walk out, turned and thanked him once again. After Peter left, Dan walked back to his cluttered desk to make some phone calls on Peter's behalf.

Sitting in his car Peter wore a sober expression on his face while he waited for the military guards to pull up behind him. Fragments of his conversation with Dan raced through his mind: never park in the same place, be aware of your surroundings, never take the same route, and on and on. Looking out the driver's window, he saw everything and yet nothing. A group of children from the same school passed by all wearing matching uniforms. The girls were in pleated skirts and white blouses with emblems on the pockets of their sweaters, and the boys wore navy pants, sweaters, and ties made out of the same fabric as the girl's skirts. They walked by all trying to outdo the others in volume, competing to be heard while laughing aloud over something. The interruption spared him for a moment from his morose thoughts but also prompted him to snap out of it. Sticking the keys into the ignition, he started the car, pushed in the clutch, put the car in first, and edged into traffic heading back towards the office. He had to pick up a few things before he headed home with his two shadows.

Chapter 26

Lucia, at this point, was knocking out her end-of-the-day to do list in preparation for calling it a day. On her way back to her desk from the mail room, she crossed paths with Sr. Gray as he stepped off the elevator. Her phone began ringing on her desk simultaneously with his arrival. Looking at him, she gave him just a minute gesture as if to say, "Excuse me," as she gave a little sprint in her heels. Her rapid little click, click, clicks resounded off the marble floors in the foyer area. Leaning over her desk, she grabbed the heavy phone handle. Lifting it to her ear, she inhaled and exhaled, trying to slow her heavy breathing from exertion so her voice would remain on an even tone as she answered, "Pradman Industries. Sr. Gray's office. Lucia speaking. How may I be of service?"

A woman on the line appeared to be in distress and hurried. "One of your employees is here. They have been in an accident, and I need to speak to Sr. Gray immediataménte!" Lucia asked more questions, making every effort to properly screen each phone call that came through. However, this lady played her role quite convincingly, stating that the employee was too injured to speak and that it was urgent that she speak with Señor Gray immediately about payment responsibility or they would not be able to treat her. Lucia's soft heart fell hook, line, and sinker. Beeping in on the intercom, she relayed the dynamics of what she knew to Peter. Then, he gave her the go ahead to transfer the call.

"Peter Gray speaking. Who is this? Who is hurt?"

When they heard Peter's voice, the voice changed on the phone, and a man's grotesque voice spoke, "Your days in

Uruguay will soon be over! Mark my words, Pig. We are going to kill you!" The line went dead.

"Damn it!" he blurted out loud, slamming the phone down. Pineda looked at him with an "I told you so" look. Today had been enough. Grabbing what he could work on at home, he stuffed it in his briefcase. He dispensed Pineda without the benefit of an explanation for his outburst and left.

Driving down the Rambla, he decided to pull over and take a walk on the beach. *To hell with them. Bring it on,* was the kind of mood he was in. He pulled the revolver out of his briefcase and stuck it in his coat pocket. Slipping off his shoes and socks, rolling up his pant legs a bit, he tossed the shoes back in the car, proceeding to walk across the well-worn cobblestone sidewalk, which was a testament to years of salty ocean breezes and usage by people. Looking back, he saw the guards out of their car standing and leaning against the side of their vehicle. By now he sensed they thought he was nuts doing this. His feet stepped into the cool sand, sinking slowly in. Needing to relax some before going home, before breaking the news of the guards, and before explaining that the Snyders were leaving to return to the States—all these 'befores' spurred him forward in a solitary state of mind. Paula was going to be something to contend with. A few birds zeroed in on him, hovering around, a few dropping down in front of him, cacawing as if to demand a feeding while the remainder who were less brave stayed in the air, letting the breeze of the ocean keep them in the air in a somewhat stationary float. As he walked through the flock of birds that had landed, they scattered quickly and took off in flight as he kept his pace, inching his way closer to the spot where the waves met the driest sand, before inching backward by the tug of the undertow. At one point, he paused, facing the ocean, taking in the peaceful serenity it offered; all the sounds, the smells, and the tingling sensations as the breeze came in billows and then pausing as quickly as it arrived. Looking back from the direction he came, he saw the long path of footsteps he left in the wet sand, with each depression now filled with water where the rush of a recent wave deposited it, with the sun reflecting colors off of it like a kaleidoscope.

Paula was going to be depressed when she learned Phillip and Margaret were leaving. Bending down, he picked up a shell, throwing it into the ocean, seeing a small blip of a splash with no sound. Sitting down, he squeezed the sand back and forth between his toes. Grabbing another shell, he drew patterns into the sand with no rhyme or reason, over and over. He knew it wasn't wise to have come, and yet, he remained in his go-to place, where he could always put his troubles into perspective and prioritize what mattered. Mission accomplished; all that mattered was to be assured that Paula and the children remained safe. Afterwards—hopefully—all would fall into place. Standing up, he dusted the sand off his suit pants and slapped his hands back and forth, trying to remove the rest. Time to go home; then, he would sit down and fill Paula in on everything up to this point; about Phillip, Margaret, Pedro, and then, the matter regarding the guards. Hopefully, that would give her some sense of security. It was a long shot, for it was normally difficult to appease a headstrong, stressed-out redhead.

Chapter 27

Paula heard the sound of Peter's car pull into their beautiful circular driveway. She still got excited every time she knew Peter was home; it never got old. Meeting him at the door, smiling, she greeted him. "Hi, handsome!" She stood there puckering her lips, waiting for a kiss just as she took in his companions. Looking back at him he shook his head. She understood he would explain it when he could.

Peter laughed, bent down, and planted a chaste kiss when he suddenly heard a big "EWWWW," coming out of Bergen's little mouth. While he closed the front door, she spoke up "Mommy and Daddy were kissing!" she yelled so her brothers could hear. She gave her dad a hug as he caught her mid-run.

"How was my little stinker's day at school?"

Bergen grinned and wiggled. "Well, Bobby got put in the corner for putting a frog in Mrs. Horn's desk! Isn't that something? He isn't afraid to be bad."

"What else?" Peter responded.

"Um, Dane has a girlfriend, or I think he does. Ummm... aaand... Loba wipes her feet now when she comes in the house 'cuz Mommy taught her! Isn't that sooo neat? Oh! I gotta go tell Jack what I forgot to tell him before!" She tried to jump down.

"Woah there, sounds like you had a pretty exciting day. Okay, sweetie, go tell Jack your news. I'll talk to Mommy for a bit."

"Ok Daddy, but don't take long talking. I'm hungry and you promised you would play soccer since you've been gone so much."

"Okay-okay, Bergen, honey, I need to talk to Mommy now. Go on, I will call you three when it is time for dinner."

Bergen ran off. As she did, she bellowed in a singsong cadence, "Jaa-acck!"

"Boy, that hit home," Peter muttered. "Well, I feel like a heel!"

"So..." Paula prompted him to get back on topic.

"So, I will just get to the point. From now on you we'll have two guards by day and two at night with us." He began filling her in on all the details of the meeting he had earlier with Dan and what lead up to the decision to assign protection for their family.

"Things aren't that serious, are they?" she asked alarmed.

"I do feel it's necessary, Paula. Please, don't disagree with me over this. Just try to understand. I am not trying to frighten you, but we have to be smart, be one step ahead just in case things do get serious."

"Fine, Peter, we'll do whatever you think is best for us. I trust your decision. Frankly, I will feel safer. Just a minute, I need to let Claudia know she can serve dinner, and before she steps out to go home, I need to alert her about the guards so they don't scare her to death. My only hope is that this does not scare her away. Go change out of your suit. We can talk more when big ears aren't around." She gave him a peck on the cheek and quietly walked into the kitchen.

This was almost too easy...Peter mulled. This had him more worried, Paula was so complacent. He half expected her to freak out a bit and yet she took the news like a champ. The night was young, and her attitude would change, for he still hadn't mentioned their friends upcoming departure.

The kids had been tucked into bed for over an hour. Peter couldn't unwind, so he stayed up, working. The revolver was on the seat next to him under a pillow. If one of the kids got up, he didn't want it in open view. He stood up and walked to the large windows in the living room. Looking out, he took it all in to see if he saw anything suspicious. He started laughing to himself. You're getting paranoid, Gray. Get it together. Back in his chair, he swiveled around towards the desk when he abruptly turned back around, grabbed the draperies, and drew them closed. Somehow, that made him feel better. Earlier, Paula had gone to bed with the remnants of tear tracks down her face and puffy eyes upon hearing that her dearest friend was choosing to return to the United States. Peter stayed, comforting her until she fell asleep.

A bloodcurdling scream ran through the air, coming from the direction of Bergen's room.

"Bergen!" Peter yelled out. "Daddy's coming!" Thinking it was just a nightmare, he got up to see to her, letting Paula rest. As he neared her room, he heard what had caused her outcry: it was the volley of breaking glass. There were several cars that passed by, and as they did, bottles were hurled onto the tiled roof of the Gray's house, some shattering on impact and others landing on soft patches of leaves, bouncing back and forth on the tiled roof before eventually crashing on the stone driveway below, shattering shards of glass everywhere. Being that Bergen's bedroom faced the street and to the left of the front door, naturally she was the recipient of the loudest brunt of the noise, as bottles and rocks of all sizes began to hit the roof. She was terrified to say the least.

The guards ran to the front of the house with guns drawn as they purposely spaced themselves to cover the area evenly. Without looking at each other they continued to communicate what they saw or didn't see all the while they had their guns ready to use. Peter had opened the front door in a panic without really thinking, to talk to them, but they barked orders at him to get back in and to lock the door. Little did the Gray's know that this was a precursor of the future daily nocturnal visits to come. The purpose of these visits became apparent. It was meant to keep them awake, frightened, and exhausted, and to chip away at their sense of security. Bergen was inconsolable at that point. Paula recognized that this was more than a nightmare. When she first heard her screams, as her mother she instantly knew what the sounds meant of each of her children's cries. When the thugs started throwing the bottles at the house, it mainly was just in the very front, so Peter and Paula from their bedroom did not hear the initial crashes; but they heard Bergen! Trying to keep up with Peter she was slowed by the battle of running and attempting to put her robe on for the benefit of modesty, in front of the guards.

"Get it!" She snapped at Peter.

"Get what? Peter asked confused and then realized she referred to his gun. She hadn't been happy about having a gun in the house, but now, her opinion had instantly changed. No longer would Peter have the nightly debate of *'It isn't safe to have a gun around the children argument."*

"Bergen," she began, "honey those are just bottles being thrown by kids that should be home in bed. Don't worry. Mommy will stay here until you fall back asleep."

"PROMISE?"

"Promise! Here's Fluffily, let's snuggle with him and let me tuck you back in, now close your eyes." Fluffily was her favorite stuffed animal. It was a Cavalier King Charles Spaniel that had been loved on and carted around so much that its head no longer stood up on its own. It was completely wobbly at the neck, but this did not matter, for he was loved by a little girl, who especially now took great comfort in having him to sleep with.

"Mommy, kids don't drive cars." Bergen was too keyed up to give up on being awake. How could one beat the logic of a child smart beyond her years? Another car drove by the front of the house, causing them to tense for a moment, but nothing happened. Probably one of the neighbors arriving home, Paula wagered. Whoever was out there succeeded inflicting fear. Peter was talking to the boys since they woke up hearing Bergen's screams. Nothing was done by happenstance but would soon be known to them as purposefully orchestrated assaults, so that Peter's family never could completely relax. The message was loud and clear; they knew where the Gray's lived, that their nights were no longer theirs for peaceful slumber, and without a doubt, they were never far and they were not going away...

Early the next morning, both of the maids were outside, sweeping up the broken glass from the driveway, and the gardener was at task removing the glass and rocks out of the flowerbeds and grass in the garden. When the guards arrived around half past seven, they saw the bustling staff hard at work. Quick introductions were made and they went immediately into asking Peter to carefully relay every possible detail about the previous evening; what they saw and what direction the cars were coming from etc. There were many cracked roof tiles. Peter had already pulled the left-over tile out from the garage and stacked them on the driveway with the expectation of a repairman coming.

Peter, addressing Claudia, asked if she would go in and get Paula. "Si Señor!" she replied as she put her dustpan down and leaned the broom against the house. It was ingrained, she didn't dare go through the front door, but entered through the side kitchen door, which was the servant's entry. Minutes later they both came back out. This time because she was following Paula, she came out the front door as she followed her. Gathering in the circular driveway, they had a small discussion explaining how they would operate during the day, and night. After the previous night's turn of events, the Sargénto sent a couple of extra guards. One guard would be inside the house, one in the garage and the other two circling around the exterior of the house, always on opposite sides. Not to get complacent they would alternate their shifts daily on who stayed inside and who remained outside. At nighttime, there would be an extra guard on the rooftop. Paula took great comfort knowing that the same guards would be assigned to them, so they would become familiar; they eventually became like family to them.

Other orders mandated were that food would be purchased from only one specific market and butcher. The Gray's also would be responsible for feeding the guards at all meals while they were on duty. When all was covered, Peter left for work, and Paula experienced her first day of taking the kids to school with a guard driving— posing as their "chauffeur." All the while, she fended off what seemed like fifty questions from the children. The hardest part having them keep mum about everything! That being said, it was especially going to be a challenging daily reminder for Jack and Bergen. On the drive to school, she leaned her head back on the rear seat, realizing this was the most relaxed she had felt in a while, all thanks to their new security team.

Chapter 28

Peter stepped out of the elevator at work. No sooner had his polished Florsheim shoes stepped off the carpeted elevator onto the marble floors did Lucia stand up, leaving all office decorum behind and practically ran over to Peter with a wobbly, scared voice she told him, "We've been robbed!" She was so afraid that he was going to blame her and since she was absolutely dependent on this job, she feared losing it.

"What do you mean?"

"Our equipment is gone, every bit of it: the typewriters, the adding machines, the Dictaphones, and the telephones!" At that very moment, he realized his error. The only rational culprit was Pedro! In the confusion of his arrest, Peter could not remember if he got Pedro's set of keys back! Thinking to himself, *could it be him? After all, he was in jail, wasn't he?* Peter held onto that thought but quickly dismissed it being devoid of logic as he went into his office to survey the losses and begin the inventory. As she had said, the typewriter, phone, intercom, adding machines, and Dictaphone— all were gone. Not just his office but everywhere. Everything that was useful for daily operation was gone; every telephone on his floor except *his*. Odd - and yet how would they torment him if they took his phone? He really didn't know for sure if it was him, but he would call Mitrione to see if Pedro was still jailed. Lucia stood in the doorway. Peter put the phone back where it belonged. He dialed Jairo's home number, and then, covering the mouthpiece with his hand, he asked her to close the door.

Jairo answered the phone. Peter brought him up to speed on this morning's findings. "Peter, just let me handle it for now,"

Jairo said. "I will follow up with the police department, and then, if you feel the need to call Mitrione, feel free to do so."

While he had been on the phone with Jairo, Pineda made his appearance, poured himself a cup of coffee, and sat on the couch, pulling a croissant out of a paper bag as loose flakes fell everywhere. As he ate and more crumbs fell, he single-handedly wiped them off his shirt, purposely aiming for the floor. Scowling, Peter tried to ignore the brute, mentally noting if he needed to meet with any clients, he would make sure to use the conference room hopefully avoiding him. On the days that Coimbra was there, at least he seemed more civilized.

Jairo called back as he said he would. Cutting to the chase, he informed him that Pedro had been released. According to the information he got, it appeared there was a mole within the department that enabled his release. Everyone knew there were Tupamáros infiltrated in politics, businesses, and apparently the Carrasco Police Department wasn't above being involved either. At least the police began an investigation due to the recent theft at Pradman Industries after Jairo filed his complaint. It was now difficult to decide who was legit in there. At least, he knew Mitrione could be one he had complete faith in. One of the officers suggested that Peter check the local pawnshops in attempt to find his missing equipment. Thank God this guy seemed genuine. Not all could be bad, right? Deciding to lend a hand, Peter joined in the quest, putting work above his own safety he helped in the search for his missing equipment. He had a lot of work to do, and this frustrated him, frankly, that precious work hours were being affected because they were missing necessary tools for work. The office staff looked up to him for his leadership. Until everyone could get back to work, it was bad for moral. So he drove from pawn shop to pawn shop. Disappointed, he had to leave it to the professionals. Peter was due at a scheduled meeting with a prospective client at their offices. Fingers crossed, he hoped something would turn up.

Towards the end of the day, Lucia gave Señor Gray some much-needed good news. Immediately after taking a message from Detective Araujo, who was assigned to the Pradman theft case, she informed him that his office equipment had been located in the barrio of Pocitos, one of the oldest barrios in Uruguay. Pocitos was going back to the colonial times when the women would gather to wash their clothes in the holes in the ground that collected water. The vast amount of colonial architecture remained intact all around, and every square inch was still in use, albeit some areas looked worn and tired. It was in one of these tired-looking street front corner shops that the equipment was found. There were two big windows to the left and right in which showcase teasers were displayed—in hopes of tempting customers to come into shop at Antenor's Casa de Empeño. Earlier Lucia had taken a phone message for Peter. He was asked to come down immediately to Antenor's so that he could identify certain equipment as possibly being Pradman property.

Getting back the equipment was a heavy weight off his shoulders; it would have been a large expense to start from scratch, not to mention an enormous headache. Jairo was notified and, as a legal back up, accompanied Peter, as did Lucia, who he deemed an essential role. It was she ultimately who would be more familiar with the equipment, ergo being one of the secondary lead secretaries. It was her specific duty to order any and all secretarial and office equipment. Consequently, as soon as Jairo was able to break away, they all left together to rendezvous with the detective in the barrio of Pocitos.

"What on God's green earth do you mean buy back our own equipment from him?" Peter declared in total disbelief, facing Jairo as his hands pointed towards Antenor.

Jairo tried to smooth his ruffled feathers so that he didn't piss off the guy and then have the proprietor refuse to sell the items back. It was a gross abuse of the situation, but there wasn't much Jairo could do in this case. There weren't laws in place for such situations either. Peter was informed by the proprietor that if he wanted to retain any of the pieces of equipment, he would have to pay him the same amount of money he had given Pedro, plus a ten percent overage for his troubles.

Antenor knew he was losing the profits he envisioned, but since there was a lawyer, a detective, and a multi-million-dollar company involved, even he was nervous about trouble coming his way. Ten percent wasn't much. The guy had to make a living, and he wasn't going to be completely devoid of making some loose change. On the other hand, Peter was still livid, but from Jairo's nod of his head and expression in his eyes—as if saying, 'Don't make this your fight right now'—he decided to keep his anger in check. He stepped outside, went next door to the little eatery, and got himself a cup of coffee while Lucia finished inventory on the equipment, picking out what was theirs and what wasn't piece by piece. When this task was done, they tallied up the expenses, and Jairo gave him a check. Gray knew even if he paid what they gave Pedro, it was still cheaper than buying everything new, but he was just angry; he was not really faulting the proprietor, for he was just a businessman that unfortunately got caught in the middle. His real anger... well, it remained not just toward one person or one thing but toward the entire situation he was in... Why? Why did this have to be what he was dealing with instead of focusing on his career and family? He felt this was such a futile waste of an important time in his career, his life.

Lucia finished distributing the equipment, returning them to the correct offices. It had been a monumental task that took half the morning since she had to check the serial numbers off her lists to see who they were assigned to. Now that that was done, she began focusing on putting her space back in order. Bending down she plugged her phone back in, rearranged her typewriter, adding machine and replaced a new roll of adding paper within. Once she felt satisfied, she collected her purse out of the drawer, so that she could go grab some lunch. Purse hanging off her wrist, she pushed her chair in and then the phone rang. Lifting the receiver, she answered as usual. Thinking she was talking to someone familiar; she patched the phone call into Peter.

Unfortunately, it was just someone who was excellent at copying voices.

"How did you like playing hide and seek with your equipment?" This time it wasn't Miguel, "Pedro", it sounded like a much older person. "Too bad all of it wasn't there. It's Imperialist Pigs like you that take jobs from our people. Watch your back....and your family's." The line went dead.

Pineda was in his normal useless position, completely reclined on the couch and snoring. Rearranging the room everyday seemed to be exhausting for the big lug. Even the distinctive sound a rotary phone in use didn't rouse him. *Some bodyguard!* The revolver on his hip reflected the sunlight that streamed in through a small gap in the curtains as the wind softly parted them. Peter preferred to leave the window open to circulate some air, even though the curtains remained pulled shut. *Better he be asleep than awake*, he thought. *If he was awake, it meant he would be just an annoying distraction.*

Thank God he was able to get some work done this afternoon due to Pineda's exceptionally long siesta. The constant disruptions were making his days longer and Peter felt his productivity was on the same level as before. Peter had toyed with the thought of calling Mitrione for several days. After they last met, initially he thought that perhaps he had moved too fast. So, for the time being, he had decided to refrain from procuring more armament for the house; however, after the other night when the drive-bys terrified the kids, his mind was changed. He just didn't feel like he was capable of protecting his family without extra provisions. If strangers were getting too close to the house, what was to say they wouldn't try breaking and entering? The last thing he wanted was to visibly be wearing a gun in front of the children, so in his mind, if he strategically placed them hidden throughout the house, he would be more at ease knowing that he was better equipped. He could also contribute along with the guards, some form of protection for Paula and the children.

Carrasco '67

Chapter 29

Lucia hunched over as she stored her purse in the bottom drawer of her desk. She had met her mom at a little sandwich shop down the street for lunch. Time had slipped away from them as it always did when they got together; as with most Latin mothers and daughters, they were extremely close. Her mom was petite in stature and a bit full figured; the effects of having birthed many children. Conversation flowed as it always did when the two were together, causing Lucia to lose track of time. As they were having their demitasse coffee after their meal of milanesa and rice, she happened to look down at her watch and realized that she was about to be late getting back to work. Hastily getting up, she fished money out of her wallet and placed it on the table. Kissing her mother goodbye on both cheeks she gave her a big hug and took off in a brisk walk back to the office. Presently she felt frazzled, she had three large blocks to cover within ten minutes, barely giving her enough time to get back within her lunch hour. Generally, the close calls were due to the constant traffic in this building and the issue with the elevators—if only there were four instead of two. As she returned her purse to the desk drawer, her phone began to ring. Without missing a beat, she pushed the drawer closed with one hand, reached out with the other, grabbing the receiver and said a little faster than was meant, "Good afternoon. Pradman Industries. How may I be of assistance?"

"Good afternoon, I am Mr. Steinhauf, and I am interested in discussing a possible audit by Señor Gray for my company. Would Mr. Gray possibly be available?" His voice came across as very friendly and intelligent with a hint of a German accent. Lucia in her haste, was remiss following the proper protocol that was now in place. The call was transferred. She could hear him as he answered his phone since his door wasn't completely closed. Coimbra was on duty today and he had gone down the hall to get a snack out of the kitchenette that was provided daily for the employees. Having worked with Peter for a year now, Lucia understood his facial expressions when he was annoyed, pleased and the sound of his voice when he was losing patience; and this is exactly what she heard this afternoon.

Clutching the black graphite handle, he announced himself.

"Peter Gray speaking." The voice on the other end of the line began with a friendly tone, but soon changed. "Hello, Mr. Gray, I heard a lot about you, including how you met a Tupamáro, you SOB, and how you are stirring up trouble for one of ours. Unfortunately for you, he was imprisoned. You Gringos, this is why you are not wanted here."

Peter interjected, "Haven't you better things to do than waste your time calling me? Quit trying to blame me for Pedro's actions. He got himself fired; I didn't cause the situation!"

The Tupamáro replied tersely, completely ignoring what Peter just said. "This is why we will rid Uruguay of all of you foreign pigs! You take our jobs, the money that should be ours, your companies profit from us, from our people's labor! Now, you have interfered with one of our own! It's all just a matter of time-your days are numbered. We are going to kill you!" The phone went dead. Peter continued gripping the handle tightly as his hand trembled. The disconnected line surreptitiously snapped him out of his momentary shock as it rebelled at being off the receiver. How could they blame him for Pedro's unethical actions? Never in a million years had he expected this of him, and yet, Pedro's actions were his own choice. Peter could not be held culpable for that. If their guy was in jail, so be it. It was up to their lawyers to get him out. It was not his problem, or so he believed—regrettably, this was but a prelude to many, many more calls to come.

Peter immediately pushed the button on the phone to get a clear dial tone. Dialing Mitrione's number, he informed Dan of all that transpired during the last phone call and the personal threat towards him. It was then that Dan decided measures were necessary to close the circle on Pedro.

Chapter 30

Too many distractions. Peter's spirit remained heavy today as he left for the office. He had to admit to himself that trying to put on a façade of indifference in front of Paula and the kids and orchestrate everything about the situation with the police at the office was beginning to affect his performance level. Being the perfectionist that he was, he expected a lot out of himself. Today, though, enough was enough. Peter decided it was what it was, and he was not going to allow himself to dwell constantly on the situation, nor was he about to break out in a Doris Day song such as Que Sera! There had to be a happy medium, a 'turn the page' type of moment; presently he would focus only on the Briner Company's account. He summoned Lucia into his office to dictate some letters that needed to be mailed that very day. His sole focus would be putting the finishing touches on the flow charts for the Briner presentation. By midday he began to feel productive, a bit like himself, remaining engrossed and devoid of distracting, harassing phone calls, for the moment, giving him a brief respite from his troubles.

A call came in the next day from a Sergeant Manuel Fonseca—Sargénto, as he was known by his peers in the force. The purpose of his phone call was to convey to Peter that the department was short on vehicles. Sargénto wanted to know if the department could use his car in the attempt to catch Pedro. At first, Peter thought it a bit strange to borrow his car, but the more he thought about it… eh, why not? There was one catch the driver would be an officer disguised to look like Peter. He was amused once he was asked to loan them a few complete outfits of his, specifically work clothes, but then, they also mentioned a couple of casual outfits. Within the military department they had handpicked a fellow officer, that fit his build and height. The measures were detailed down to having the officer dye his hair blonde.

The irony of the situation was not lost by Peter. The fact that he was loaning his vehicle to the military, so that they could in turn impersonate him in an attempt to catch the very terrorist that was threatening him. Well, this was straight out of a fiction novel and too incredulous for any normal human being to believe!

Miguel and Mata met again to discuss the latest within their movement. Up until this summons, Miguel had been lying low for the most part at his place, except for his limited role organizing the nightly terroristic assaults on the Gray's home and the phone calls to Peter. He never made his presence known as none of the others did either. Whenever a call came into the Grays' household, the person making the call would not utter a word, sometimes allowing whoever answered the ability to hear their breathing. Long enough to disrupt whatever Paula or Peter might have been doing, and then serving the purpose of disrupting their peace of mind. Paula's nerves were fraying. At first, she wasn't putting two and two together, but the nightly visits increased in frequency and by day more calls were made to the house while Peter was at work. One could now hear a tinge of apprehension and fear in her voice. It was today's call that pushed her to her emotional limit. She finally lost control and screamed into the phone, telling whoever called to stop calling. Miguel broke out laughing the minute he hung up. Turning to Mata, he said, "That's what she gets for sleeping with a foreign pig!"

Mata was somewhat humored but not as much as Miguel. He was concerned by how much of a live wire he was. Fanatics always had fractured personalities to a certain extent and many were also known to be a major driving force behind the Tupamáro movement. The real buzz currently was that a big mission was being carried out today by one of their cells. He wasn't privy to know the details; it wasn't his group, or he would have known of it in some fashion. However, it was known when a mission was planned, or an action was carried out. It usually made the evening news and, many times, the papers. Making the most of their downtime, they continued to toy with Paula. Miguel knew their efforts were working. She was showing signs of great distress. For this reason, they were relentless. Even with trepidation Mata relented to Miguel's suggestion, and gave the green light for Bergen's kidnapping.

Chapter 31

Mornings now had a new routine in place at the office. First thing was rearranging the furniture in Peter's office. Then, Pineda would hit up Lucia to go get him a snack to have with his coffee and to discuss a favorite daily topic, courtesy of Pineda. Today's topic of the day was women. Most days, it was about women, or at least, it circled around back to his obsession with women. He was so crude, and this disgusted a cultured man like Peter to no end. Lucia was spared for the most part since her desk was in an outside cubicle, and now that Peter shared his office space with Pineda, he was the lucky recipient of listening to Pineda's dialogue.

"Is your wife the frigid type or do you have a woman on the side, one to give you what a man really wants?"

"No, and don't you dare speak of my wife in that manner! Kapeesh?" Peter indignantly answered, and yet, Pineda kept on, either by stupidity or bravery—so far, it was a toss-up.

"I like my women to have big breasts and a big round butt. What does your wife look like? What's your type?" Pineda tossed some peanuts in his mouth and kept talking away.

"I find this conversation tasteless, and I would appreciate it if you would just address me when there are necessary topics. Let me work in peace."

"Okay, Señor Gray," he said with a hint of disrespect, but even then, he still couldn't hold back one more jibe. "But you don't know what you're missing. There is always room for a little woman on the side." Chuckling, he shuffled through the newspaper in front of him, picking out the sport page as he tossed the other pages on the floor. Peter felt like telling him to shut the hell up, but his phone started ringing, so he got in a bit while it rang. "Pick up those papers off the floor, and I would appreciate it if you kept your feet off the furniture. You aren't here to trash my office." Turning his leather chair around, he said into the phone, "Peter Gray speaking!"

"Peter! Oh, Peter, I am so glad you answered." Paula was in an extremely agitated state. "The bowling alley, Peter… it just was bombed! They strongly suspect it was the Tupamáros! Peter… Peter? Peter, did you hear what I said?"

"Ye-yes, of course, I did. Where did you hear this from? From what source?"

"It's on the television. They interrupted the show that was on. The boys, Peter… if it had been just a little later, our boys could have been there!" She was crying at this point. "They had plans to go today," she added. "Do you think it was on purpose?"

Peter interrupted her train of thought since she was working herself up to being on the verge of hysteria.

"Paula, enough. I know it is horrible but get yourself together. Just be thankful that they weren't. We cannot dwell on the if's; we must work with what we know and keep our nerves from getting the best of us over every little thing. Not everything is Tupamáro related—"

She cut in, "On top of it all, I've been getting a lot of calls today. I have tried to be brave, so I didn't want you to know how many. I know someone is there; I can hear noises, and sometimes I can hear someone breathing. When is this going to stop?"

"I don't know, Paula. Sometimes, I don't have all the answers. Just keep it together… please, for me? Listen, I love you. You have the guards. You are safe. Don't let the kids go anywhere. Distract yourself by baking me something special for dessert tonight, and I will come home early, okay? It will get your mind off things. You do that for me, Rusty, okay?"

"Yes, I… Oh…" She cleared her throat. "Okay, I'll try. It's just… just… well, I—All of this has just worn on me today. I guess I'll let you go. Please, be extra careful coming home. Please, be vigilant of your surroundings, dear. I love you, Peter. Please, please, be careful… I love you!"

"I love you too, Rusty. I'll be home soon. Don't worry. I'll be fine." Hanging up, he looked up and noticed Pineda, who was watching him more, listening into his conversation, and was grinning like a Cheshire cat.

"Rusty? Aww... pet names. How touching? I bet I know what she calls you."

"Can it!" He barked. Peter needed a break from this clown they had assigned to him, so he decided to step away from his office to go have a coffee with Jairo. This momentary respite from Pineda gave him the opportunity to go over a few things with him too. As Peter was walking out of the office though, Pineda got up to follow him as was expected. However, Peter pivoted around and, short of patience, snapped, "Don't! Just don't."

Pineda understood and backed off as Peter informed Lucia where he would be if she needed him, and then, he would be leaving early to run an errand and then have lunch. The barber was only a few blocks from the office, so he planned to take a walk, enjoying some fresh air while dispelling some of this nervous energy he was carrying. Sitting in the barber's chair he enjoyed the friendly banter with Diego who had been cutting his hair ever since they first moved to Montevideo. Besides receiving a decent haircut, he appreciated the convenience it afforded being so close to Pradman's. Another bonus he liked, and only if time permitted, he would get his shoes shined. A permanent fixture in front of the barbershop was the shoe shiner with his tall chair set up and awaiting its next customer. Most of the time, he tried to take advantage of this service so that there would be one less thing Paula would have to contend with, but every rare once in a while, she would drive there like a trooper after dropping the kids off at school and wait while he shined his shoes. This made him think of her again with the awful day she was having; he wasn't sure how he could make it up to her. Everything was pretty much out of his control—and hers too, for that matter. He felt confident that the military police would take care of things and things would go back to normal now that they were in charge. For now, though, he would continue to stay the course and remain on top of any news so he could be in the know. He observed the shoe shiner as he went about his task of buffing his shoes. He somewhat envied him, for he was so upbeat about everything and just talked up a storm, as if he had not a care in the world. The man had a small hunch on his back due to years of bending over on the job. His clothes were old but clean, his nails stained from years of working with shoe polish, and yet no one could be as content with life as he. When finished, Peter stepped down. He thanked him for another excellent shine, and after paying him he started to walk towards the little bar up the street. The barbershop had been a bit busier than he anticipated, so instead of eating at a restaurant, he chose to pick up a quick bite from the local bar located a block from the office.

Juggling his drink and lunch in a wrapped to-go container, he left the bar, moving ever so carefully. He decided on simple fare of black beans and rice, but he was leery of keeping the plate level. He could not afford getting bean juice on his suit. It smelt so good. If he were a dog, he would have been drooling profusely.

Reaching the corner, he waited on the cars that were passing. Looking at the building ahead, he noticed a car parked in front of it sideways. It was blocking exactly where he would have to pass to get to the front steps of Pradman Industries. Two guys were standing near the car while the driver remained behind the wheel. Their demeanor and body stature didn't match the clothes that they wore, nor did the weather merit the heavy, long coats they wore. His gut instinct told him to flee. He tried to recall all the things Dan had said regarding sizing up if someone possibly were a Tupamáro, like someone appearing to be out of place and not quite looking the part. What lay before him seemed to fit the criteria. He would even bet his Mercedes that they were not only affiliated with the Tupamáros but were possibly hiding guns under the long, 'too-soon-for-this-weather' type of coats. *Why was he second guessing his instincts?* He remained at the corner to observe them. After a few minutes, deciding to chance it he began crossing the street towards the front door. As he walked past from the opposite side of the street, he observed that they were no longer leaning on the car but had stepped away and were crossing the street towards him. Instinctively, he shoved his lunch in the hands of a street corner beggar. As he tried to thank him, Peter didn't stay to listen, for he knew that proceeding to the front of the building would most likely get him nabbed. The elevator would be a hindrance since one never knew how long it could take to arrive at ground level. After shoving his lunch in the beggar's hands, saying, "Dios te quiere, God loves you" he took off running with all his might.

The chase was on, and the thugs were after him. Crossing the street, Peter dodged cars; some screeched to a halt, blaring their horns, while not stopping his momentum. Peter just put his hands up, shouting, "Perdón, sorry!" The guys were catching up; at that point, he couldn't exactly stop and explain himself to every person he passed, as the thugs continued to trail his steps too close for comfort. Peter waited until they almost reached the same side he was on, and then he sprinted forward, hoping they would not be able to stop their momentum and secure an opening between traffic as the cars kept coming. Dodging back to the other side from whence he came, he repeated the same strategy again and again. If he ever doubted he was being possibly set up he now clearly had no doubt he was being followed. Realizing they were not backing off he aimed for a group of women he had spotted earlier that were window shopping. They were gaining on him, and he hoped he could make it. He always considered himself to be in prime shape, but these guys were running in full coats and keeping up! Only a bit further, and he would reach the women. It was at this exact moment that a family with umpteen children walked out of an adjacent store, blocking the entire sidewalk. Slowing him down and giving him only one choice, he had to dart back out between the parked cars toward the street, running parallel to them. Each continuing their forward movement, constantly looking back and forth at each other, assessing each other's next move, never losing sight of one another. As he passed the family, he darted back through another set of cars. Reaching the women, he pushed himself right in the middle of them, grabbing onto them by way of linking arms with them as they let out a shriek. In a loud voice, Peter quickly spoke to them in Spanish, pleading for help as the Tupamáros were trying to get him. Being winded, he was breathing really hard as he tried to convince them to help, describing the three thugs that were after him. Pointing them out, he told them, "See? They're the ones wearing the long coats. Please, for the love of God, don't leave me, or they will get me. I have a wife and children!" As he pleaded to the ladies, he had to stop and catch his breath, so if this didn't work out, he would be able to maintain another bout of running.

The heftiest woman of the bunch puffed up. Without fear, she turned around and sought out the men Peter was describing. Zeroing in on them, she stared them down with a 'go-to-hell' look. Then, with the added confidence of the rest of the women, she made it clear that they picked the wrong group of women to mess with. The men pretended to be window shopping across the street from them, but continued to stand there, waiting for their opportunity to nab him, believing that the women would eventually give up and leave, but they underestimated the ol' gals. Things weren't turning out as planned. The women consoled Peter and assured him that they would not leave him as long as those men were there. Like the Hatfield and McCoy's, they continued in their unified front, each on their side of the street, all the while sizing each other up. Thirty long, nerve-racking minutes passed when the lead guy made a signal. As the men had separated, Peter could only guess that he might be less inclined to try and leave. After the signal, they all immediately turned and walked back towards their car. As they turned the corner, they were out of Peter's sight, and yet, he was leery to move, so he remained planted. He didn't trust that they weren't hiding somewhere out of sight. Thanking the women profusely, he asked if they would do one more thing and just walk with him a bit of a ways towards his office so he could get a better view around the corner. Edging up as far as he could so he could see and yet be able to retreat, he scanned left to right, slowly back and forth many times until he felt assured that they were gone. The adrenaline he had was crashing, and he began to feel like a ton of bricks had hit him. Turning to the women again, he thanked them, and with that part over, he took off running as fast he could up the front steps and finally back inside the office building. He didn't wait for the elevator but took the stairs, two at a time, all the way up. Sweating again, he entered his office, closing the door behind him and locking it. Pineda looked up and asked, "What is going on and where have you been?"

"Just listen, would you? I don't want to say the same thing twice. If you have any questions after, then so be it." Picking up the handle to his rotary phone, he dialed the numbers to the police station.

Chapter 32

Dan's secretary was a portly woman, extremely efficient, but her girth slowed her down. Using the back side of her pencil, she leaned forward, smashing her large bosoms against the desk just to punch the intercom button; without it shortening the distance for her, it would have required her to get up just to use the intercom. Dan had already mentioned to her that, until further notice, he would accept all calls from Peter giving her permission to immediately forward them.

"Peter, hello!" Dan greeted him expecting the call to be about gun acquisitions.

"Dan, *they* tried to get me just now. Get some guys over here now. For all I know, they are just waiting for me to leave work!"

"Where are you and how many were there?"

"Just outside my office on the other side of the street. He replied. "There were three of them. They dressed the part but looked a bit out of place, as you suggested they might. Dan, they stood out to me despite their clothing and long coats, they seemed too rough-looking."

"Peter, their coats probably concealed weapons."

"That's what I was guessing. Have you been able to find more guns for me?"

"You're sure about this?" This was said more as a confirming statement than a question giving Peter another opportunity to re-think.

"Yes," he replied with such affirmation no one would have questioned it.

"Well, let's see. I bought two off an Air Force guy going back to the states this morning. I have that so far, and they have been cleaned too."

"Dan, I don't just want two, which I am very grateful for, but I want more so that every square inch of my house is covered. I will even take rifles if that is what is available."

"I completely understand. If it were my family, I would do the same. However, I have these two for now, and then, I can loan you one for the meantime until more can be purchased. I believe I can get some rifle loaners from the Military. Be prepared it isn't chea—"

Peter interjected, "Price isn't an issue. Don't worry about that; plus, at this point, is there ever really a dollar amount someone else in my position wouldn't pay?"

Dan continued. "No, you're right, there isn't where family is concerned. Peter, I hear your angst. I myself must consider my family due to the nature of my job. My wife learned long ago that bodyguards for each our six children and for us was to be the norm. This saddens me that your family is experiencing this strife. Just know this, that I truly understand, and that I will be with you each step of the way."

"Thank you, Dan, this support is immeasurable to me. It is difficult knowing what to do and keeping a lot from Paula, the phone calls, their attempt to have me kidnapped, just so my family is spared. Well, all of this you can say has kept me occupied," Peter muttered sarcastically.

Dan busted out laughing, to which Peter responded with a smirk. "Gray, you've got one twisted sense of humor! Better to laugh than go insane over the situation." Dan respected him; Peter had balls. "I know I would," Dan said while inhaling a drag from his cigarette. Blowing out the smoke, he jabbed the cigarette into the ashtray, not quite putting out the fire but breaking little sparks that danced up a little before floating down. Dan continued, "Anyway, Peter, these people need to be controlled, and damn it, I am not giving up. They think they can intimidate civilians, kidnap, bomb or extort businesses, and get away with it? … They will be caught eventually-all of them. This will not be one of those overnight success stories. I could see it taking years! Stay put in your office. Is Coimbra or Pineda with you?"

"Pineda took over about an hour ago, evidently Coimbra had something he had to do." Peter replied.

"I will see if the Sargénto can round up some men to escort you home. Sargénto can bring the weapons we discussed. If he is unavailable, then I will."

"Once again, Dan, thank you for all you have done. I know you have a lot on your plate with other families and people needing you." Peter choked up, embarrassed at the thought that a man like Mitrione might have picked up on it.

"No problem, Gray. I might see you in a bit. Until then, amigo."

Once he hung up with Dan Peter summoned Lucia into his office, then asked Pineda to step out so he could have a word with her privately.

"How are things for you, any calls?" he asked.

"A little scary, but I'm calm," Lucia answered. "When the phone rings, I do get a little tense. I get nervous that it will be one of those horrible people. I know I shouldn't think this way, but I do. Today it just has been relentless while you were out. The calls are not only being transferred to me, but they are coming into everyone within the building!"

"I am sorry Lucia," he added. "I wanted to express how very much so, and how I appreciate everything you are doing to help me. This is insane and dealing with this shouldn't be on your plate. Unfortunately, I need you and without your help screening these calls, I wouldn't be able to get any work done. Having someone here I can trust is immeasurable. Now, if you ever need anything, all you have to do is ask."

"You don't have to thank me, Sr. Gray. I am happy to help, and I am good. Really, I am. I just worry if I don't catch someone, and I transfer one of them, that you well, might get with annoyed me."

"Never, take that thought out of your mind completely. I know they are cunning. Listen, I wanted to tell you that I had a bit of an encounter with some Tupamáros that followed me today," *even this he downplayed on her behalf,* "So I am going to stay here with Pineda until some soldiers arrive that Dan Mitrione is sending to escort me home. Afterwards, I am going to call it a day. So, if you would like, feel free to go home early and enjoy your afternoon. You deserve it. Go have some fun, I am just going to pack up some things to work at home." He said with a reassuring smile.

"Oh, thank you!" Lucia broke out in a big grin. "There is a movie I wanted to see with my friend! Excuse me then, I am going to call her and see if she can go!" Taking off in a whirl, Peter watched her while he tapped his pencil methodically on the desk, as he anticipated Pineda's return. He envied her. He longed for the mindless days of yesterday. What he wanted was a rewind button, so that he could return to last year. He wondered if he had missed an obvious detail. He further pondered could he have done anything differently? Could he have avoided hiring Pedro?

Pineda walked into the room while letting out a belch. Peter looked at him with disgust. "Señor Gray don't forget my offer is always good," he chuckled. "That is, for the right price." Rubbing his full stomach, he added, "I shouldn't have eaten as much as I did, but since Pradman is paying to feed me, I am going to eat like a king!" Laughing as he leaned over the coffee table, he grabbed a magazine. Sitting back, he began to thumb through it, occasionally licking his thumb and fore finger, whenever he wanted to turn a page. Such a disgusting habit Peter thought, how he cringed knowing every page of the magazine would be covered with this man's spit. What a waste of money on a perfectly good magazine since it would now end up in the waste basket. He then addressed Pineda.

"Just stick to doing your job. Since you will ask, I am going to Jairo's office for a minute-alone. Watch the elevators and stairwell," he felt he should say, "while I am in there."

Chapter 33

The weather was great. Driving across town on such a gorgeous day wasn't so bad; the sun, the clouds, and the birds were pleasant. Peter's arm lay restfully, hanging out the window of his car. The wind whipped against it gently, almost soothingly upon his skin and through his hair. He could smell the light saltiness of the ocean breeze. At the red light, he perused his surroundings. Times would never be the same. His family weighed heavily on his mind. *Always be prepared...* wasn't that part of the boy scout motto, or something like that? Following the path of the beach front the next song that came on the radio happened to be his all-time favorite, the theme song of a Summer Place by Percy Faith Orchestra. Looking to the right, a beautiful young girl in her school uniform was walking arm in arm with her friends erupting in laughter at something that had been said. The light turned green. The asshole behind Peter immediately started blaring his horn before he even had a chance to accelerate, ruining a perfectly relaxing moment. One haphazard jerk of a wave later, he drove on towards Dan's office. Trying to relax to keep the dread at bay, he thought *was this to be his daily ritual...stress?*

The meeting was eventful. Dan had superseded all of Peter's hopes regarding the acquisition of more guns. Motioning to take a look at the armaments laid out on the table. Dan proceeded to review the mechanisms of each of the guns to include the two rifles which were an added bonus. Most of

Peter's knowledge was already honed while in the Brazilian military himself, but he did not interrupt as Dan, always thorough, left no instruction unreviewed. Dan did take the opportunity to discuss the updates on a worst-case scenario preventative plan. They had to start somewhere, and what amazed Peter at this juncture was learning firsthand how many details went into the planning of an operation as such. The Uruguayan military had already coordinated their tactical soldiers in the event that an escorted escape was deemed necessary; but for the time being, the operation's sole purpose was to protect the Gray family, at least until things settled down. Their meeting had left him with a sense of peace.... His emotions recently tended to go up and down like a car on a roller coaster, which he hated. Nonetheless, this cold steel that he acquired today was yet another reminder of the ultimate lengths he would go to defend his family from the unknown threatening presence. Knowing that he had protection within a fingertip's length gave him some security.

The way to success is patience, and I have all the time in the world, Miguel mused. I will get that rat bastard! He was good at taking his time. He made a habit of it, not for the strategic benefits but because it added to the level of excitement. He was an adrenaline junkie. While he waited, he thought, *why not entertain myself a little? The idiots don't even know I am here.* Miguel had hunkered down in front of the chimney in the "V" area up on the roof where the joists met.

Nestled between a row of other older homes, prior to the growth of the area, this home was a testament to the endurance of time. It had large, fully developed trees and tall hibiscus bushes, making a perfect wall of privacy around its circumference. It was the perfect spot for Miguel. He had the chimney to his back providing cover, and the eve of the roof was just so that he could rest his binoculars on the crested point to observe Peter's office and the front entrance of the building.

They were being sloppy, he thought. They were leaving the curtains cracked open. Sometimes, he could see the figure of

Peter pacing, as he habitually did while talking on the phone. How Miguel wished he could be even closer and that he had the ability to read lips. One never knew what Peter's conversations could give him regarding where the families whereabouts would be on any particular given day.

Chapter 34

Lucia walked out of the building. Turning right, like she did most afternoons, she headed towards the bus stop. She was a tad bit earlier than her normal time. *How, convenient for me,* he thought. Hanging the binoculars around his neck, he quietly made his way across the tiled roof, careful not to slip or knock any tiles loose— exposing his presence to the tenants living in the house below. He also did not want to divulge his location to anyone that might notice him from the street. Going to the edge of the roof, he stepped over onto the ledge of the wall that surrounded the house for protection. Some of the houses had broken glass embedded in the cement at the top as added protection discouraging thieves from trespassing. Thankfully, this one didn't. Moving along the wall, peering over, Miguel looked for the tree he knew would be there. Leaning over, he reached up and over into the couple's yard and proceeded to lunge towards it grabbing the limb, and as he did he swung off of it doing a bit of a dismount as if he were a gymnast, onto the sidewalk below. Rating the dismount, a ten, he laughed as he walked down the street towards his parked car. Climbing in he slammed the door shut and started up the engine. It wasn't the newest Volkswagen, but it sputtered to life, however reluctantly. Jamming it into first, he looked to see if any cars were coming, then pulled out quickly. Turning at the next corner, he made a rolling stop and switched into second as he continued. The car hummed along, making the ascending noises as it neared time to switch into third gear. To him, a vehicle was only a means to get him from point A to point B, so he wasn't exactly very gentle with his vehicles. Plus, for anonymity's sake, he tended to discard them after certain missions. Reaching a high velocity, he switched to fourth gear. The windows were down, and the salty air whipped around his face, causing the sleeve on his shirt to flap relentlessly. Arriving home, he entered his apartment and locked the front door, tossing his keys on the couch. Grabbing a beer, he went upstairs to the closet he had soundproofed. Picking up the phone, he pulled it into the closet with him. He kept the light on that he had wired into the closet area so that he could see. Most closets of this time didn't have any lights within them, so this was a definite addition. He began dialing the number he knew now by heart that rang directly into Peter's office. The phone began ringing.

"Peter Gray," Peter answered. He could hear breathing on the line. "Hello? Damn it! Habla! Speak!" Slamming the phone down, Peter groaned with exasperation. Pineda had a feeling of who had been on the line, but he just smirked from across the room and kept silent. Miguel waited about five minutes and rang again. Just enough time to allow him to relax and then start up again. Peter answered, immediately barking, "Hello?"

A muffled voice spoke. "You think you are *so* above everyone, you miserable *Imperialist Pig!* We *know* where you live. We *know* where your kids go to school. We *know* everything about you! You better drop the charges against me, or your kids are next!"

Peter started to say something back when the line disconnected. He did not waste time. Racing to the window, he peeked outside, looking to see if he saw anyone. Not feeling like he had the time to observe, he went out of the building via the service elevator. Maneuvering through the work areas, the staff looked at him with puzzled looks. He mumbled an excuse of being in a hurry and that he had parked close behind. He jogged to his car, all the while keeping his hand in his pocket with his finger around the trigger. The downside about driving a stick shift was he had to let go of his revolver. He had to be creative and plan an entirely new route home, which meant some increased drive time. He pulled into the driveway rather abruptly, which caught the attention of the guards. One of the night guards approached the car. He knew something was up by the way Peter pulled in. Peter scrambled out of the car, all the while blurting his comments to the guards. "I got another phone call.

They mentioned the kids. I just had to get home and make sure everyone was okay. "Why don't you get inside? The guard suggested. It isn't good for you to be standing out here. We can talk there."

"I will be in as soon as I talk to the other officers; I suggest that the kids no longer play outside."

Peter unlocked the front door and entered the house.

Putting on a false air of 'everything was hunky-dory,' he walked into a rather frenetic greeting. "Daddy's hooome!" Bergen drug out the syllables, squealing in a high pitch. She had been playing with her dolls in the living room. Hopping up from the carpet, she ran to hug her Daddy.

Paula walked in. "Hey, you! Kind of early, aren't you?"

"A little, just wanted to see my girls. Is that a crime?" Grabbing her, he swung her around as if they were dancing. Then, he bent over and gave her a big kiss as he dipped her downward and then brought her right back up. Paula laughed and swatted at his arm. The phone rang. Peter stiffened momentarily. By then, Paula had stepped to the side to smooth out her dress and pat her hair in place, as if to recompose herself. Before he could get to the phone, Paula, still giggling, reached for it and answered the call. Her laughter was cut short. "Grays' residency," she said into the receiver. Not a word was spoken, but she could hear a distant muffled sound of a radio. "Hello?" she said again. Peter, by then, reached her and took the receiver out of her hand and slammed it down on its cradle.

"It was them again. Wasn't it, Peter?" Tears immediately pooled in her eyes threatening to spill over.

"Probably. Just, if the phone rings again, do not answer it, okay? I got a couple of calls today at work. I didn't want to tell you and upset you, but now, I might as well. They are just trying to get in our heads, and we won't let them."

"You did?" she said incredulously. "What did they say? Could you make anything out?"

"Once, they spoke, but other times, nothing." He followed her into the kitchen. "We need to talk to the kids. You know that, right?" Peter said somberly.

"Oh, Peter, do we have to? I don't think it is good to tell them all of what's going on. The children do not need to worry or have that kind of stress in their lives." Pleading, she added, "It will only instill fear!"

"Yes, but meanwhile, we need to prepare them, mentally and emotionally. We do not know what is going to happen next. What if they did get to them? Have you thought about that? They need to have something to go on. We need to teach them what to do if they are approached, as well as the worst-case scenario... What if they did get one of them? We are dealing with Tupamáros! If they have a little bit of knowledge, it might save them and empower them, knowing the whys and what to do in a situation. This is a potential reality, even though we are doing everything possible to avoid that scenario! They will not take us seriously if we do not share how serious it truly is, Paula! I am about to tell them they can no longer play out front for Christ sakes! If you think the boys won't try and pull a fast one on us and go out, you are sorely mistaken. You know how Dane is, he tries to act like he is as tough as nails all the time! You are going to have your hands full making sure they don't go outside as it is." Cupping her chin in his hand, he lifted her chin gently so that she was looking him in the eyes. "You do understand, don't you?" he said softly. She tried to pull away, but he gently held on so she remained looking at him while he added, "And why we cannot hold off anymore?"

Nodding in understanding, she softly said with a defeated whisper, "Let's get this over with." Wiping tears from her face, she morosely walked over to the sink, ran cold water over her hands, patting her face. Picking up a clean kitchen towel she gently patted her face once again and dried her hands. Paula turned around and nodded as if to say "ready." God, she was gorgeous. There were very few women he had come across in his lifetime that were as beautiful, with or without makeup. One thing for which he would never forgive himself was the image of the contorted agony on her face, and he felt responsible for it.

They walked together into the living room, as Peter called the kids by name. "Come on, kids. Family meeting all three of you-now!"

"Hey, Dad, you're never home this early," Jack remarked. "What's going on?" he asked always suspicious. "Are we in trouble? Don't tell me we are moving again? 'Cause if we are, I'm not going. I just made friends, and I like them, and I—"

Peter cut him off before he rambled on some more. This was Jack's way: never short of words and always perceptive too. "Whoa there, cowboy! One, we are not moving… yet, and two—"

Jack butted in again. "Good because I am not going. You can, but I don't want to. I like it here. Right Mom?" He looked at Paula for reinforcement.

Right at that moment, Dane walked in over-hearing Jack's last comment. Questioningly, he looked over at his dad with extreme irritation and retorted, "Moving? Again? Awww, come on, Dad. We just got here! For Christ's sake, Dad!"

"DANE!" Paula snapped at her son. Dane looked sheepishly over at his mother.

Peter looked toward Paula in exasperation. "For the last time, we are not moving—well, at least, not for now!"

Bergen, by then, was the last to make her entry into the living room with her baby doll and all its necessary accessories. She practically packed a suitcase full for her babies which were as real as real could be to her, and they just might need something. Her eyes were big as saucers, it was hard to not hear what Dane said as he delivered his opinion loudly. "That is good, Daddy, because I don't want to leave my school!"

"Children," Peter said, "come sit down. We need to talk about some particularly important things." They each plopped on the couch, and Bergen situated her Madame Alexander baby doll next to her.

"I know you have wondered why some of the changes have taken place at home and also why so many weird things have gone on. Frankly, I did not think it was something you all needed to worry yourselves about, but now, I have no choice but to share." They nodded in unison as they looked at one another with apprehensive expressions. Dane, however being the eldest, wasn't fooled. Peter went on, "So, the questions have been why the phone rings, and no one talks on the other line, why people drive by and are breaking bottles on the roof, why rocks are being thrown too, and why we have personal drivers, and—the last question—what is the reason we have guards around our home. First, I want to say that we are all okay, so I do not want you to worry. Leave that to the grown-ups. However, that is why we are doing all these things: to make sure we are all safe. It is time for us to tell you the reason why. There was a man at work that I caught who did some bad things, and he got into trouble for it."

Bergen tattled, "Like Jack does when he talks a lot?" Jack stuck out his tongue at her, and she did the same right back.

Peter spoke out, "Enough!" They all snapped to attention. This was not like their dad to raise his voice—ever! Dane had yet to sit down. He remained stoic, leaning against the wall with his arms crossed in a defensive posture. Peter began again, "Like I was saying, this man got into trouble, and he lost his job because of his poor choices. He is very angry with me and has begun to make some threats. He is just being a bully and is just trying to scare us. So, all we have to do is be smart and cautious until he goes away."

Bergen asked, "What's cautious?"

Dane blurted, "Means be careful, Bergen. I bet he's a Tupamáro, nobody would have this much going on if he wasn't!" This was hitting him the hardest. Being the oldest, he saw through this little charade his dad was putting on to downplay the situation and not frighten his younger brother and sister. Nothing fooled Dane. He was sharp.

Peter began again, "Dane enough! Bergen, we must be careful. That means all of us! Understand? So, we have to give up doing a few things in the meantime."

"NOOOOO!" the boys said in unity.

He put his hand up, signaling them to stop. "The first thing is no more riding your bikes around the neighborhood or playing in the front yard of the house!"

Dane spoke up first, "Aww, come on, Dad. You have got to be kidding! I can take care of myself. You know I can ride my bike fast; no one can catch me. Anyway, Jack has had to share his bike since mine got stolen, so I don't get that much time as it is!"

"No, Dane, this is not up for discussion. For now, this is how it has to be. You are going to have to trust me on this. I have one last thing I want to say, and this is very serious, so listen carefully. This is only in the event that someone ever did get any of you: I want you all to be calm. You must stay strong, and you need to be very observant of everything you see and hear. I want you to make sure you know all our phone numbers and home address. Bergen, Mommy is going to practice with you every day to learn the address and phone numbers of my work and the house— thankfully you boys, I believe, already know, but you do need to learn my work information along with Bergen. Unfortunately, Bergen needs to learn all of it. If you were to get caught…" Peter paused, getting choked up at the thought. He cleared his throat and tried again. "This is serious: *GAIN THEIR TRUST!* Make them think you would be too scared to run from them. Do everything they say. Do not, I repeat, do not annoy them ever! Doing these things… they might lean towards not wanting to harm you and might save you. Not doing so might anger them. Turning specifically towards his son, Peter said, "Dane, no shooting your mouth off and no tough guy stuff either! Don't allow yourself to get weak by refusing food just because you're upset. If they offer it, eat. If they ever do leave you alone, then—and only then—try to find a phone. If there is one, call us. Describe where you are or what you see outside: a street sign or a name of a store… so that we can find you. A name you remember they called themselves. If they ever take you outside for any reason, remember your surroundings: the color of the building or if there is a number on the door. Stuff like that. If they have left you alone, use your best judgment before you do anything to try and escape. If you are able to sneak out, check to see if anyone is watching the building first! If you can get out, run as far away without looking back, until you are tired and then hide. When you are hiding, look around. Find someone that looks kind, if you cannot find a policeman, ask for them to hide you, and give them my numbers to call me. You can tell them a huge reward will be waiting for them! If they do not have a phone, have them bring you to me if possible and tell them that I will pay for everything! Do you have any questions for me?"

In the silence that followed, one could hear a pin drop. He knew then that this had sunk in on the deepest level. None spoke, nor did any want to. Dane just stared—there was a mature melancholy that came from him being the eldest. He really understood that this was much bigger and that his father was not even sparing Bergen. Speaking again, Peter gently said, "I think this is enough to digest for one night. Any questions?" All three shook their heads morosely. "Ok then, go on, but try not to worry, most likely none of these possibilities will ever happen. I just needed to be honest with you that there could be a time you might need to know these things, and, if you find yourself in a tough spot, God forbid it, that you would know what to do and would be prepared. Oh, and one last thing - leave the answering of the phone to your mom or one of the maids, at least for a while."

"Dad, about riding my bike—"

Peter cut Dane off a little more sharply than he had intended to. "It isn't an option, son!" Dane took off furiously to his room and slammed his door. Peter stood there for what seemed to be an eternity. Normally, he wouldn't have tolerated a scene like that and would have reprimanded him on the spot, but under the circumstances, he chose to let it slide. He could be a bit hot headed, and all his buttons had just been pushed. Deep in thought at what had just transpired, Peter felt a tap on his arm. Looking up at Paula, she handed him a drink. "Thank you." He kissed her on the forehead and rested his to hers. With his eyes closed, he took in her scent. Somehow, just being with her relaxed him. He kissed her again. "Hey, let's eat. I am starved after all."

"I see where Jack gets this." They both laughed. It felt good to laugh; they needed to laugh.

Chapter 35

Dinner was rather quiet as the kids were preoccupied with their own thoughts. Afterwards, the boys chose to stay in their rooms not wanting to be socializing. Bergen hung around a bit but then decided to go join her brothers.

Paula, while making some after-dinner drinks, remarked, "So, where are the evening guards hiding out? I haven't heard them yet."

Peter snapped his head up. "What do you mean?" he said a little more tersely than planned.

"Well, I looked outside just now when I let Loba out, and no one is out there!"

Peter got up and strode to the front door, jerking the side window curtain aside, first from the left and then to the right of the front door trying to see all angles. Not seeing anyone, he risked going outside. Briskly, he walked the perimeter of the front side of the house and found nothing; not one guard, Paula was right! Walking back in the house, he re-locked the door, he asked Paula, "Are the kids still all in the house?"

"I just heard them, they're in the back garden with Loba," she answered. The tension was immediately back permeating the air like a see-through veil cloaking the air.

"Get them inside and lock the back doors while I check the complete perimeter of the house. I'm calling the police station this minute. Maybe, they are just late." He sat at the phone desk in the corridor. Opening the drawer, he pulled out the small telephone book, where he had jotted down the number of the police station. Dialing was a frustrating thing when trying to do it quickly. There never was a quick way to dial a rotary phone. The mechanism always took its time spinning back to its original position before the next number could be selected. No amount of griping changed the outcome. As in anything, one day he supposed that someone would invent something easier. He was sweating on his upper lip. The thought ran across his mind that he was so glad he had the guns. Damn it! He could feel the tension in his shoulders. When he got home, the lead guard never mentioned to him that the night shift would not be available.

The line rang and rang. Finally, the receptionist answered. "Estación de la Policía."

Blurting ahead of himself, he began and then reigned it in. "Sargénto. I-I need to speak with the Sargénto please. This is Peter Gray."

"One moment, Señor." The call was put into No Man's Land for a minute.

Then, he heard the voice on the other end. "Mr. Gray, how may I be of service?" Sargénto said in a deep, gravelly voice.

"The guards are not here, and it is after dark! Is there a reason for this?"

"Give me a minute to figure this out." Sargénto put him on hold and then called back up to the front desk. He spoke with the officer in charge of scheduling special ops. "What is going on with the guards assigned to the Grays' home?"

The officer stood up and walked over to the master calendar on the chalkboard. "Sargénto, they were pulled for tonight. They were needed on a stakeout. From one of our sources, we received a promising lead today that there is going to be another hit in the southern section of town. We have been trying to nab these thugs for eight months now. When we are shorthanded, we have to pull our men from smaller cases." The Sargénto snapped, and the guy's eyes opened wide. It was too bad Peter couldn't see that.

"Smaller cases?" Sargénto said in disbelief. "Smaller cases! Why wasn't I notified? This isn't a babysitting job! This is protecting a family from the Tupamáros. Who in the hell made this decision without my authorization? This could be a purposeful deflection just to leave this family vulnerable. Who was the idiot that approved this?" The officer tried to reply but was shut down.

"I need Dan Mitrione to call me tonight, this cannot continue." This was insane. He knew times were hard, but one would think the government could afford to keep more officers employed and know the distinction on assessing what was important when assigning officers.

God, he didn't want to tell Peter they weren't coming, but he had to. Sargénto, after talking with Dan, walked into his office and closed the door. Picking up the phone, he continued his conversation with Peter.

"What did you find out?" Peter said. "How much longer before they get here?"

"I am ashamed to say this, but they won't be coming," Sargénto answered, disappointment dripping in his voice.

"Won't be coming?" He said incredulously. "I hope you're kidding! We cannot be left without security! The assholes already called me at work and at home today!"

"Peter, they were pulled on another assignment. A bad call was made somewhere that it was more important than yours. I am not happy about this, trust me! I was not informed, and this was done without my authorization. I will deal with this tomorrow. I can assure you! Not sure if this will make you feel any better, but I spoke with Dan. We decided that your protection will be completely in the hands of the Uruguayan Military from now on. We need to be consistent and as tonight proved, the Police Department isn't reliable for long term protection."

"Not happy? No disrespect, Sargénto, but this isn't about happy or not. We are living in a fishbowl from hell here. They know who we are and where we live, and we don't have the same privilege!" Due to frustration, he raised his voice. "We are sitting ducks, ready to be picked off if they so choose. I don't have time to waste here, for all I know, they might decide to trail my family and not just me! They've already threatened my kids. You're talking about my kids—my wife, Sarge! Find out what is happening. Fix it, for God's sake please!" Peter cradled his head in his hand. He was weary. "I don't care how, I don't care who, but find some guys and get them here, even if you have to pay them extra."

Sargénto was a good man, and he was ashamed of his unit at that moment. He was one of the few that had a heart—a real conscience. "Señor. Gray, I am terribly sorry. I will do my best. Do you have your guns in place?"

"Some," Peter said. "The minute we hang up I will get the new ones ready."

"Make sure that you have plenty of ammunition in each area, so you are covered, if needed," Sargénto added. "I hope your evening is peaceful and that nothing happens. I will do my best from my end. I will personally come out if no one is found. God be with you."

"Thank you, I appreciate that, goodnight." Peter slowly hung the phone up. Pensively, he looked over and then up at Paula as she walked in the hallway, shaking his head from left to right, communicating that no one was most likely coming, answering the questioning look in her eyes. "Paula, I picked up some extra armaments today. We will be okay. I wasn't going to tell you that, but now, I think it should make you feel better. I want you to double-check all the doors and windows making sure they are still locked. Would you also make sure the curtains are closed tight too, please?"

"Of course, Peter." Paula said.

He continued, "I am going to load the new guns and decide where to place them. Don't tell the kids that we have as many as we do, or they will be freaked out."

"I wouldn't dream of it, Peter, but I am worried leaving loaded guns around the house, especially with the children." He could hear the worry in her voice.

"We don't have any other option. I need to protect you all! God, Paula, it looks like we're on our own tonight. I will have to talk to the kids. They shouldn't have to know what fear is, or at least on this level, but they do! At least, now, they have to—all because I had to take this damn job here."

"Peter, please, stop that!" Paula said with a plea to her voice. She cupped his face in her hands as he remained seated in the telephone chair. "Look at me! It is not your fault. It's theirs, the Tupamáros. You did not cause this," she said as she gestured to open air.

"But I had to hire one," he said bitterly. "I should have been more careful during these times. He was too good to be true. I should have caught that!" Continuing to beat himself up he added, "If I had been only a little more suspicious about everyone, I interviewed…" Getting up, he walked over to his briefcase, eventually he would retrieve the rifles from the trunk of his car, it would be a risk going outside tonight albeit necessary.

"There is no way you could have known, Peter. They are brilliant at deception."

"I'm going to go load these in our bedroom, and when I finish, we can decide where best to position them. Just keep the kids occupied. If they come near, I don't want to explain why I have the door locked. I will eventually need to show you how to use one of these, just in case, God forbid, you needed to protect yourself."

Softly, she said, "Okay. If you think it's best." He embraced her with one arm, as his other hand still held his briefcase. Letting go he went towards their bedroom, locking the door behind him. Paula decided to bring the dog inside. Loba was excellent about letting them know if someone was outside, but she wasn't about to leave her in a vulnerable position where they would try and kill her to silence her. She could still do her job from indoors. Opening the backdoor, dutifully, Loba walked forward, wiping her front paws on the mat. She took a few more steps forward, and then wiped her back paws before stopping and looking up at Paula, waiting for the acknowledgment of a deed well done. Paula scratched her behind the ears, while talking in a baby voice to her, "You are a dear, Loba. What would we do without you? We wouldn't leave you outside, would we?" Wagging her tail all happy, Loba trotted off towards the voices of the kids. That dog was amazing, knowing how to wipe its paws! She locked the back door and worked her way from one side of the house to the other, checking every window and door making sure they were locked and that every curtain was drawn closed. She had even taken to hanging noisy spoons on a ring and hanging them off the doorknobs too. She had seen that in a movie. Peter, at first, laughed at her paranoia, but now, he was not laughing anymore. It actually wasn't such a bad idea.

Peter rushed through the task of loading the guns and rifles, then he began the process of placing the newly acquired guns in their strategic spots. He found that he had to reconfigure the distances so that they were evenly dispersed. Walking back to the kitchen, he felt rather good about things. Retrieving his forgotten glass of wine, he took a final swig and put his glass in the sink. Flipping off the light, he headed towards the master bedroom as he heard the first volley of glass bottles crashing onto the roof tiles above, followed by several more. This time was different; he could hear two different cars accelerating past at delayed intervals, and they were early. He was unaware that some guards had shown up until he heard them yelling at each other. He said to himself *God bless the Sargénto! Better late than never!* He continued being comforted by hearing their raised voices. Due to their military training, they knew not to leave their designated sides they were assigned to cover, but to communicate as best as possible. Ever the professionals, they also knew a side would be compromised if one left it unguarded, and that is exactly what those characters kept hoping for. Bergen was crying. Jack had fallen asleep on top of the covers in his clothes and slept on, oblivious to the chaos. That child could sleep through an earthquake. The only other child to consider was Dane. Their eyes met, and he had the saddest expression, as if aged by an experience only an old man could have. Turning around, Dane walked back into his room. Paula began comforting Bergen by singing her a lullaby. Peter walked back into the boy's room, worried about his sons. Still seeing only Dane awake, he spoke, "Son?"

"Yes, Dad?" he answered quietly.

"It's going to be okay. The guards are here. All those criminals can do are these small scare tactics." *He wasn't sure, if he was trying to convince Dane or himself with those words.* An afterthought, he wondered if he was trying to convince himself more than Dane.

"Yes, and break all the lamps around our house and the streetlights! It's not going to stop, Dad, and making us be stuck in this house without our friends stinks!"

"I am sorry, son. Trust me, I will do everything in my power to—" He stopped due to a lump forming in his throat. Fighting to gain emotional control, he then continued, "—to take care of all of you. Try and get some sleep now. They have probably had all their fun for one evening at our expense. I am going to let Bergen sleep in here tonight with Jack, and tomorrow I may squeeze her bed into here so you all can be together. I need to get her away from the front of the house. I have my own ways of protecting us too. We are covered-trust me! Dane, he paused then added, son, I love you. You don't have to be tough all the time you know. If you need me, I am here. Capiche?" A few seconds passed, then he heard Dane's reply.

"Capiche," he almost whispered back to his dad.

Peter walked back to check on Bergen. Paula put her fingers to her lips, signaling him to be quiet. She pointed for him to go to the bedroom. Quietly, she got up and pulled the blankets up and around her little girl. It was hard getting her back to sleep, but since she did, it was best to leave her for now. Later she definitely would have Peter move her bed into the boy's room. Paula took a quick peek out the curtains in Bergen's room. Staring into the black abyss of the night, her eyes had adjusted to the darkness. Nothing could be seen except the distant glow of a streetlight. Looking to the opposite side, she saw the fire light up as one of the guards took a long drag from his cigarette, which gave her comfort, knowing he was just outside of Bergen's bedroom window. Well, at least some guards showed up. Better late than never. Bergen was finally sleeping soundly. Paula had lingered a while to make sure. Giving one last kiss on Bergen's head, Paula went to kiss the boy's goodnight. Dane was still awake. "I am so sorry, Dane. Dad told me he was going to bring your sister in here to sleep, but since she fell back asleep, I wanted you to know I am just going to leave her for tonight, in her bed. Please, try and sleep now, love," Paula said lovingly to her eldest child. Dane nodded, not saying anything. This was his way of shutting down. She bent down and gave him a kiss on the head. He would never be too big for her to do so. He rolled over. His body language said the conversation was over, and she would respect that. He had enough on his shoulders for a young boy. He needed to drop the subject to survive emotionally. No matter how manly and tough he acted, he was still a young boy trying to be a man.

Chapter 36

Miguel, I want Gray shut down." Mata made his comment to the group gathered. "He is a distraction, and he will create a needless focus upon us by the authorities, especially by not dropping the charges against you."

"Miguel? Miguel!" he yelled at him. "Are you listening?"

"Yes, yes, Señor. I just was thinking of how."

Mata harrumphed at his answer and turned to face the men again. "I want pressure put on them tonight. Don't let up, and tomorrow... well, tomorrow, I think the time has come for our little visit to his daughter at school." Miguel started chuckling, and the others joined in while Mata continued, "I have the specs of the roads surrounding The British Schools behind me on the board." Standing up, he walked over and started drawing arrows to the directions and positions of the folks involved. "I want Miguel to guard the front gate; Sal, the back gate; and Paco, Rafa, and Mario will go in and nab her."

Paco spoke up first. "What is the time frame, and do you have an idea of the school's schedule?" Mata walked over to the left of the chalk board and started jotting down what little he knew. "The name of the child is Bergen. She is eight years old, and their schedule is simpler than the older students. At two o'clock, they go out to the west field for what they call a "recess." It is what the English call a break time." He began passing out a copy of a picture of Bergen to the men and continued. "Here is her picture. Memorize it. You will all go in as a crew of repairmen. Tonight, we will snip the line to the electrical box, and tomorrow, you will show up to fix it. We will divert the phone call to us when it comes in. When you arrive, you will be expected, so act casually. I want you to angle the vehicle outwardly so you will be ready when leaving. Make sure there is chloroform to quiet the girl. I want no harm done to her, but she needs to be quieted immediately. I cannot stress how valuable she is to us. We will extort lots of money, and then, we will take care of her—teaching that Gringo a valuable lesson. You will go three blocks, turn right on Calle das Rosas, and enter the Pontifica Garage from the back. Pull in behind the third bay door and, when they open the door, do not waste time. Enter immediately. The attendant—a brother of the cause—will close the door. Quickly transfer her to the other vehicle in the second bay, change your clothes, and then head out to the rancho. One of our Tupamara's named Deusalinda will ride as your wife, Rafa. You will look like a traveling family. The car will be full of petrol. We will keep her there. There will be snacks and water in the car as well if she wakes up. Your maps will be in the glove box. Stick to the route mapped out for you. It will take you two days to get there. Only if she causes a problem, do you use the chloroform again. She is an exceedingly small child, rather on the skinny side, and as I said before - nothing must happen to her. Understood?" He said that more as a warning and not a question. "Report back to me as soon as you arrive at the rancho. Flavia will be there to take care of your needs. After this, I want you to stay out of view for a while. We will contact you. Dismissed." Without looking back, in a low monotone voice, he said, "Don't fail."

Chapter 37

The car came down the street without its headlights on. A hand came out the window, and an object was thrown. The streetlight's glass shattered onto the asphalt on the street below. The guys cracked up in amusement as they hit their target. Tires squealing, they turned the corner sharply and rapidly made their turnaround so that they could repeat their barrage once more before leaving. The second streetlight was busted, letting out a small flame that immediately went out. A volley of glass bottles followed, all aimed for the roof above the children's bedrooms. They took off with every intention of returning. They would wait long enough so the Gray family would just begin to relax, thinking it might be over and wham, the assault would begin again! This continued as ordered throughout the night, only calling it off around four in the morning.

Paula was shaking, holding on to Bergen. Bergen was whimpering, exhausted; her tears soaked her pajamas. "Peter, please, this has to stop—Peter, what if we moved? If we move, they won't know where we are!"

"I think they would find us wherever we went, despite our attempts to hide. Stay here. I'm going to check on the boys again." He walked out of their room and ran into the guard that happened to have the same idea as Peter. Things were bleak. He was feeling helpless. The stress was starting to wear him down, and he began to doubt his ability to protect his family. Tomorrow, if all the guards weren't back at night, he made plans to take Paula and the kids to stay at the hotel. They would stay there until he could figure out what to do. At least, there, they would be in a public venue and within a fortress of the stone walls.

Morning came, and everyone was quiet at the breakfast table suffering from exhaustion. Dane spoke up first. "Dad, let me keep my BB gun loaded, and whenever they come by, I can shoot at their tires!"

"NO! I mean, just no. Sorry, son. I did not mean to snap." Dane looked at him, surprised. It was so unlike his dad to lose his composure. "I am sorry Dane. We all are tired and a little on edge from the lack of sleep. Well, that is, except Jack." With that comment, they all busted out laughing for he never woke up.

Dane continued. "It's okay, Dad. I just wanted to help. I am a good shot! I can even get birds while they are in flight, Dad," he said with hope.

"Still, I don't want you anywhere near the windows. No BB guns! We will leave any shooting up to the guards. That is what they are here for." Peter's word was final and Dane didn't even argue with him. Turning to Paula he asked, "Do you think the maids could handle carrying the twin mattresses of the boys into our room?

"I think they could, if not I am sure two of the guards could help."

"Good deal. I am thinking if we put theirs together on the floor perhaps all three could fit and sleep in our room. I don't think we could fit Bergen's in there." Dane scowled in the corner choosing to keep silent.

"Give me a hug goodbye." They stood up one by one and embraced their dad before he went out the front door. Bergen stood in the bay window watching as the guards searched the undercarriage with large, oversized mirrors. These mirrors reminded you of the ones the dentist's used but way bigger! They were searching for any possible bombs that might have been placed overnight. Peter asked the lead guard on duty,

"Why the hell weren't you here last night at the beginning of the shift? You wouldn't have to do this if one of you had been here!"

"Sometimes, we are pulled for other high priority cases. We don't make the call. We are not a big estación; we are a small station. Anyway we have been given orders that we are to check your car every day from now on."

"High priority!" That bit into Peter. "What else is as high of a priority as protecting my family from potential Tupamáros! Those criminals were a joy last night—ask my wife and my frightened kids!" He got in the car and slammed the door.

The guards went nuts. "No, Señor Gray, we must start the car!" Peter let out an explicative, stepped back out, and walked away from the car. Fuming, he waited at what they perceived as a safe distance to be. The guard continued circling the car carefully finishing their inspection of the undercarriage for the potential bombs. Once the inspection was finished, one of the guards got in as the others stepped away; only then did he start the vehicle without issue. No bombs today. For the first time it dawned on Peter, that this man too probably had a family wanting him to come home, and yet here he was putting his life on the line, just for him. Humbled he thought, *these guys didn't deserve his earlier outburst, for they were just following orders otherwise they would have been here.* As he drove out of the driveway, with his bodyguard in the passenger seat, Peter happened to catch a glimpse of Bergen in his rear-view mirror as she stared out the front bay window. *Damn it,* he thought to himself, *no kid should have to watch their dad's car be checked for bombs.* He wondered just what could possibly be running through her mind and if this would leave any lasting emotional harm.

Chapter 38

One of the guards, affectionately known as Perro, had developed a friendship over time with Dane. He felt for the boy, especially since he had a son the same age, and he had great empathy that a boy his age was experiencing a situation like this. Dane had confided to him long before he broke the news to his parents that his bike had been stolen a few months ago, after he left it outside overnight. Living in an affluent neighborhood did not mean necessarily they were shielded from petty larceny.

Perro had a gut feeling that it was a local kid that probably nabbed it. So, every day as he came to work, he purposefully took different routes through the neighborhood making it his mission to find Dane's bicycle. On a hunch, Perro searched the neighborhood around the Arocena Bowling Alley and slowly worked his way outwardly. It so happened that a bike that looked similar to Dane's was only ten blocks away. First of all, Dane's bike wasn't your average Uruguayan made bike, but stood out like a sore thumb, as it was American made. This particular bike was unique, for it had an angulated seat with ridges. Perro noticed that the color wasn't the same as Dane's, but the rest seemed the same, so he devised a plan to further inspect it closely. Taking a few days, he had an opportunity as the boy riding it carelessly left it outside his home just as Dane had. Stopping his car across the street, Perro grabbed his Swiss knife. Quickly crossing the street, he crouched down where it was then he noticed that it had been repainted. In an inconspicuous area, he scraped away the navy-colored paint, exposing the original light blue underneath-this was the exact color of Dane's bike! Pumped, he got back in his car and continued to the Gray's house hoping to catch Sr. Gray before he left for work to share his finding's.

As Perro drove up to the house, he blocked the driveway so Peter couldn't pull out. It was a good move since he had just been given the go ahead to leave. Perro got out and jogged over to Peter's driver's side door. He explained his findings and the measures he took to find the bike.

Peter asked him, "Will you ride with me and point out the house?"

"Of course, of course, let me move my car and then we can go." Climbing in the back seat of Peter's car, he gave him the directions, explaining that the house where the bike was found was about ten blocks from the Arocena Bowling Alley and more than likely being an American bike made it a hot commodity. They pulled in front of a well-kept house. Their maid was outside sweeping the walkways. This was a house that in Peter's mind could afford a bike for their child, so why steal? Getting out he asked the maid if he could speak with the owner of the house. After she went in, Perro, who decided to step out, pointed at the area he had scraped the paint away revealing the original color. Peter knew it was Dane's and before the owner of the house came out, he asked the guard to place the bike in the trunk of the car. As the man of the house came out his front door, he saw them loading the bike in the trunk of Peter's car. Ignoring Peter, he began yelling. "What the hell are you doing?"

Peter interjected, "That is my son's bike, and I would like to know why it is at your house and why it has been repainted?"

The man argued, "This is my son's bike and he bought it from a friend, I gave him the money!"

"I don't think he bought it from anyone. I think he stole it. It is obvious it's been re-painted." Peter added. "Come over to the car, I'll show you."

"My son doesn't steal" The man replied.

"Then how do you explain this?" Peter showed him where the guard had scraped the paint revealing the original paint color. "I have pictures showing my son with this very exact bike!" Precisely at that moment there was a commotion at the front door as the man's wife came out, verbally reprimanding her son in Spanish as she pulled him by his ear, towards his father; all the while the boy cried out due to the discomfort.

The woman spoke to her husband as she let go of the boy's ear, "Marcos, I believe our son has something to tell you about this."

Speaking to his son he asked him, "What do you have to say? Did you have anything to do with taking this man's son's bike?" The boy just whimpered without coherently speaking as he continued to rub his throbbing ear. "Answer me!" He commanded. "I am only going to ask you one more time son. Did you or did you not take the bike?"

Finally, afraid of further angering his father, he said softly, "Si Papa."

Speaking to his wife, he asked her to take him in the house as he turned to address Peter. He offered, "Let me know how much it costs for you to have your sons bike re-painted and I will cover the expenditures. My son will have consequences for his actions, I am sorry for your troubles." The man was so agitated he just turned around and went back inside his house without saying anything else.

Now that the bike was repossessed, they drove back to the house so he could drop both Perro and the bike off. Peter asked Perro to refrain from mentioning anything to Dane. He wanted the opportunity to address the consequences for leaving his bike outside.

Presently clueless to what was happening across town, Peter went on to work. The Tupamáros assigned to this mission, were outfitted with matching uniforms. Patches that bore their names were sewn on each uniform along with the insignia of the local electric company. Paco tapped the windowsill, nervously as they drove along. Looking out, he could see shop owners opening their businesses, some throwing buckets of hot soapy water as they scrubbed the outer sidewalk outside of their establishments. All this effort in preparation for yet another day of work. Everything was going as clockwork. By the time they rolled into the city, enough time was allotted for all to get situated. Then, the waiting began until the moment the students were released for recess.

"Yes sir, yes, I understand," said Peter. It was already almost 10:00 a.m. He had been on a long-distance call to Canada, speaking with the senior partner of Pradman Industries, Carl Vener. "I just wanted to inform you that things are rather tense here. In fact, they are getting worse." This was such an intense phone call he had lost track of the time.

Carl listened to Peter and then chose his words carefully. "Please, give this some time. You now have security in place. I need you here, Peter. Let's be practical and give this some time. More than likely this will blow over and they will move on. There is no one else with your expertise and language skills that can handle the Uruguayan area. I am pleading for you to be patient. We can increase the manpower if we need to, bring in some outside help, I'll sign off on anything that will make your wife comfortable."

"Carl, I cannot make any promises, nor can I guarantee how much more my family can take, even with extra help. You really don't understand what it has been like here. To be clear, I will not jeopardize my family or my wife's sanity at this point. If it gets to the point where I am not willing to go further, I will leave. You can talk with Dan Mitrione. He will tell you these are some very scary people. Perhaps, the two of you can iron out some details. I do not run from scare tactics, but this is on an entirely different level, I can deal with a lot but when it comes to my family again, I draw the line. I am not ready to give up just yet, but I will not make promises that I cannot keep. I have always been a man of my word."

Chapter 39

Miguel drove past the school. All seemed normal—in place. He drove further down the road and met up with the guys behind an abandoned building. Rolling down the window, he spoke to them. "All is clear. I am going down to block the entry. Let's go." Driving off, he headed back towards the front entrance to the school. Pulling in, Miguel blocked the entrance as he said he would and pulled a map out. He staged the scene as if he were a lost soul in town just studying a road map, all the while keeping an eye on the back-street gate. He saw Rafa as he turned the corner moving down the side street towards the back entrance of the school. Once he got so far, Miguel briefly lost site of the van. Rafa entered slowly as the gate was opened for him. As he pulled forward, he circled the van around so he was facing the exit and yet was adjacent to the school's playground. Mario remained hidden in the rear of the van, ready with a rag and a bottle of chloroform. While Mario waited, Paco and Rafa stepped out of the van and went about with the farce of pulling out their tool kits as if ready for the day's work. He greeted the secretary who came to say hello, presenting their falsified credentials as employees of the electric company. She was satisfied and showed them where the breaker boxes were. Further explaining the problems they were having, the men went along with the ruse, acting as concerned workers. Already knowing exactly where the breaker box was located and why the school was having issues this morning, they were hoping she soon would be satisfied that they were legit and return inside the school. After thinking that things were being handled, the secretary did in fact return. Things couldn't be going any better. Paco scoped out the location of the phone line. He planned to cut the line the minute they got Bergen so that no one could call the police. That would give them time to get away without the police crawling out of the woodwork. So far, so good. One of the teacher's started clapping her hands loudly, signaling to her class it was time to line up. Rafa and Paco pretended to be oblivious to the kids and only focused on their work, while digging a hole next to the fence. The students walked in single file towards the back door and soon entered as the next lot began streaming out.

Paco looked at his watch saying, "It's time, this should be her class coming out." Rafa nodded in agreement. Several shrieking girls went by while the boys ran straight for the futbol field, passing the girls as they ran towards the little playhouse. "Do you see her?" said Paco.

"No, not yet." Rafa responded.

"Wait, who's that coming out, holding the teacher's hand?"

"That's her!" said Rafa. They waited for them to move closer. At that exact moment, the director happened to come out with his assistant.

"Damn it!" Rafa whispered to Paco. "I observed their routine day after day, and the director never comes out, so why the hell is he now?"

"Let's wait just a minute longer," said Paco. Dr. Miller began walking towards them. This was not in the plans. *We're going to have to abort this job*, Rafa thought. *Damn it!* They waited. As Dr. Miller reached the "workers" he greeted them, "Hello! I just came to see how long you anticipate the repairs could possibly take?"

"Won't be long, perhaps an hour tops and we'll be finished. I just need to re-splice a wire that looks like it was chewed by an animal and some preventative maintenance making sure no other areas were affected. Then we should be done." Rafa explained.

"Good, good. This was just so odd there was absolutely no previous signs, of any issues! Anyway, carry on then." Hoping he would go back in the building proved to be a disappointment. Dr. Miller walked back in the direction next to where the girls were playing to watch the boys as they played futbol. Paco spoke up, "Let's pack up and go. This mission is aborted. I will make the call and take responsibility for it. To continue would be too risky."

"I agree." Rafa said. Going through the motions of being hard at work, one by one, they put their tools in the back of the truck and jumped in. When the kids were cheering loudly, he started the motor to the van and stayed put until he knew for sure that the director was fully engrossed in the game and not paying attention to them. When Paco felt the time was right, they took off. Now it was just a matter of time before they discovered that they were not who they presented themselves to be.

Chapter 40

Peter had a meeting in town with one of his clients. They were upset, hearing rumors that we were involved with the Tupamáros and he didn't want any bad press for his company by association. The man further believed they could lose a lot of business. So due to the serious nature and choosing to not heed the previous advice given regarding conducting any business outside of the confines of Pradman Industries, he ventured out. It was a touch and go meeting in which their relationship hung by a thread. Somehow, he managed to retain them in the end as a client. During a lunch break, he consumed a lot of coffee, trying to put some sort of an artificial fortifier to counter the lethargy he was feeling. He was exhausted and he looked forward to going home. It really was a blessing that he was oblivious as to what was going down at the children's school. If he had known, he would have come unglued!

"Rapido! Fast vira, vira! Turn, turn here!" he yelled. They kept swiveling in their seats, checking to see if they were being followed. All three were on edge. Once they got far enough away, then they would focus on the fall out of the failed mission.

Mario was being tossed around, like a ball, in the back. The interior of the van was an empty shell with only the blanket and supplies, which had presently landed on him. He pounded on the back and yelled, "Mierda! Toma mas cuidado! Shit, be more careful!" The last thing he needed was the bottle of chloroform to fly out of his hand and break. Pulling up to a red light, they stopped after spotting a police car. Rafa mumbled, "Shit." Thinking they were caught. He just knew it. Rafa asked, "Where did he come from?"

"I don't know. I didn't see him," answered Paco. The police car, instead of pulling behind them as expected, pulled up beside them. The engine of the van idled loudly—it was the only thing breaking the deadly silence.

"Don't make eye contact," said Rafa. He started laughing while he said, "Laugh back. Pretend I said something funny." The light turned green, and they took their time moving forward. The police car moved forward first. They both looked at each other, reading each other's body language. Cautiously optimistic, they held back to see the direction the police car went, and then, they went the opposite direction.

Still unaware of the day's events, Peter picked up some trip brochures, toying with the idea of a getaway. If they could get away for just a little while, he felt like it would be a much-needed breather for a sense of normalcy. After touching base with Dan, he knew it was all just another wish that would remain just that - a wish. The intercom rang. Leaning over, Peter spoke into the speaker, "Yes, Lucia?"

"A Mr. Ranoldo is on the line. May I transfer?" Ranoldo was one of their oldest clients from long before Peter began working for Pradman so Lucia didn't question anything.

He did not waste time getting on the line to attend his needs. "Sr. Ranoldo, how may I be of service today?"

The voice on the line broke out in a sinister laugh.

"Who is this?" Peter shouted. No answer, but the laughter continued. "Speak, what do you want, or I am hanging up."

"That would not be a good idea, and you think you are so smart. Eh, Gringo?" he said. "You have a lovely daughter."

"You leave my daughter out of this. This is between you and me, not my child!"

The voice continued, "Oh, Mr. Gray, but it is indeed all my business: you, your wife, your sons—"

Peter interrupted, "What do you want today? What is of so much importance to disrupt my day? Why am I so important that you spend so much time focusing on me?"

"She was so cute today," he continued. Peter had to really listen to hear him. Pineda was asking him questions, and Peter had to wave him off so that he could hear. The man went on. "She has the bluest eyes. Funny they're just like yours, right?" He laughed acidly. "Cute little girl. Too bad the uniform is a bit drab; wouldn't you agree? I've seen those ugly brown boots on many a nun. You would think the British had better taste."

"Where is my daughter? What have you done with her?"

Ignoring his demanding questions, the voice continued. "Her teacher is quite the beauty too; long legs, big breasts..."

Peter forcefully said, "Where is my daughter—what have you done with her?"

"Your daughter is fine, just fine," he paused and then added, "for today. Just so you know, you Imperialist Pig, we can always have what we want, when we want."

The line went dead. Peter came unglued and screamed into the phone, even though he knew they'd hung up. "You sorry son of a bitch... Bastards!" Frantic, his next thought was to call the house. Peter was the ultimate gentleman, always in check, always distinguished. Today was his undoing. Today he crested that peak that most never experience in a lifetime. Most people experienced sorrow, or the loss of an elderly loved one, but nothing compared to the violence of a kidnapping or the potential kidnapping of your children and death threats. Finally, to shut Pineda up he gave him every detail, that he could conjure about the phone call, then he began dialing the number to his house.

Claudia answered, "Residencia Gray. Como—"

Peter didn't have time for courtesies, so he interjected, "Claudia, donde está mi esposa? Where is my wife?"

"Sr. Gray, Sra. Gray left to pick up the niños from school. I will ask her to call you when she gets back. Si?"

"Thank you. Don't worry, I will be leaving the office early." After hanging up with Claudia, he decided to call the children's school.

"The British Schools," said a pleasant feminine voice.

"This is Peter Gray. Have my children been picked up by their mother? We received another alarming call giving me a hint that Bergen was possibly being watched today."

"Please hold. I will find out." She put Peter on hold. It seemed like an eternity, but it was actually only a few minutes before she was back on the line. "Mr. Gray, your wife just picked up your children. Can I help you with anything else?"

"No, no, thank you," he said, as if he had no air to speak. "You just gave me great news, thank you." He hung up, and Pineda was on him wanting to know if the kids were ok. Peter let him know they were safe with Paula. Without any explanations except to say that he would be in Jairo's office, Peter took off to talk to him. The door was ajar, and Peter could see that he was on the telephone. Choosing to respect his privacy. He remained just outside the doorway. Jairo becoming aware that he stood there waved at him so he would come in. Cupping the mouthpiece with his hand, he said, "Just a minute more and I'll be off." Returning to his phone call he said, "Si, si, yes, very good. Thank you. Until next week." As Jairo hung up the telephone, he looked across at Peter saying, "What's up?"

"Another phone call." Peter added glumly.

"Aaannd," Jairo dragged out the syllable in a questioning manner.

"They were watching Bergen at school."

"Crap!" Jairo said, exhaling.

"I don't know if it is a good idea for the children to remain at school or how long I can manage to stay here in Uruguay. Even I am starting to lose a handle on the stress. It is getting too close, too personal."

"Peter let's think this through rationally. Even if, let's say, you pulled them out of school or you decided you want to move, nothing would move quickly. In order to leave the country, it would take anywhere from two to three months minimum in order to get the necessary paperwork. Visas are not easy, nor are renewing passports internationally. Your boys and wife are American citizens. Plus, getting slotted to ship your belongings via cargo ships is a 'first come, first serve' deal. Back to the kids, I doubt they would try anything with all those children and teachers around. There are too many people, I bet they were bluffing. If they hurt children, that would make them look bad. The negative attention would be detrimental to their public relations. PR is just as important to a cause, even neurotic ones!"

Peter bypassed answering his argument.

"Jairo, please, advise our higher-ups as to where we are now. I need to focus on work, on my preparations for the auditor's training. I want you to work on getting all my family's documents in order just in case."

"Speaking of monotonous," Jairo added, "the Fiesta account is still on us for the damage Pedro did. They want another meeting but this time with their lawyer's present. I mentioned it to Mr. Pradman. He said that they would get back with us for the final meeting. I guess we will have another meeting about that, but for now don't forget what I asked."

Peter stood up to return to his office. As he was walking out, he said, "I can't make promises I may not keep!"

The sun was starting to get that last burst of sheen as it does just before dusk. Peter had asked Lucia to hold all calls and visitors, so he could work uninterrupted. All his specs pieced together and most of the flow charts samples were all ready for the auditor's annual training. It was shaping up. Pleased with the outcome so far, there was very little left to do. His only concern at this point was being out of town and leaving Paula and the kids to fend for themselves while away on business. He knew they wouldn't be alone; at least technically. Dan had assured him that an extra detail of guards would be in place. He had to go on faith that all would be fine or else go mad.

Chapter 41

A muffled clicking sound emanated from Dan's telephone. Recognizing the distinct sound, he learned it meant that a transferred call was about to come in. As the shrill of the first ring began, Dan picked up the receiver.

"Mitrione." He said in an all-business fashion.

Peter greeted him, "Dan this is Peter Gray, I called to let you know that I just spoke with the Sargénto and he plans to stop by shortly to see you. I just happened to be talking to him, so I let him know you were seeking to speak with him as well."

"Great, I appreciate it." Not wanting Peter to know quite yet, Dan had spent the morning continuing to study the maps of all the neighboring barrios from the Rambla Hotel in route all the way to the Carrasco International Airport. Even if they never had to escort the family out, they had to be prepared with a plan in place, avoiding being caught off guard. He felt invested in Peter's situation. Why, he had no idea. He wasn't the warm fuzzy type of guy, but he did give a damn about people. Always the professional, personal and client relationships never crossed paths. His office door was closed when Sargénto arrived. He rapped quickly twice on the heavy wooden door, announcing himself. Having been seated, working for a long time Dan's legs were stiff. He quickly did two squats by his desk trying to re-activate the circulation back in his legs as he bade Sargénto to enter.

Upon seeing Dan's predicament, Sargénto found it amusing and started laughing. Dan looked up at him saying, "Hey low blow." They bantered back and forth good-naturedly, as he too found the situation amusing. "Cut me some slack," he said. "I've been working for hours on this little gem; guess I should have moved around some. Two more raps on the door and three soldiers came in to be a part of the meeting. They were here to listen only, not having much room they squatted down and leaned against one of the walls in silence.

So, I want to show you something. Look at this," he said as he pointed to the bulletin board. Pointing at the board, Sargénto could see the map of the city with lines drawn down through the streets. "So," he continued, "remember when we talked a few weeks ago about devising an escape route for the Gray's? Well after you left, I thought a lot about it. I thought where we should hide them if we needed to move them to a safe location?"

"Ok, what do you suggest? A hotel, a rental, what?" Sargénto asked.

"Precisely what you said first," Dan said. Pointing at the map, he put his finger where the Rambla Hotel was situated. Resuming, he said, "For this exact reason I thought the Rambla Hotel would be the best location. It is obscure, in an older part of town, the outer walls are thick blocks of stone. It is a proverbial fortress. There are only three areas where anyone could gain entrance, therefore minimizing the number of guards needed. You want to know the irony in this?"

"I'm game, tell me." Sargénto replied as he sat down.

"This was the hotel the Gray family stayed in when they first arrived in Uruguay!" Tracing his outline with his finger he explained, "We start at the hotel, avoiding the paths expected I thought we'd turn on Avenida Arocena, go up to Avenida Gral Rivera, turn right on Rafael Barradas going up until it splits, and we go via the Salida Luas Fabbri. After that we can turn up Avenida Italia where it will intercept at Avenida de las Americas, which will then be a straight stretch until we get to the tricky part."

"What do you mean by that?" Sargénto asked.

"What I mean, is from that point on the choices of roads are few, and so we become more visible. We have no choice but to head north until we get to the Rotonda Aeropuerto which splits into the Ruta IB and last the accesos Aeropuerto will take us to the concourse. This is where I need you. How do we gain entrance directly onto the tarmac? There isn't a problem having a plane ready to go but getting on to the tarmac needs to be fluid and fast. So, help me here. I need you to study this and tell me if you think any particular street on this route is flawed in any way that would increase our chances of an ambush."

"What are you doing tomorrow?" Sargénto asked pensively, as he leaned against Dan's desk, crossing his arms.

"Are you thinking what I am thinking?"

"I believe so. Let's give this route a test run. We need to take a closer look at what advantages and disadvantages we could have from the rooftops of the buildings or from down below from the street. What do you think?"

"Sounds good."

Sargénto walked over to the conference table where other maps were spread out. "Well, the first thing before we go any further, I must insist that this has to be a closed job. *Only* the most trustworthy men will be a part of this operation and we will hold back telling them until a few days before. I have some pull, so they can fly out on a military craft under assumed names. I can take care of that part. The mission must be executed during the night. They must be moved at nighttime so there is reduced visibility as well. As far as getting the side gates open to the tarmac, arrangements can be made. I just need some time to be able to talk to a few trustworthy people. Have you thought about how we can transport them?"

"Yes, I figured using one of the armored vehicles that are usually used for transporting your political figures. The color is even perfect being all black. The only thing to do is remove the flags and plates on it and put a decoy plate on. Since there are five in the family and we want a guard within the vehicle, it will be a bit of a squeeze for sure, but this isn't about comfort; it's about getting out safely. A regular vehicle would present other problems. We would have to worry about making it look old, unpretentious, forgettable. Another idea I floated in my head was painting the car to look like a taxi.

"What?" Sargénto said as if he were crazy.

"No, follow me on this. One, no one would question seeing one at an airport and two, they are always hanging around at any airport, and at all hours of the night. This is just an idea. I am just throwing out ideas."

"Well, I am not sold on that. I agree it would be expected," Sargénto added, "but being bright yellow...I am just not sold on the idea."

"Fine, we can stick with the black armored car then. Then what? Once on the airport grounds, I do not foresee any problems, as long as we can fluidly gain access to the gate getting us a direct beeline to the plane. Getting there remains the main issue."

"The woman is going to want to bring her things, a lot of baggage. How are you going to deal with all that?"

Looking up, Dan said, "That would be Mrs. Gray, and she will not be allowed to. One suitcase *only!* One change of clothes for each family member can fit in one suitcase. That is being generous in my view. We shouldn't even be dealing with that. More would be ridiculous. This is a mission to save their family, I am sure she can do without. I seriously doubt at this juncture she will complain, and if she does, well she can go shopping later. I will take care of organizing a standby vehicle, but I would like to have you come up with an alternative route; that way, if they run into trouble, there is a Plan B." Dan re-read the notes he jotted down on his yellow writing pad, looking to see if he left anything off.

"I can definitely work on another route, no problem. Let's just say for argument's sake, that things do not improve - you get that funny feeling, an inkling that things are taking a turn for the worst, then I have three guys already in mind to help us lead the operation. These men, I would trust with my life, not to mention that all three are excellent marksmen too. When you are ready, mind you, and hopefully we never get to that point, but if we do, let me know. The day I hear from you, I will bring them in for a meeting. Then we can further discuss the breakdown of the operation. What about you? You have worked with plenty of the guys by now, are there any you would recommend?" Sargénto said.

"Honestly, that's the issue. I have one man besides you. Haven't been here long enough... You can only go so far on body language. Plenty of guys have the fight and the stamina, but knowing which side they are on, not so much. This is my disadvantage."

"Well, that's four people, and with me, that's a total of five. One more lead person and that is more than enough to do a quiet job. We need one more then we can screen the top military police officers to line the roads. This must be executed with precision. Clearly our goal is to move in a manner that those around would not expect this to be anything out of the ordinary."

The more Dan and Sargento exchanged ideas, he seemed more at ease as each idea collectively now formulated into a solid plan. When Sarge was finished, Dan added.

"...and with my contacts I can make sure we have the south gates of the airport open allowing our soldier to drive directly onto the tarmac, right up adjacent to the plane's staircase. This gives us the ability to a) board the family quickly, and b) get the plane in the air immediately. Meanwhile Sarge, if you could work on the back-up emergency route, I will take care of the aircraft and transport vehicle.

"Absolutely! The guys started to get up thinking they were finished. Sarge immediately spoke loudly to get their attention. Hey, hey! One more thing I need to emphasize. Each of us involved must be willing to commit to this mission, for the next couple of months, to spell it out this means *being on standby at all times.* If anyone has a problem, you have until tomorrow to let Dan or myself know. After that, we consider you committed. Who knows maybe none of this will play out?

Chapter 42

The hair on Peter's neck stood up. He felt as if he were being watched and yet he did not know from where, or from which direction this intrusion originated. Nowadays, he was becoming jumpier as his nerves were beginning to fray at the edges. Peter kept walking. Rationalizing in his mind if this was for real or just his imagination running rampant again. Meanwhile he worked his way towards the street where he had parked. The downside of not taking a taxi was not getting a close parking spot, but with a taxi, he could be dropped off at the door right in front of Pradman Industries, or anywhere he did business for that matter. Furthermore, this meant Peter didn't have to sit there trying to dodge trouble for self-preservation either. One of the main streets near Pradman Industries was a street called Nove de Julio; it was one of the most picturesque, gorgeous avenues that stretched on for miles and miles! It was so beautiful to look at and drive through with the occasional ray of sun that broke through between the branches of the trees lining the street. The trees were strategically planted years ago directly across from one another. Once matured, they had the thickest trunks, and their branches stretched out like long lost lovers reaching out across the avenue towards each other, meeting in the middle, as they interlaced their fingers obliterating most of the light in their path. The area was definitely not built with expansion on its mind, nor for the modern-day number of vehicles on the road.

On the days that Peter parked on the street Nove de Julho, he used the protection of the large trunks to hide behind. Once out of his car, he quickly sought the shelter that the closest tree provided. Peering occasionally from his vantage point, he remained there for at least five minutes behind each individual tree, as he examined the area over and over. Then again, at times fear set in, taking over, removing all sense of logic. Second guessing himself, sometimes he found himself frozen in place, terrified to move toward the next tree. The moment he felt confident things were secure, only then, would he breach the shelter of the tree he presently hid behind only to sprint to the next. Subsequently this pattern repeated, depending how far back it took to find a parking spot. At times he wondered if any of the residents ever noticed his peculiar behavior, or if any ever came close to calling the Police Department on him! As he came to the last tree, which was the closest, and also catty-corner to his office, his building came into view. On the days he came this route, and only after he felt relatively sure that the coast was clear, did Peter even emerge from his wooden shelter. Decision made, then it became the sprint for his life; only stopping once he was inside the confines of Pradman Industries building.

Chapter 43

The telephone's high-pitched ring disturbed their slumber. Paula reached over and tapped Peter on his back. "Peter, Peter," shaking him again she repeated, "Peter!"

"Whaat?" he said sleepily, as he started to fall back asleep, until Paula shook him again.

"The telephone, I do not want to answer it, you do it. It rang three times about twenty minutes ago, but it stopped. What if it's Dan? Maybe he knows something?"

"It is probably another one of those calls," he said as he sat up on the side of the bed. "I'll go get it." He said annoyed, not with her but the phone disturbing their sleep yet again.

"Hurry, it's going to wake up the kids!" Paula pleaded.

"Okay, I'm going." Slipping his robe on and stepping into his slippers, he headed down the hallway towards the phone. "Hello?"

"Well, it is about time," Pedro said, "I thought you were avoiding me. I really do not think you want to, especially since we have built such a close relationship." He said caustically, as he continued. "I almost thought I needed to send another drive-by wake-up call to your house!"

"What do you want? I know you have my number at work and obviously everyone else's, so why not call them? You don't have to terrify my family. They have nothing to do with this."

"Aah, but they do Peter. Paula is married to the Pig and the pig has piglets. It's all in the family now." Pedro added.

Growing impatient and not wanting to wake the kids by raising his voice, Peter continued to speak in a low but controlled manner. "So, what is it this time? What is so important? Your goons have already been by twice tonight. My daughter is so stressed out she is barely sleeping. So, unless you have anything to say I am hanging up!"

"Not exactly a wise choice Pig. This is over when I say it is over, or I will keep calling." Peter felt his blood pressure rising and one of those headaches was starting to make its presence known. "Since you are in a hurry to get back to sleep, I will get to the point. We were at the Armazen today around 5:00 pm and the funny thing is, there is a man that looks absolutely the spitting image of you! Can you believe it? Oh wait, I am sorry, my mistake, it was you!"

"Leave me the hell alone and leave my family alone! I am warning you!" Peter spoke with veracity.

"That is funny, what a coincidence we both have warnings. How nice. I just want to bring you up to speed; we almost got you again today, but we can always try again tomorrow! You have become our newest play toy. Mark my words all the Imperialist Pigs like you will be gone soon. We will rid Uruguay of varmints like you!" Before Peter could reply Pedro had hung up.

The next morning it was business as usual. First Claudia and the other maid, Cida, would spend time cleaning up all the broken glass outside the house before entering to make breakfast. They both wanted to remove all evidence as quickly as possible to help make the Gray's day start a little bit better. Claudia was now in the kitchen with Bergen. Bergen loved to help out and Claudia never seemed to mind. The task of feeding the guards became like having a small restaurant daily, or so it seemed. Even Cida had to rush through her chores so that she could help Claudia with the dishes. Paula even jumped in and began to help with some of the household duties, working alongside Claudia to offset how time-consuming cooking all three meals had become. As Claudia fixed their plates, she would personally deliver them to each guard going back and forth to the kitchen to retrieve another plate. When it came to taking Perro's plate, who was holed down inside the garage,

Bergen began begging Claudia to let her help. "Por favor Claudia!! Deja-me ayudar?" As she begged her to let her help.

"No mi amor, tiene que hablar con su mamá." Bergen ran out of the kitchen with a mission in mind. When she found her Mother, she was relentless until Paula caved, feeling extremely sorry for her daughter's confinement; taking a risk against her better judgment, she allowed her outside of the confines of the house. Skipping alongside Claudia, she jabbered on happily as she carried the towel that kept the rolls warm within, while Claudia carried the plate and glass of tea. Sometimes concessions made things better.

Chapter 44

Peter had been warned but no one ever expects things like this to come true. This was the stuff that movies were made of....and yet a simple trip to get his glasses adjusted proved to be a mistake. Damn dog. He loved Loba, but he could ring her neck about now for having pulled his glasses off of the nightstand and bending the frame. The children had just about taught her to fetch and bring them everything, so it seemed a great idea for Loba to bring him his glasses, when he went to get in the shower.

The eye glass doctor was a bit further in town, not terribly far from Pradman's but on foot it seemed to be, and he wasn't as familiar with the area. After getting his glasses fixed, he had walked not but a half a block and he realized he walked into the middle of a real mess. No sooner had he turned the corner had he singled out the two guys. This was becoming a second sense to him. Not counting on him being as lithe as he was, he started to walk faster and faster then he found himself running again. Hot on Peter's tail, the pursuit began. He crossed the street in a tactical method. Dan had suggested if he ever found himself in a situation within town, to move in and out, changing sides of the street. Presently, there were more people on the other side of the street, then from where he was, so moving in a diagonal angle, he made his move. Peter slowed down not by choice, but long enough for several cars to pass. Darting through the cars, he moved to the other side hopping back on the curb. Casually looking over his shoulder, he noticed a couple of guys that were crossing the street in just as much of a hurry. Peter continued walking up the sidewalk for half of a block slowly, this was no longer his imagination. Whenever he picked up his gate, so did they. Cars were moving again as the light turned green, and for once, this was what Peter hoped for: using the chaos of moving cars, he jumped out into the street zigzagging back from whence he came. Horns started blaring, tires screeched, and men screamed obscenities out the window at him for jumping out in front of them. Presently stuck in the middle of the street, he took a few of the insults up close and personal, and all he could do was apologize as he stood there helpless trying to find an opening between the cars. The guys were making strides, advancing on him but parallel from the vantage point of the sidewalk. He decided to keep walking up the center line of the road, keeping a distance until he found a brief opening so that he could push through. Once Peter made it, he took off running. Every so often bumping into people, some almost dropping their packages. Some folks yelling back their indignation! Every step took on a life of its own. Pounding step after step on the pavement, he could feel his revolver banging against his hipbone. The guys trailing him made it across to the same side he was on. Peter, again darted back out, zigzagging into the traffic toward the side which he just came from. The horns were blaring. Now, people began to watch, stopping to be front row spectators from their safe vantage points. His heart pounding, and now sweat saturating his shirt, it was a miracle he hadn't been hit by oncoming cars. His mind was reeling, trying to recall all the advice that Dan had given him. Multi-tasking on this level was a bit of a challenge even for him. He tried everything to ditch them, and yet they were still keeping up. If he could just make it to the next street, he knew of a business that he frequented before that had a rear exit into an alley. Most of the businesses on that street had a back alley. He was hoping that this one would exit precisely or close enough to be caddy cornered to the taxicab hub for the area. Surging forward he jumped back in traffic, broke left half-flipping over a car, all just to make it across again. The second he stepped on to the sidewalk, he made a beeline right into the front door of the small retail business, running through the building and out the back, while he maintained his pace, all the way to the taxi hub. Peter started yelling at the cab drivers, saying he was being pursued, and asking for help. He realized none of them were willing to help.

They just waved him away calling him loco - crazy. Trying to climb in a cab, the driver pushed him away telling him to go - get out. Damn it! Looking back to see if he could see the thugs, thus far it appeared he had made some headway. He couldn't see them. He cut through to a nearby alley, wanting to gain more ground as he did. Like an old movie reel, he quickly thought of places he could go. Most he quickly dismissed, and then BINGO! *The Presidential Palace! That's it!* There were always guards stationed outside. In fact, they also had guards dressed in decorative period uniforms out front, just like Buckingham Palace in England.

He could tell he was running out of steam, exhaustion was setting in. Running in a suit was a disadvantage. They were tight, cumbersome and retained heat. At this juncture Peter wasn't sure if luck was on his side or if the guys actually had lost his trail. Choosing to continue his pace for three more blocks, he finally made it to the grounds of the Presidential Palace. Approaching the guards that were on ceremonial duty, he pushed himself right up in between them. Talking right now was a challenge. Trying to catch his breath was difficult, but he tried to speak anyway. "Tup… Tup… Tupamáros," He gulped in air. "Two of them… They're after me. Dios Mio ayuda me. My God help me! Please, let me stay - don't make me leave."

Bent over trying to catch his breath, he kept glancing back from the direction he had just come. Shit! Just then they appeared but chose to remain in the background, not taking their eyes off of him. Even Peter wasn't worth being caught and arrested. Not willing to leave his spot nestled between the armed guards, he stood still. They might be ceremonial, but they were real militia, wearing real working pistols on their belts. Thankfully they didn't kick him out, but neither did they acknowledge him. Five, ten, then fifteen minutes passed, and the Tupamáros remained stoically in place. Twenty minutes went by, and the asses were still there! By then, Peter's breathing began to emulate a more normal rhythm. As his breathing improved, his ability to speak coherently did too, and he rattled off everything to the Palacial guards. Peter, not knowing when they started their shift, was concerned for he didn't know how soon the changing of the guards would take place. What if say one set would completely leave before the other came? Or would they meet out front to exchange spots? Wanting to be sure that they would continue to provide a sense of protection, he decided to give them the full account of what was going on. An hour passed; then, two. Legs cramping from dehydration and afraid to sit down, he remained like a third wheel. If the guards withstand it, then he could man up and deal with it too. At one point, he amused himself with the thought that they should bring him a uniform. He had been there long enough. *Good grief, Gray! You are pathetic.* Three and a half hours later, to be exact, Peter's pursuers abruptly turned and just walked away, and yet, Peter remained with his two overdressed buddies a while longer. On all accounts and in his opinion, Tupamáros were not trustworthy. Who is to say they would not be waiting further on down around the corner?

Dusk began to show signs of nocturnal life. Shadows grew deeper in color, and shades of light and dark became more obvious as they streamed through the heavy iron gates of the Presidential Palace. Time had marched on, and there were no longer any signs of the men that pursued him. Peter vacillated back and forth whether he should stay or make a break for the main road. Nighttime held another beast of an animal. If he didn't go, his visibility would be greatly affected. Yes, your eyes can adjust in the dark, but it also made it extremely advantageous for those that hid in its recesses. At least, for now, he could see, so he took his chances.

Peter could not wait to make it back to the office to call Dan Mitrione. He had his personal phone number written down at work and at home just in case. He didn't know it at the time, but he had jotted his number down with a brief message and stuffed it into the gun case he had handed over to him when he got his first gun; it was later on that Peter found the note.

After several blocks, Peter slowed down from running to a fast-paced walk. He kept that up until he spotted an open cab. "Indústrias Pradman rapido, fast!" he instructed the driver. He slunk down into the seat to where he could look out the window but could not exactly be seen. The driver looked in his rearview mirror, believing the behavior to be odd, but he said nothing, until he arrived at their destination and told him how much was owed. Peter finally spoke asking, "Pull around back please."

"Si, Señor."

Paying the man, he exited the cab and ran into the building from the service entrance. Peter began to tremble from the letdown of the adrenaline that had pumped through him for the past four hours. Lucia had long been gone, and really, only the cleanup crew remained. He thought they may question his disheveled appearance, but no one had the audacity to ask. He had to freshen up. He was not about to go home like that, for nothing escaped Paula's vigilant eyes. Opening the side dresser drawer next to the window, he pulled out a clean shirt. He always kept extra white shirts in case he spilled something on one. Walking into his en suite bathroom, he stripped the pungent shirt off, and proceeded to attempt to wash the source of the odor. Paula could smell sweat from a mile away; to say she hated the smell was an understatement. She had a bonafide aversion to it! He scrubbed his face, neck, and underarms and then dried off. Redressing, Peter put the same tie back on, combed his hair, and headed back to his favorite vantage point to assess the view of the street before attempting to exit the building.

Later that evening

The children had had an exhausting day, so much so that all, including Paula, had gone to bed earlier than usual. Working late into the night, Peter chose to finish the report he didn't finish during the day. He sat at an ornamental desk he had purchased in Brazil years earlier. It was made of dark cherry wood and was ornately carved all down the legs and the side lip of the top. It was exquisite. The only house phone location was changed. Due to the barrage of non-stop phone calls from the Tupamáros the phone now was housed on his ornamental desk, and for that reason, he was able to catch the phone call on its first ring. "Hello?"

"I see your light on. You are home, eh Gringo? Too bad. Hey, pig, how did you like your little exercise this afternoon? Enjoy your evening, your days are numbered."

"Leave us the hell alone," Peter said in a low, controlled tone, not wanting to wake the family. The man on the other line broke out laughing and hung up.

Chapter 45

The following day, there was no time to hash out the previous day's events. He did not even have time to talk to anyone except for a five-minute conversation to touch base with Dan. He updated him on the latest happenings, and Dan informed him that his meeting took place and plans were being perfected, if the need ever arose, for them to leave in an emergency.

Morning was over, and a brunch meeting for the auditors was scheduled at one of the local hotels. It was centrally located, which benefited most in attendance. The brunch ended by one, and Peter was glad that he had the time to make it back and finish a few more things before heading home. It was unbelievable how just one afternoon could set back his already tight schedule. As if on cue, the phone rang briefly after Peter had arrived back. It was uncanny how they knew. Either someone else was involved—perhaps even in this building—or he was being watched by someone he least suspected.

"I would not hang up if I were you. We are not finished, you Imperialist Pig," the voice spat out. Instantly Peter recognized the voice. It was the same one from yesterday, but now he was angry. "You are very lucky, somewhat like a cat, but you are losing most of your lives, and so will your family."

"Leave my family out of this. It is me you want, not them. They have nothing to do with this situation! Nothing!"

"As I was saying…" He chuckled and then spoke in a menacing way, "You and your little girl have been a little challenge to get. Maybe it is Gringo luck?"

"Ah—" Peter began but didn't get to finish.

"Silencio! Silence, it is your time to listen to me. You will be the last killed, for you will first know of the deaths of all those you love. We will start with your dog Loba, next Bergen, then Jack, Dane and last your dear Paula. Just cannot decide if we will play with her a bit first before we kill her slowly." The line went dead.

Chapter 46

Lucia arrived at the orphanage. She always arrived at the same time, on the same day of every week as she had for the past two years. "Good morning, Sister Tereza," she said.

"Good morning, my child," the sister responded with a loving look. "Have you had a good week?"

"Yes, Sister." They continued in silence, walking down the hall towards the arched doorway ahead. The door was wide open as the windows spilled in light from all around. The décor was simple: a worn couch in the corner and wooden chairs made for little children lined up at a table low to the ground. The table had originally been beautiful in its day but now showed the marring of time. Everything was showing a little wear, but everything was also clean, and the place was spotless. As soon as Lucia stepped out into view, the children cried out her name and began to run towards her.

Sister Tereza spoke, "They never grow tired of your visits. Let us show our manners. Manolo, your hands are muddy. Wash first, darling. Then, you may hug Lucia."

"Si, Señora." He ran over to the outside tank to wash. Lucia looked around but could not find Monica. Her heart pounded a little faster. No one knew her secret, not even the sisters at the orphanage. "Sister, where is Monica? I do not see her. She hasn't been…" She couldn't continue, or her voice might quiver. Her mind was screaming no! She knew it always was a possibility that the child would find a home, but she wasn't ready to see her go. She had grown attached.

"Why, our precious Monica is up in the infirmary. She has been running a small fever. She will be fine and be back with the others in no time. It is very thoughtful how you care so much for that little one. Such a shame you are not married yet or I do believe she would have a home!" Lucia snapped her head up, looking first at the nun and then looking away quickly—circumventing that the sister see the blush that had crept upon her face.

Chapter 47

Hell—oh," Paula finished with a faint exhaust of air as she was sharply interrupted by her husband, Peter.

"Don't—" his voice broke. Regaining his composure, he continued with measured force, "don't talk. Just listen! The children—us—we are in danger!" Instantly, her skin prickled, and the room buzzed as she felt it implode, growing smaller by the second. The stress in his voice was biting. Peter wasn't the type of man that raised his voice to anyone. "Do you know where the children are?"

"Why yes, I—" Once again, he butted in.

"No, Paula, I mean now, at this exact moment?"

"Yes-yes, I do—but Peter, what's happening?"

"Not now, I don't have time to explain, Paula!" He knew he was being harsh and rather dickish, but time was of the essence. "I need you to go get the kids right now - enter through the service entry! This is serious. When you leave the school, take the route we normally take via the Rambla whenever we go to the beach and meet me at the first place we stayed in when we arrived."

"Peter, what is happening?" she said with a tight voice.

"There is no time to explain. Our lives have been threatened; now, go! I will meet you there!"

Paula hung up and looked slowly around the room. She felt the effects that the shock had on her body. Gradually regaining her wits, she began running towards the bedroom while shouting instructions for Claudia to get the kids a change of clothes and shoes. Grabbing a suitcase, she began throwing a change of clothes in for her and Peter and some toiletries. Claudia brought their clothes into the master bedroom along with an extra bag with their shoes. After arranging the children's clothes in the suitcase, she closed it and carried it to the car placing it in the trunk. Paula grabbed an extra suit for Peter, keeping it on the hanger to avoid wrinkling it, then headed to the kitchen. The car was parked up the driveway near the door that entered directly into the kitchen. Meeting Claudia on her way back in, Paula advised her that she did not know exactly how long it would be before they would be back home. She handed her money so that she would have enough to buy groceries. It was a real undertaking feeding all these guards for both shifts, and yet Claudia managed. Grabbing her purse and keys, she said her goodbyes and flew out the door, not minding to even lock the door behind her. Getting into the car, she put the key in. Slamming the clutch down, she started the car, then put it in reverse, and floored it. Claudia yelled out as she was backing up, "Dios te bendiga! God Bless you! Don't worry about the house or Loba. I will take care of everything. I won't leave!!"

Turning the steering wheel as she reached the street the tires screeched as she slammed on the brakes. She then shifted into first, took her foot off the brake easing her foot off of the clutch, as she pushed down on the accelerator, she actually burned some rubber before taking off down the street, leaving the evidence of her assault on the street with two big, long black streaks of rubber. She drove like a mad man, careening around cars as a race car driver would. The light was red up ahead. Damn it! She knew she couldn't deviate from the route in case the car didn't hold up, Peter would know how to find her. The car had been randomly acting up. The past week Peter dismissed the issue assuming it was due to her being a novice stick shift driver, not to mention Miguel's friends had kept him quite busy.

Speaking to the car as if it were human while patting the dash, Paula urged it on, "Come on, Betsey. Stay with me." It was funny how she always had a habit of naming their cars. Peter always thought it endearing. As the traffic began moving forward, she rode the bumper of the car in front of her, hoping they would either speed up or move out of the way. Her nails were digging into the palms of her hand, as her grip on the steering wheel was on lock down.

The minute he hung up, Peter began dialing the school. "This is Peter Gray." Not giving the receptionist of the school time to greet him, he continued. "This is an extreme emergency. I need to speak with Dr. Miller immediately!"

"Yes, sir, Mr. Gray. Please, hold one moment," said the lady.

He felt so out of control - helpless. That was what he was. As a man, he felt like he let his family down: first, by bringing them to Uruguay and, second, by not having the better judgment when he picked the son of a bitch that worked for him. Nigel Miller's deep voice was soon heard on the other end of the line. "Peter, what has happened, my receptionist said there was an emergency?"

"They have threatened us, Nigel. They have put a death sentence on my wife and children today. We have had non-stop threats, but none seemed as final as today. I need you to get the kids out of their classrooms and hide them until Paula gets there. She is going to pull in through the service entry. Please have the gate open. She is on her way now. She will honk when she arrives, and then, if you will, rush the kids out. Please, hurry!"

Chapter 48

D r. Nigel Miller, who never raised his voice ever, began barking orders to his assistant principal, Mr. Gordon, the receptionist, and his own secretary. Both ladies' eyes were as big as saucers. "Well don't just dawdle, go!" The receptionist left to collect Dane, Mr. Gordon went to get Jack, and Nigel took off towards Bergen's classroom with his secretary. The door was ajar so he rapped on the door to get the teacher's attention, motioning her to come out into the hallway.

"Children, I am stepping out into the hallway. Continue reading. Dr. Miller?"

"Miss Dima, I need you to get Bergen and come with me now. The Tupamáros have thrown the gauntlet at this family. My secretary will stay with your class until you return, but I believe you would be of great comfort to Bergen since we need to hide her until her mother arrives." His eyes darted back into the classroom, spotting Bergen who was obediently bent over her book.

"I will get her. Can I get her things? Is there time?" she asked Dr. Miller.

"No, there is no time for that, just grab her sweater. Quickly!"

She entered the room and walked over to Bergen. Crouching down, she gently put her arm around her delicate little shoulders. Speaking softly, she said, "Bergen, we need to go now. Your mommy is coming to pick you up."

"Why? School isn't over yet," Bergen stated innocently. "I know honey, but something has come up and you need to go home with your mommy." She stood up and started to walk towards the shelving unit in which they kept their little school bags.

"No, Bergen, leave your things. Let's go, we will get your things later."

Without wasting time they proceeded down the hallway. First turning to the right, then down a way, they descended down the stairs to the first floor. They continued down yet another hallway when Dr. Miller stopped in front of the maintenance closet. He addressed Bergen. "I want you to go in the closet with your teacher. You will be hiding in there until your mother arrives. The bad guys are not being very good right now, and I need you to be very quiet. It is very important; do you understand?" Bergen nodded her head with those big blue eyes filled with fear. He continued. "It will be dark in there, but Miss Dima will be with you. I am going to go make sure Dane and Jack are on their way, and they will join you soon, okay?" Once again, Bergen just nodded and did not say a word.

They walked into the closet, and—finding a towel—Miss Dima put it down on the floor for them to sit on. The room smelled of cleaning supplies and that rancid smell that occurred when mops took too long to dry. Dr. Miller closed the door of the closet. They sat there in the dark, hearing the sound of Dr. Miller's footsteps getting softer and softer the further away he went. Dane joined them first. Bergen reached out and held onto him, burying her face into his chest as he squeezed her back with a gentle hug. "Where's Jack?" she asked.

"Shh!" said her teacher with a warning. They tensed up when they heard footsteps walking quickly down the staircase. Dane was tense and Bergen could sense it, but she didn't understand her feelings. Dane knew the reality of the situation, being older. His stomach was in knots, not knowing for sure who was coming. The knob began to turn on the door, and the bright light of the hall momentarily blinded them until their eyes adjusted.

"Jack! I am so glad they got you!" said Bergen with relief.

"Hush, Bergen," Dane said sternly.

Jack started, "Do you know what happened? What's going on Dane?"

Dr. Miller addressed them. "You need to be very quiet. If there are any noises out here… If anything were to happen, do not, I repeat, do not make any noise! The minute your mom is here, we will take you to the car. Understood?"

"Yes, sir," said Dane.

"Yes, sir," Jack added while Bergen just nodded. They could hear each other breathing, but all was quiet and dark. Jack was hoping a cockroach wouldn't climb on him, for he just knew being in the dark they usually showed up and he couldn't promise he would not yelp out loud. He was always imaginative and the most dramatic. He loved any animal but hated insects. Even in this situation, his imagination was working on overdrive. He wanted to ask all kinds of questions. He wanted a box of matches so he could light one and explore the area in which they were hiding. Time passed slowly or so it felt like it did. Bergen's teacher now had her on her lap rocking her gently, trying to provide comfort.

Dr. Miller stood by the back door, looking out while Mr. Gordon was sent to watch the front of the school.

The car sputtered as it turned the corner making that sound that was troubling again, but it continued as Paula drove onto the school grounds, honking. Paula had never prayed so hard. Fear is a powerful enemy that gives birth to terror and she was privy to that right now. Paula entered the turnaround at the back and rounded her car so that it faced towards the exit—if she only knew this was where the van had been days earlier when Bergen was in danger, she would have flipped. Stopping the car, Paula left it idling and jumped out. Speaking to Dr. Miller she asked, "Where are my children?"

"We have them well hidden, I'll get them," said Dr. Miller.

"I will come with you." Opening the closet door, all four squinted at the intrusion of light. Having been in there for close to half an hour their eyes were now accustomed to the darkness. The kids started to talk all at once to their mother when she shushed them. "Don't talk and move fast. When we get in the car, I am going to cover you up. Stay down and do not move. Understood?" Paula instructed.

"Yes, ma'am," they all answered dejectedly. Walking quickly to the car, they all climbed in. Bergen and Jack climbed into the backseat, while Dane insisted on being in the front with his mother. He wanted to help by being a lookout for her — always the little man— her valiant protector. Meanwhile Jack and Bergen were covered up by blankets that Paula brought as they lay on the floorboard of the backseat. Paula had worn a brunette wig to cover up her hair color and big glasses, hoping no one would recognize her. Paula turned around and shook hands with the men and hugged the teacher. "Thank you for everything. I am so sorry for all the grief our being here has caused everyone. We will miss you all," Paula said with her voice breaking.

Dr. Miller was the first to speak up. "It was our pleasure having you and your family. You were the kind of family we take pride in having at our school. May I speak for all: we wish you all well and Godspeed your safe return to the United States. God be with you! We will keep you in our prayers."

"Thank you," said Paula, turning she climbed into the car. Moving forward, she stuck her delicate hand out of the window and waved. Glancing one last time in the rear-view mirror she saw them waving. As the tears clouded her vision, she swiped at her face in a manner to avoid Dane from noticing. She edged closer to the street, slowly trying to see if there was anyone looking for them. Deciding that they were okay, she pulled out and she drove off like a bat out of hell. Little did the kids know that this most likely would be the last time they saw their friends, never getting to even say goodbye.

The trees whipped by, almost seeming blurry. She always had a heavy foot while driving, but this was exceeding her normal limits, especially with the children in the car. If she could only make it to the hotel safely, was all she could think of and pray for. She tried to keep a strong appearance in front of Dane. Like he said he would, he did keep a look out, constantly looking front, back, sideways and stealing glimpses at his mom, trying to read her demeanor. "Dane, slide down in the seat, at least some. I don't want you visible!" his mother ordered. They drove on through the downtown area, heading towards the Rambla Drive. It wasn't a short drive and halfway down, the noise the car had been doing became loud and the car kept doing little jerks. "No, no, no-no!" Paula begged the car before it stalled. Damn it! She started pumping the accelerator, all the while holding down on the clutch. Nothing was working. She turned to Dane. "Let's try and push the car. There is a little hill; I can use that to our benefit. When the car starts rolling, jump in and slam the door shut. Think you can do that?"

"Got it, piece of cake!" he answered her with a cocky 'I can' attitude.

They opened the car doors. Climbing out, they started to push the car forward. The strain of moving a car from a dead stop was almost more than she could handle, but her adrenaline had kicked in, and she would use whatever means she had to protect her children. The car started to move forward. Rolling a little faster, she looked at Dane and yelled, "Now! Jump in!" They both did. Slamming the doors, she popped the clutch, and the car sputtered to life. "WOO-HOO!" she yelled out. Dane grinned. She could see glimpses of the ocean ahead. This gave her the hope that she needed at that very moment. Her nerves were frayed. She wanted to fall apart, to curl up in a ball and cry her heart out until she was spent. Never in a million years would she have thought this was what her life would be. "Mom we're almost to the Rambla Drive," Dane said with excitement.

If all went well, they would be there in fifteen minutes at the most. They drove on for another few miles, and the car started to falter again. "No, no, NO!" she yelled out loud. "Not again!" The engine died. She tried to revive it like a mad woman, doing everything she knew to get it started, but accidentally flooded the car. "Kids listen, we have to get out. We are going to have to make a run for it. It is the only way!"

Chapter 49

Peter arrived at the hotel. He had less of a distance then Paula to get there. Paying the cab driver, he asked if he could wait just a minute; he might have to use him again. Popping the door open, he ran inside as his heart sunk. Upon entering, he went straight to the front counter and asked if his wife and children had arrived. The concierge let him know that the hotel was still waiting for his family to arrive. *Damn it!* Momentarily he panicked, then ran back out the door. *They should have been there by now! Where the hell are they?* Jumping back into the cab he asked the taxi driver to make a U-turn quickly and head back up the Rambla retracing the route he had asked Paula to take. *God, please,* he prayed, *let them be okay. Please, don't let anything happen to my family.* They drove for two more blocks and nothing! He was trying not to panic. They kept on for another block, and in the distance, he thought he could make out a woman and children. No, it couldn't be? Could it? He slid forward in his seat, trying to get a better look. He pointed and yelled, "There! "Hurry, hurry! Stop when you get to that lady up ahead with the kids," he ordered the cab driver. The cab pulled up, squealing its tires.

Paula instinctively pulled the kids behind her in a protective stance. When the cab had first pulled up, she thought the Tupamáros had found them, that it was over, and she would never see Peter again. She believed their perfect life together, as they knew it, was over. The lives of her children were now out of her control. Tears started to fall. She started to scream when Peter stepped out of the cab and began spewing orders. She stayed frozen, like a pillar, in shock. He yelled, "Paula, move!" His voice snapped her out of it. "Kids get in fast, move it! Now!"

The boys immediately did as ordered. Paula joined the boys in the back seat and Bergen sat on Peter's lap in the front. Ordering the cab to turn back around they headed back to the hotel. He paid the man a rather large sum of money and thanked him profusely. He felt that money wasn't enough to repay him for his help, the driver didn't have to wait for him when he first arrived at the hotel, and yet he did. Addressing the concierge, he asked him for the key to their suite, so his family could be taken straight away out of sight to their rooms. When they were safely delivered inside the elevator, Peter made arrangements for someone to go back to his car and retrieve their luggage and to take the key out of the ignition that Paula forgot, lock the doors and hide the key inside the gas tank.

Eventually, he joined the family upstairs. A lot of hugging and tears and laughter went on. Peter then pulled his wife aside and let her know that he needed to make some phone calls, and he needed her to keep the kids occupied in the adjoining room. She turned the TV on, hoping that would distract them and make enough noise that they would not be able to listen in. The children were quite fluent not only in English and Portuguese but Spanish as well, so not a lot escaped their ears. Peter first called Dan, letting him know that they had made it and then he followed up by calling Lucia about having his car picked up for servicing and ordering some room service for the family.

Thirty minutes later, food arrived for the family, and unbeknownst to the kids, the chief of police, Dan Mitrione, and men from the military had gathered in the adjoining room to brief Peter. Operation Liberty was put into place. The men met way into the early hours of the morning. One servant was assigned to bring food and coffee upstairs to the guards that held vigil outside the door. The guards, in turn, would bring the items into the meeting room. The air was tense; the tones of their voices were quiet but determined. Not a detail was overlooked. Every scenario was thoroughly worked through for all the pros and cons. Totally spent, Peter went to bed long after the kids had awakened. This would be a long, tense day. The head general of the military took over. It was the general that was going to be the one back in contact with Peter to let him know when his family would be able to return to their home.

Chapter 50

The general was up for four hours, gathering his men, and then, they headed out. It was one thing to discuss certain locations and routes, but it was another to fine tune it by actually seeing the area and timing the distance between each point along the route. A dry run was necessary, but first thing's first: mapping a course was never easy. Vantage points could easily turn into a disastrous situation. He took pride in his job, and this mission hit home base for him. He wasn't a native to this country. Where he came from, abductions happened all the time. He had experienced it firsthand when he lost some relatives as a young boy. That hatred never left him. He would be damned if another child was left fatherless or motherless, as his cousins had been.

By noon, the general had decided on two specific routes, referring to them as Cobra and Raton, the latter being an enormous rat. The names were derived from the fact that both were beings that thrived in the night and could escape rapidly from situations—at least, one could only hope. After surveillance, the men returned with their calculations to the station and began to plan their strategies. Certain points were revisited and changed to improve movement for various reasons. There was always a potential of exposure, a risk of the Grays being trapped without an emergency exit route, and—last, but not least—a danger to innocent bystanders. When the details were finalized, the men went home, only to return to the precinct at 2:30 a.m. They created two dummy convoys and began rehearsing both runs within the board room. There would be three decoy cars in the mix instead of two. The men continued to diligently work long into the night, reviewing the routes over and over until they could do it in their sleep. Occasionally more coffee was brought in and ashtrays had to be emptied along with having to open the windows to get some fresh air. Some of the guys were chain-smokers. Due to dawn threatening to reveal their presence, they quickly did a singular dry run, leaving Peter at the hotel. Then, and only then, did they call it a wrap for the night, only to begin again the next day.

Chapter 51

A few days later, the two youngest stumbled sleepily as they walked down the corridor. Dane, however, was alert and on edge. Interrupted sleep was never the best recipe when kids were in the mix. The children were dressed in dark clothing that had been sent through an envoy that had gone to the house. Careful instructions were given that no matter what happened, even if an unexpected change occurred, there was to be complete silence: no crying and absolutely no talking. The crying was aimed primarily towards Bergen since she seemed to have a short fuse and prone to tears when upset. The men in charge were not accustomed to operating missions where children were involved. Taking the service elevator, they made their way down to the kitchen of the hotel. Walking through, they were signaled to stop and wait. The soldier went outside and signaled, making a bird call, only to be answered by another and then another. The sound was almost faint due to the distance. A car could be heard approaching. The soldier then signaled to his comrade that had stayed back by the door, motioning the family to come out. The one inside whispered to the family, "It's time. Remember, siléncio, silence, and stay down in the car. Safe journey."

Somberly, Peter shook his hand, nodding a message of thanks and respect. Stepping outside, the temperature change in the wee hours of the morning was more remarkable, especially when minutes before the kids were in bed asleep. They had been made to sleep in the dark clothes that night. Quickly, they entered the car, and blankets were put on to cover the kids up. As fast as they were in and the doors closed, the car began to accelerate and turn on to the street. Very few cars were out and about, as they had hoped for. Lights twinkled off the puddles left by the rainfall that fell sporadically through the night. This was a plus since more folks would be less apt to be outside. Paula wore the brunette wig again, hiding the color of her hair to avoid standing out. With all the moisture, the windows were beginning to fog up, and they had to be cracked open a bit.

Nearing the house, they stopped at the first of the two check points now in place at the entrances of the neighborhood. Initially they drove by it several times, making sure all was clear. Then, on the last pass, they turned off the headlights of the car and the motor, letting the car roll forward until the very last rotation of the wheels. The guards jumped out of the second vehicle that followed the Gray family. The children, prior to leaving the hotel, were forewarned to be absolutely silent once arriving home. The guards moved with purpose each opening a car door escorting the family out with signals barely detectable if it weren't for the moonlight. In silence, they made their way towards the house walking directly into the kitchen. The guard that drove the Gray's home, put the car in neutral then he himself popped the driver's door open. All in sync, with doors ajar the soldiers braced the framework of the doors and with all their might began to push the car towards the house. Task at hand being extremely difficult, they managed to maneuver the car around and then pushed backwards into the driveway. The entire neighborhood now was officially blocked off. Only those that lived within could enter or exit. The neighbors were informed of the gravity of the situation and were required to cooperate under the circumstances or given the option to temporarily live somewhere else. Paula focused on getting the kids to bed. Bergen was no longer to use her bedroom since it faced the street. Dane's room was selected as the optimal place for the kids: it was the closest room to Peter and Paula and did not face the front of the house. Before they arrived, Jack and Bergen's mattresses had been moved into Dane's room, and their beds on the floor were prepared for their arrival. Not much of an argument was made. The kids were exhausted, and all they wanted was to go to sleep.

Peter was talking with the Sargénto. They were rehashing where each guard would be stationed since the number of guards now had doubled. Two sharpshooters were assigned to the roofs. One was stationed on the roof of the house, and the other on the detached garage. The car, meanwhile, had been turned around and positioned facing the street. Every square inch was a veritable impenetrable fortress. The transport was a success. No one knew the family was home. This was as they planned. Now, the waiting began: countdown to Operation Rio. The general of the military and only a few select people knew where they were headed, and it would remain that way until they were safely back in the States.

Chapter 52

It was early morning at one of the local corner bars. The smell of coffee was permeating the air intermingling with the aroma of freshly baked French bread. The morning hustle and bustle had begun. One could feel the energy. Miguel was speaking to a woman in hushed tones. It was obvious to those around, if they cared to be interested, that she appeared agitated. Lifting the coffee cup to her lips, her hand gave away her nervousness as it shook ever so slightly.

"I never thought you would force me!" she spat out vehemently. "I never said I would be a part of this."

"Well, you were the minute you began to spy for me. What did you think I was asking you? Are you that stupid?" Miguel snapped right back in his machismo way.

"Bu-but I," she stammered as her emotions got the best of her, "I didn't think you would expect any more out of me!"

"Grow up! God you're stupid. Like it or not, you are in it up to your pretty little neck. If you mess up and don't follow through with what is expected of you, you will regret it," he said in a threatening way to her.

"I- I should never have helped you!" She stuttered under duress. "Mr. Gray is a good man. Why?"

"Just do what you are told, and nothing will happen to you. Is that understood? You will report to me the minute you hear anything about their leaving! Anything! Now, get going before you are late. You are to find out what their plans are. Do you understand?" He gripped her upper arm to the point of inflicting pain and definitely leaving another bruise.

"I thought you loved me... Why would you want to harm me?" she pleaded.

"You are so weak. I don't like weak women. Why do you think I picked you? I knew you would be an easy target. You best toughen up!" He began to squeeze her arm tighter. In annoyance he snapped. "Stop that sniveling now!" he said acidly while jerking her arm.

"Okay, okay. Please, let go of my arm. You are hurting me." She quickly wiped the tears that threatened to fall down her face before they did. Standing up, she cinched the belt of her coat tighter around her waist. Turning, she hurried off, not daring to look back at Miguel.

Chapter 53

Months later...

The black cars rolled down the street single file, spacing themselves at four car lengths apart. The time was at hand. Operation Rio would be transporting the Gray family out of the country, but first, the military had to stage their people in place along the route. The only noises were the sounds of the wheels passing over the wet stone pavement. Every so often, the car would stop. Each time they did a rolling stop, two to three guys would jump out. Leaving men behind was never easy, even if they were trained. There were different assignments for each soldier. When they emptied a vehicle, it would veer off, driving away, leaving their occupants behind. The men moved with added purpose and great stealth, wasting not a moment. The marksmen were assigned to the rooftops, and the rest were ground crew. Hoisting the other up, the first man grabbed the fire escape ladder and pulled it down.

Devoid of sound, they climbed one at a time, reaching a rhythm of unison, moving up the side of the building with only brief interruptions due to the twist and turns of the staircases. Once on the roof, they positioned themselves to face the two streets on which the caravan would be traveling to include the decoy vehicles. The cars outwardly looked simple, middle-of-the-line cars. Under the hood was another thing. These vehicles were modified to reach high speeds and to handle the abuse of extreme measures. The doors were bulletproof and so was the glass throughout the cars.

Crouching down, each man quietly opened their cases that they had carried up on their backs. Inside were their long-range rifles that they began to quickly assemble together, with silencers on the ends. They signaled with hand gestures, letting each other know that they were ready and that nothing was amiss below from their vantage points. The cars continued down the road, ever so often dropping off more men on the route from the Grays home all the way to the airport tarmac. Only a select few had radios as to keep the anonymity of the operation at hand. Some men were left to hide on the street. Most crouched down in the darkness between the buildings or between—and even under—parked cars. Some of the communication was transmitted via imitation bird calls that the men had perfected. The dove sound meant the coast was clear. Another local bird call was used to alert of an approaching car or person. They hunkered down once they all were in place to wait. This, they were used to. Seasoned for missions, this was part of it. Keeping alert was easy when adrenaline was coursing in one's veins. This was a thrill by which these men thrived. One couldn't tell by their outwardly expressions; they were devoid of any. Stoic faces that had been altered with camouflage makeup stared back. Only the whites of their eyes were remotely visible.

By now, it was three o'clock in the morning. Everyone was whisked into the back of a sedan. The guys had ditched the idea of painting one of the vehicles to look like a taxi. Dane sat between his parents while Jack and Bergen were down on the floorboard. The windows were tinted extra dark, so looking out was even a problem for those inside. All they could do was rely on two senses: feeling the movement of the car and sound. Leaving the house, the car rocked as it drove off over the curb onto the street. Everyone swayed a little left and right as the car lurched forward. The wheels rolled over the payment with crunching noises as it covered the gravelly terrain. Even though they couldn't see, they could picture in their minds what the street looked like since they knew the direction they had headed out. After a while, all sense of direction was lost as they made several turns, and mentally, they were no longer able to keep up with where they were. Peter didn't even know exactly what time their rendezvous would be. Holding hands, occasional squeezes went on between Paula and Peter as he tried to comfort her in silence. As the car moved along beyond the parameters of their old neighborhood, every so many streets, another vehicle pulled in to join the convoy, each dropping back at a bit of a distance. In the end, there would be five vehicles. They were in the next-to-last vehicle.

They drove on into the night, reaching the downtown area. One of the men on the first rooftop spotted the caravan, as they came into view. A bird call done in a soft, unassuming way announced the arrival of the convoy, announcing them from one block to the next. The message was passed throughout the planned path. Peter felt his shirt sticking in the back. It wasn't even hot, but he was on edge. He gripped the handheld, leather zip bag that had all their documents within it. Bergen started to squirm, and Paula patted her back and whispered a warning to settle her back down. It was eerie how all was going smoothly. Expecting the unexpected made every moment seem like an eternity. They were so close yet so far. Anything could go wrong. The minutes felt like hours. Even though the sharpshooters could see that the cars had passed by, they would remain in place. If something were to go wrong, coverage would be necessary for the escape routes. Once again, the rain began to fall heavily, cloaking the caravan. This certainly wasn't easy for the driver. Decidedly it could make the task all the more difficult or perhaps be their saving grace. Time would tell.

Chapter 54

The sign up ahead read *Carrasco Airport.* The entire route, they drove with their headlights off. It was amazing to Peter that these men operated as if they had a higher sensory ability. With extreme precision, they executed their jobs, joining the surveillance of the caravan when necessary and dropping off to remain behind when called for. Estimated time of arrival was forty-five minutes from start to finish. The driver of the Grays' vehicle was clutching the steering wheel with a death grip. The muscle in his cheek flexed with tension. So far, so good. They were close, but even that wasn't cause to celebrate or for that matter, to relax. Anything could happen anywhere along the way. The lights up ahead glowed and twinkled on the tarmac, illuminating the paths for takeoff. Security was blocking the back-gate entrance to the airport. As previously arranged, they were set to enter through the rear and drive directly onto the tarmac. Peter was lost in thought. He had loved every minute and had been genuinely happy— totally content both professionally and family wise— while living in Uruguay. It was only when this mess with Miguel started that things soured. What a shame. Such a loss for his family and for him professionally.

A private jet was waiting on the runway, fueled, running, and in position, ready for takeoff. Coming to a stop at the check point was risky. Being at a dead stop made them easy targets. After credentials were shown, the barricades were moved, and the guards unlocked the gates and pulled them aside, allowing them to enter. The cars pulled forward quickly, and the gates were closed behind. The men moved back into place, blocking anyone's entrance. The lead and rear car escorted the Gray family. Moving forward they pulled onto the tarmac. Once they reached the plane, the driver did a semicircle stopping directly adjacent to the stairs of the plane that were already lowered in place just waiting for them. Guards rushed to the car doors, whisking Paula out. She tried to turn around and reach for Jack, but they grabbed her arm and pulled her towards the staircase. She began climbing up, all the while looking back at her children with turmoil of being separated. Another man was already leading Jack and Dane to the stairs. Peter had Bergen. Helping her up, he fell behind, followed by yet another guard. Once inside, they were met by a female guard that began directing them to sit down immediately and to put on their seat belts. As they were doing that, the plane's motor began revving up to a higher speed. The windows in the plane were closed, and the only interior lights were the faintly glimmering floor lights. It was just enough for them to see what they were doing. The cars fell back but remained. The plane began moving forward as the two guards were pulling the staircase up and locking the door. They had just barely enough time to sit when the plane lifted off, into the pre-dawn darkness.

Chapter 55

The kids had fallen asleep; however, their parents were on a seemingly endless adrenaline rush. One of the guards approached with two coffee mugs, handing them each a small token of normalcy. "Thank you. Any word on what's next?" Peter asked her. He could see her name sewn on the uniform. It said M. Braga.

She spoke softly but was self-assured. "When we reach Brazilian airspace, then our pilot will turn over the reins to our co-captain and come back here to update you on the next step of your journey. If you are hungry, I have snacks."

Peter waved and shook his head politely no, but he did ask, "About how long before we arrive?"

"We are due to cross into Brazilian territory in about three hours. Just call me if you need anything; I am Lt. Braga." She stood up, walked to the back, and sat down. If it weren't for her uniform and the gun strapped to her waist, one would have thought she was a normal stewardess just communicating with a fellow passenger. The plane bounced a bit, sending more butterflies to its passengers' stomachs.

Paula always hated flying, especially since they had experienced distress on another flight when the engines failed. Luckily then, the captain was able to get them restarted as they began to spiral down toward the building tops in New York. Paula shuddered at the memory. "Peter how long are we staying in Rio before we fly out?" she asked, trying to just make small talk.

"I believe we will remain at the airport until we are able to get a connecting flight. We should be fine once we get there, but we are not in charge. We need to continue to let others be in control of our safety."

"We have made it this far, haven't we? The worst is behind us, right?"

"I think so, but the Tupamáros are powerful, and I will just feel more comfortable if they see this all the way through and we get back to the States." Peter continued to talk quietly. As long as the kids were asleep they could speak openly. He looked over at the children one by one, feeling a bit of a failure. Admitting that he couldn't protect his family alone, made him feel less as a man. The plane bounced up and down again, sloshing some of the coffee onto the carpet. The turbulence was at best patchy with the increasing storm. In the distance you could hear thunder and lightning which peaked Paula's curiosity as the shades were still closed.

Paula called Lt. Braga over. "Could we raise the window covering to look out at the storm?"

Braga answered, "I believe for now, yes. Once we announce we are about to land, please lower them again." Having said that she retreated back to her seat. *She definitely is suited for the job,* Paula observed. *She is all business and not big on small talk.* The only thing that showed her femininity was the evidence of long hair, but even that was sleeked back into a tight, neat bun.

Paula raised the shade halfway. Lightning bolts wickedly illuminated the sky. If it had not been so intense it could have been entertaining, but for now, she just stared out the window at the play of lightening in the sky as thoughts drifted through her mind of the past couple of years, everything they had hoped for and everything that eventually transpired. Eventually she succumbed to sleep.

Just about the time Paula awakened, the door to the cockpit opened. A tall, muscular man stepped out as he settled his hat on his head. He was wearing a military uniform. *Interesting,* Peter thought. He knew that they had their hand on everything, but since this wasn't a military plane, he was surprised it was not a normal pilot that walked out. He walked towards them with a definite masculinity to his gait. He was all business.

"Mr. and Mrs. Gray," he addressed them as he nodded. "We will be arriving in Rio in about ten minutes. Once we touch down, a car will be waiting for you to take you inside the airport terminal. Once inside, you all will be escorted to a private room where you will be able to eat something and rest. You will not be staying overnight; we have a plane, after all, that will be finished fueling, and the pilot should be ready to go shortly after that. I will be passing over the reins to him, and he will see you through your next leg of your journey. It has been an honor to have been of assistance to you and your family." He shook hands with Peter and Paula.

"Thank you for putting your life on the line for us," Peter said sincerely.

"It is what we are trained to do. God be with you." He touched the rim of his cap and stooped his head in a military salutation. He then turned and went back to the cockpit. That was the last time they would ever see him.

Peter and Paula woke the kids up to secure their seatbelts. They were about to land. By now, it was morning in Rio, and the light was bright. Paula secured the scarf around her head again, being careful that no stray red hair was visible, and put her sunglasses on. She was done with the wig. Surprisingly, the kids were not talkative. It was funny how their kids acted when they sensed danger or real stress, how they altered their behavior. At this point, they were in landing mode and were just purely exhausted. The plane lowered and lowered. It was odd to not be able to look out, so the moment of landing was elusive to them until they felt the connection. The impact of the wheels touching down lurched them forward while the rumbling of the plane rocked them in an attempt to slow its speed down the runway. The plane came to a normal speed and continued moving and, after several turns, pulled to a stop. Lt. Braga spoke in a radio to the ground crew. She began to lower the stairs. A black Sedan pulled up to the staircase. Approaching the family, she said, "Please, exit now. Your vehicle is here, your suitcase will be on the next plane. It has been my pleasure serving you. Then she was gone."

Peter went down the stairs first with Bergen, followed by the boys and then Paula. Reaching the bottom, the family, one by one, entered the awaiting vehicle. Standing by the car door, Peter only entered after everyone was in. The minute the door closed the car moved forward towards the corner of the airport concourse. Pulling in under the enclosure, they were met by more guards that escorted them to a nearby elevator. Once inside, the female guard spoke, "I am Roni. It is my pleasure to be of service to you today. We will go upstairs, and lunch will be served any minute. We should have about an hour before your flight will be ready."

"Thank you," both Peter and Paula said. The elevator door opened.

"Follow me, please," Roni said. Upon exiting the elevator they followed her down a short hallway to the first door on the left. Pulling out a key, she unlocked the deadbolt and the other lock below it. Opening the door, she held it open while all entered. There was a sense of levity. The kids believed that their problems were now over and started to talk a little more, even beginning to joke around a bit. A short rap on the door announced lunch had arrived. The male guard who stayed outside, unlocked the door allowing several carts to be wheeled in with covered food trays. The waiter set the food on the table and proceeded to uncover the trays, leaving the minute his task was completed. They were starving. Having skipped breakfast, no prodding for the kids to eat was necessary; this soon became a race to the last bite.

The phone in the waiting room rang. The guard answered it immediately. "Sim, eles estão quase acabado com o almoço. Yes, they are almost finished with lunch," he said in Portuguese. "Voçês estão pronto pra eles embarcarem no avião? Are you ready for them to board the plane?" He repeated, "Tá, tá," which meant "Okay, okay," before hanging up. Turning around, he faced Mr. Gray and spoke Portuguese again, knowing that Peter knew the language. "Tá na hora, por favor se vocês podem pegar as suas coisas e me seguir. It's time; if you would please, get your things and follow me."

Peter began, "Come on, it's time to go home! Grab your doll, Bergen. Remember, no talking and just walk quietly until we are on the plane. Understood?"

"Yes," both Jack and Dane piped in at the same time.

"Yes, Daddy," said Bergen. "Daddy, after this, can we go outside and play again like before?"

Peter chuckled, "Yes, once this is all over and we are back in the States, then yes!"

"Finally," Dane said with sarcasm. This was met by a warning lift from Peter's eyebrow that quickly shut that small rebellion down.

They moved back down the corridor the same way that they had originally entered, riding the same elevator too. When the doors opened, the same car awaited them, except someone had turned it around to face in an outwardly direction. After entering the vehicle, the door was closed by the guard and after tapping on the roof twice as a signal, they were once again in motion.

They drove back onto the tarmac towards the plane that was in the first position for takeoff. Stopping next to the plane, Paula read the words 'Pan Am' in bold English. The fluke of this was not missed by her that they had also arrived in Uruguay, by Pan American Airlines as they now prepared to leave. They could see the baggage being loaded in the underbelly of the plane. Getting out, Peter and Paula thanked everyone for their help. Shaking hands, they then turned and started the ascent up the stairs and entered the plane. A gentle, warm breeze was in the air as the afternoon sun was high in the sky. It was invigorating. The airplane hostesses greeted them and escorted them to their first-class seats. The plane was rather light on passengers besides the Gray's on board this Pan Am flight, purposefully. The procedures were already beginning for takeoff. The air hostesses were giving all the instructions on the safety features since they would be traveling over water. It was amusing that at this point in time, crashing over the ocean seemed like a day at the park, compared to what they had been through. The mood on the plane was lifting every mile they were further away. The kids were enjoying being spoiled by the first-class air hostesses.

Jack popped his head over the seat. "Hey, Mom, can I go to the bathroom?"

"Yes." Jack started to walk towards the back when Paula stopped him. "Jack, you are going the wrong way. There is a bathroom in the front."

"But, Mom, someone just went in that one, so I was going to go to the other."

"Fine, just don't forget to wash up and don't sit and play with anything!"

Jack took off down the aisle towards the rear of the plane. He passed one of the stewardesses, and he quickly did a double take, for he thought he had seen someone he knew. Right when he did, she had already turned her back and started walking towards the center of the plane. Dismissing the notion since it would apply too much effort to go after her to take a look, he continued on toward the restroom. As was Jack's routine, he was in the restroom a long time, much longer than he should have been. He was enjoying his newfound freedom, even if it was thousands of feet in the air within the confines of a plane! It was, not to mention, fun checking out all the gadgets in the compact bathroom. He couldn't resist flushing the toilet and watching how the mechanism worked with the suction and air of the plane. Watching the inner flaps open and close and being able to see the insides of the plane, his inner voice took over, and he tossed wads of paper into the toilet one at a time and flushed, over and over. He was a gadget boy. When he got tired of that, he started looking at all the nooks and crannies, and then played with the water. Someone knocked on the bathroom door. Startled, he remained silent. That same persistent person knocked on the door again. This time, he answered, "I will be right out."

"Son, this is Dad. Wrap it up and get to your seat now," Peter said with pure, calm authority. Jack sure didn't waste time then. He knew he was going to get it from Mom.

Jack stepped out of the tiny enclosure of the bathroom and looked up at his dad sheepishly, saying, "Uh... hi, Dad!"

"Yes, indeed. Hi back to you. You know your mother said to not play with anything. Now, come on." Jack walked out first, and then Peter followed him up the aisle. A rather large, portly man was getting up and blocking their way, so they stopped and stepped back into an empty aisle to allow him passage. For Peter, he had to stand with his neck bent so as not to bump his head on the overhead cargo area. A minute went by, while all of this was going on, then the door to the second bathroom opened, a stewardess began to step out. That was when Jack made eye contact recognizing the person, he thought he had known. Pointing in her direction, he yelled out, "Miss Lucia, Dad! It's Miss Lucia!"

Peter's head snapped up toward the direction Jack was tugging him. When he himself processed that it was Lucia, he greeted her with confusion. She moved quickly into the alcove of the kitchenette area and reached into the bottom drawer. Peter reached the area right when her hand made contact with the item she sought. She froze upon hearing Peter's voice.

"Lucia?" His voice was full of consternation. "What is going on? What is the meaning of all this? You were just in the office yesterday."

Lucia began to stand up, and as she did, he saw tears rolling down her face, which added to the confusion. Her hand that was hidden in the drawer soon emerged with a gun that she soon pointed at him. This wasn't how it was supposed to be. She was there to identify him to her allies, not be directly face to face with him. "I am sorry," she whispered with a shaking voice, "so very sorry. I didn't mean to."

"Lucia, put the gun down. Jack, go to your mother," Peter ordered.

"No!" The other woman dressed as a stewardess snapped. "We cannot let you. Sit down now, Mr. Gray." She pointed at the stewardess seats as Lucia pulled the privacy curtains closed. Peter's mind was reeling. The other woman continued, "You should advise your child to shut up. Now, we are going to finish this little trip, and then, you are going to instruct your wife to remain quiet as well. We will bring her back here for you to instruct her. When we land, however, you will come with us. We expect you to cooperate, especially if you want no harm to come to your family. It is you that we want."

Peter turned and spoke directly to Lucia. "Why?"

"I am so sorry. I didn't want to. I had to." She was sobbing at this point. The other woman turned, waving her gun at Lucia. "Stop your blubbering! You are being weak." Turning to face Peter again, she stated, "Lucia will bring your wife back, and you will instruct her to stay seated and to do exactly as we say. When all is over, we will release the boy."

"No! I will not allow you to take my son from me!" He started to stand up, and that is when she backhanded him across the face with the pistol. The corner of his mouth split open, and blood began to run down his chin and onto his white shirt. By now, Lucia had bound Peter's feet together and tied his hands down his sides to the seat. Lucia then placed the seatbelt around his waist and ordered Jack to put his seatbelt on as well. Lucia looked at her and said, "Magda, please! Let the boy go!" she begged. Finally, the mystery woman had a name.

"You have your orders. Quit being weak. Go get his mother and bring her back here alone."

Lucia quietly walked through the curtains towards Paula's area. A passenger asked Lucia for a blanket, so playing along with her role, she said that someone would bring them one shortly.

"Mrs. Gray come with me. Leave the kids," Lucia spoke softly.

Paula had only spoken to Lucia on the phone, so she didn't recognize her. "What is going on?"

"Please, don't ask questions and follow me." Alarmed, Paula jumped up and instructed the children to stay put, while she quickly walked towards the rear of the plane. The plane bumped as it encountered a little turbulence, catching Paula off balance. She grabbed the nearest seat, righted herself, and continued towards the back. When she opened the partition curtain, she didn't notice anyone at first. It was after she had stepped through, that she noticed Peter and Jack tied up, and Magda's handgun pointed right at them.

"Be very quiet, Mrs. Gray," Magda spoke. "As you can see, we have things to our advantage." She laughed a bit and then continued, "This is how things will proceed. You will do as I instruct, and your son will be returned to you."

"Untie my husband and child, or I will not cooperate!" Paula said with steel determination. There was something to be said about redheads: they could be all brass.

"Oh, really?" Magda answered smugly.

Peter spoke up, "This isn't time to be my champion."

"Do as she instructs, for Jack's sake." Lucia said urgently.

"We have all these people around us. How do you expect to get away with this?" Paula still wouldn't back down.

Magda tapped the side of Paula's face with the pistol, taunting her like a slap. She ignored Paula's words and continued explaining how Paula would return to her seat, when the plane landed. She was supposed to disembark and leave the airport to a bogus destination to await Jack. However, Paula didn't know this was bogus, but regardless, she was to follow through with her demands. All her attempts to find out what they planned for Peter were ignored. She began to have a panic attack and her voice was rising. Magda was caught up, warning her to get composed.

Magda made a critical error, by focusing on Paula so much so, she failed to notice the hand that pulled a corner of the curtain aside. He looked in, assessing where everyone stood. Paula had been pulled into the kitchen area to separate her from Peter when she tried to reach out to him. A moment was all it took for Dane to lunge in and smack Magda as hard as he could with a metal coffee pot that was on the counter. She began to fall to the ground. At the same time, the gun went off, as Magda crumpled to the ground, out cold. Paula grabbed the gun and held the women at gunpoint, even though it was redundant at this point being that one was knocked out cold and the other was shot. Dane, rushing to his dad's aid, began to untie him. Peter looked over as Lucia slowly slid down the wall, landing on her bottom on the floor with her legs splayed out. Her hand was clutching her chest. Through her fingers, blood pooled, saturating the pale blue fabric of the uniform that lay beneath. By then, Peter was loose. He untied Jack and then walked over to Lucia. Crouching down, he looked into her eyes but didn't speak. He looked at her as if he didn't recognize the person before him. Lucia whispered to him as tears rolled down her face, "Ple-ple-please…" She was suffering through every breath, trying to talk. She had to tell him something, even though it was excruciatingly painful. "For-give me."

"Why?" That was all he could say, nothing else measured up.

"I…" She moaned and began to cough. "I had… to." He noticed blood on the enamel of her teeth. She was filling with blood, and her skin was looking pallid. She labored to speak, "He has my daughter… ha-ha, I had," she started to slump over. She inhaled one last time and finished saying, "…to save her." With that last effort, she took her last breath, and lifeless eyes stared back at Peter.

Peter stood up quickly and ordered the boys to go sit down. He grabbed Magda and tied her exactly where he had been. Taking the gun from Paula, he asked her to notify the pilot. Before she walked through the curtain, he reached out and grabbed her hand, turning her around. Grabbing her chin gently, he rested his forehead to hers, briefly closing his eyes for a solitary moment. Lifting his head, he brushed his hand through her hair, and cupping her chin, he gave the softest kiss on her lips. She turned and headed up the aisle towards the front. He looked down at his hand, studying the gun he held like it was a vile object though necessary. He marveled at what life had brought his way. He made a vow that he would find Lucia's child to provide for her; the poor thing didn't deserve the life she had either.

Success had its ways of gifting others with accolades. For Peter, it gifted him and his family an encounter with hell and a second chance at redemption, at living, a rebirth so to speak, and that was exactly what they were going to do from that day forward. They were simply going to live, and they did!

Epilogue

Within the year after the Gray family escaped, the Uruguayan Military apprehended Miguel De Luna. Eventually he was committed to an insane asylum where he remained.

Dan Mitrione Chief Public Safety Adviser, while in Uruguay, was a U. S. Government anti-guerrilla torture techniques advisor. The year after the Gray family escaped to the United States, he was kidnapped by the Tupamáros. Due to a most unfortunate miscommunication during the ransom exchanges, a message erroneously was given that no ransom would be paid. Subsequently, Dan was murdered on August 10, 1970 in Montevideo, Uruguay at fifty years of age, leaving behind a wife and nine children.

Peter Gray genuinely terrified of being pursued, forbade his family from ever mentioning or discussing anything about their Uruguayan experience with friends or amongst the family. It was only in 2017, that he began to share the true horror of what he personally experienced with his wife and children.

Peter, Paula, Dane and Bergen all adjusted and healed with time. Sadly, Jack did not fare so well. He suffered from extreme anxiety through the years culminating as an adult being diagnosed with PTSD, which contributed to an advanced stage of early onset Dementia.

Peter after arriving in the United States, had his attorney's secure documents making financial arrangements for the long-term care and education of Lucia's daughter. Upon finding out she had a granddaughter, Lucia's mother petitioned for custody of Monica with the help of Peter. She was awarded Custody six months later.

About The Author

Elaine Broun is a wife, mother of four, and grandmother. She has lived in many different countries, speaks several languages, loves to travel, read, collect antiquities and presently lives in Texas.

Made in the USA
Coppell, TX
28 June 2022